And It All Came Tumbling Down

Hannah Allman Kennedy

2021

For information about this title or to order other books and/or electronic media,
contact this publisher:
The Watershed Journal Literary Group
thewatershedjournal@gmail.com
thewatershedjournal.org

ISBN: 978-1-59539-057-8

Cover Image: Greg Clary

Table of Contents

Dedication

To the land hiding so many forgotten stories.

Acknowledgements

This book is ten years in the making. Ten years of growing up, learning, settling and being unsettled, and all that time thinking and thinking and writing and writing. Along the way, numerous people have believed in me and in this book, and without them I'd probably still be thinking and writing in a corner somewhere.

To Jess Weible, Sarah Rossey, and everyone at The Watershed Journal: thank you so much for taking this book on and for loving it as much as I do. I'm incredibly grateful for the opportunity to tell stories about the region we all know and love with you.

Thank you to everyone at the MFA in Creative Writing program at Carlow University for your endless support, encouragement, and mentorship. To Joseph Bathanti, Evelyn Conlon, and Karin Lin-Greenberg especially: thank you for your invaluable guidance in bringing this story to life.

Thank you to my friends: to the El writing group, for being a supportive and enlightening space to share work and writing inspiration. To Jenny, for your excitement as I wrote my *manuscript*, and Tim, for answering all my law enforcement questions and only being mildly concerned. Thank you, Dr. Dan Williams, for reading the first iteration of this story and seeing the good among the truly terrible. Thank you everyone who encouraged me and asked, "how's the book doing?"

Thank you to my parents and family for nurturing my love of stories from an early age, and for always cheering me on. Mom and Dad: this book isn't about you, but I hope you still like it. To the Kennedys and Mansfields and the other various relations, thank you for your excitement, your support, and for always inspiring me to write about the small stories.

To Alex: thank you for being a safe place of love and laughter, for having confidence in me, and for challenging me to challenge myself. I could not do this without you.

And finally, thank you to the land which will always hold my love and fascination. I will never tire of reading your stories.

Chapter One

Outside the window, the sky is a wash of white. The bare, black tree branches scrape against it like bony fingers on marble. The sound puts a vinegar taste in my mouth. We're on the second floor of this funeral home, and all I see of the world outside is the sky and the branches. The whole world is bones and marble.

"I'm so sorry for your loss," says somebody. I look up. It's a man in his sixties, salt-and-pepper mustache, black suit that looks too big in some places and too small in others. I don't know who he is, but he isn't talking to me. He's bent down in a little bow towards Nanna Mae, who's in the chair next to me.

"Thanks, Frank," she says. Her green eyes are muted, desaturated. "We just… can't believe it."

Now he turns to me awkwardly, with the look someone gives you when they know who you are but aren't sure whether you know them. I smile politely; this whole weekend has been an exercise in re-meeting people. Nanna Mae grips my shoulder. "Frank, this is Amy," she says. "One of my granddaughters. And her sister, Laura." In the chair next to me, Laura, my fraternal twin, stiffens in response. "Girls, this is Frank, my cousin."

Frank smiles kindly, sheepishly. "Of course. Amy. Laura. I met you once. Moons ago. I'm so sorry for your loss."

We nod in reply, as if we remember him well, as if he is the closest of relatives, as if our loss is not as bad as all that. Laura turns back to her husband, Theo, in the chair on the other side of her, and Nanna Mae and Cousin Frank pick up a conversation. While they chat, I stare down our line of chairs. Nanna Mae to my right. Laura to my left, Theo next to her, then Grandma Nancy and Grandad George and Aunt Maeve and Aunt Sophie next to them. We all sit in black folding chairs neatly arranged on the green geometric carpet, faded from years of foot traffic and shampoos. We are like *The Last Supper*, sprawled out

8

and leaning into each other and somber and angelic as hell. Who's Jesus, I wonder. I count to the middle. Theo. Theo is Jesus. Obviously.

Of course, *The Last Supper* is very colorful. That's something I've always loved about it. All those guys have the most beautiful clothes. In reality, a dozen peasants from the first century Roman-occupied Palestine would be wearing various shades of gray and brown. They'd be all dirty and uncouth. They would not be a tidy collection of Irish-Americans in black funeral clothes. But, oh, in the painting they look so splendid. So ethereal. So not like us.

Theo, of course, is Jesus because Theo is calm and collected and quietly funny, and he always has something wise to say. Laura is John, *the disciple Jesus loved*, because they just celebrated their second anniversary two weeks ago. I guess if you're going to be strictly biblical, I should be James, because James and John were brothers. But today, I feel more like Judas, who in the painting is craning his neck, furtively glancing around, wondering if he's been found out yet.

I've always thought funerals were terrible shams. I never understood the reason for throwing a party because someone died. In our case, two people. The cause of death is always various shades of tragic. In our case, an accident. Out of the blue. Two people lost in the vast forest of rural Pennsylvania, their car fallen into a steep ravine and smashed up like an accordion. And now we're all throwing a big, stupid party on the second floor of an old Victorian mansion, and people are talking and laughing and all the staff at this funeral home are far too cheerful for their own good. And two urns sit on a table on one side of the room, and we are sitting in a ridiculous parody of Renaissance art on the other side of the room: "Ode to a Grecian Urn" versus *The Last Supper*.

And those people were my parents.

Ever since I got a garbled call from Theo the morning they were lost and found; since I made the two-hour drive from Pittsburgh to this town of Haven and sat for hours on end with Laura, who was crumpled and crying on the couch; since I helped my grandparents put together the funeral, I've been compiling a list of "Lasts."

The Last Time I Saw Mom and Dad Alive: a month and a half ago, at the end of August. We had a cookout on the back porch, and Dad made bratwursts, and Laura and Theo talked about houses they were looking at, and Mom lamented that they shouldn't leave, because she and Dad loved having them there in the same house with them. I said something snarky about how the chicks have to leave the roost sometime, and Laura gave me one of her looks that darken her green eyes and dehydrate me like a wilting plant. Mom said there wasn't any shame in living with one's parents as an adult, especially when one's mom happened to be as badass as her. Soon we were all laughing, and Mom proved again that she could make everything better.

The Last Time I Talked to One of Them on the Phone: Two weeks ago. Dad called on his way home from work at Catawba University to tell me that he'd seen a mountain lion in the woods, even though the official stance of the state Game Commission is that mountain lions are extinct in Pennsylvania. We chatted a bit about bureaucracy and conspiracy theories, and how Paul McCartney might actually be dead.

The Last Text: A few days ago. Mom texted me, "Sorry I missed you. Call back. Love!" This leads my mind to assemble a list of "Would-Have-Been Lasts" or lasts I missed because, well, I am Judas.

What Would Have Been the Last Time I Talked to One of Them on the Phone: Less than a week ago, Mom called me. I was driving home from work and stuck in traffic, and I could have answered because I was parked, but I wasn't in the mood to talk. She left a message—her voice always sounded like the color orange—that began, "Hello darling!" as always.

What Would've Been the Last Time I Saw Mom and Dad Alive: The reason she called me, and then texted me, was because they were planning to spend last Saturday shopping in Grove City, the halfway point between Pittsburgh and Haven, and they wanted to meet me for lunch. I already had plans, but I forgot to text or call Mom back about it. Because my week was so busy, I didn't even think about it until Friday morning, when Theo called me and said they'd been in an accident, and they were gone.

I was numb; I barely remember what I did next. I shouldn't have been allowed to drive. I left my apartment, dashing off quick texts to my roommates and boss. Some part of me, still, wondered if it wasn't a hoax, or if maybe I had misunderstood Theo. Perhaps I had imagined the part in which they were actually dead. Perhaps they were only in the hospital. In my head a kind of chant took shape, over and over: *It's fine. They're fine. It's fine. They're fine,* for the first half of my journey up.

But when I passed the Grove City exit, the shimmering lights of the outlet mall, and the sign of the restaurant that was our perennial meeting place, I suddenly burst into tears and pounded the steering wheel and screamed the worst words I knew. I began a new chant, out loud: "I'm sorry, I'm sorry, I'm sorry, I'm sorry," and rolled into Haven Pennsylvania, Established 1859, Population 10,452, crying apology after apology. I drove up to my parents' house, my house, my home, whimpering *I'm sorry I'm sorry I left.* Theo met me at the door and said my sister wasn't doing well. I stopped the mental apologies right there, stopped crying. I swallowed everything and kept it in the bottom of my stomach. Because despite the fact that my sister and I are twins, I've always felt older, and I've always felt it my duty to take care of her.

Laura was crumpled on the couch, staring at the TV even though it was off. I hugged her and told her that everything would be okay. When the jealousy that she had gotten to see Mom and Dad in the past twenty-four hours came up, I swallowed that too. Because it was my own fault, not hers, and it was my penance to serve, not hers.

And then, as each hour passed, I knew with greater certainty that everything would not be okay. The police were in and out of the house, asking us all kinds of questions again and again, and I felt like I knew too much and far too little. We heard how the car had been found: on that Friday morning, some guy who owns land outside of town had been doing a routine drive around his many acres, and he found Dad's bright blue SUV plummeted down a wooded hill, at the tight hairpin curve of a dirt road, in the middle of the woods. The only reason the man even saw the SUV was because the leaves had fallen enough that the little scraps of blue showed through the vibrant reds and oranges and yellows of the thick forest. If he hadn't driven by, if the leaves hadn't fallen to just the perfect amount of visibility, we wouldn't know where they were at all.

On my first day home, that Terrible Friday, once the realization hit me that this was actually happening, and the second realization hit that I would have to take care of Laura through it, two officers came to our house to ask us questions. They were both big, muscular guys I knew by name. Two of Haven's ten-person police force. I went to school with them; they were high school seniors when I was in second grade. We rode the same bus to the Haven Area Schools campus, the elementary and high schools, which sit on top of a hill like a beacon of hope against hope that perhaps education can solve a few things. I used to have a crush on one of those guys. Cory Landers. In high school, he was very blond. Now he was Officer Landers with graying hair and he did not remember me. We sat in the kitchen around the table: Laura and I on one side and the officers on the other, Theo beside Laura, with his hand on hers.

"Their car was found on Frasier Church Road, about three miles from the Route 322 intersection," said Landers. His voice was harder now, not loose and carefree as I remembered. He went on to tell us how it had rained the night before the accident, so the dirt roads in the woods had turned soft, hillsides eroded. Going just a little too fast, driving a little less carefully, could spell disaster. And it did. Dad's car was crunched up, flipped over. Our parents had died from the trauma of the crash. Landers went on, "They were found on private property. Do you know why they would be out that way?"

Laura was incoherent, and had been all day. She shook her head, and the rest of her shook along with it. I racked my brain trying to think of why they would be miles outside of town, on Frasier Church Road, on private property, on a Thursday night. There's nothing out that way, no one they knew who lived there. The answer was simple, stupidly simple.

"They were probably going to see the waterfall," I said. "They liked to take drives and look for nature areas." I knew exactly the place the car had been found; we had driven there once as a family. The road was treacherous, and it was private property, but it had one of the most beautiful waterfalls in the area, because the curve of the hills was so steep and there were so many huge rocks left over from the glaciers long ago. For Dad, that would have been enough of a reason to take the risk. He always asked for forgiveness rather than permission when it came to exploring the wilderness. He was of the mind that the trees were God's trees, the rocks were God's rocks, the water was God's water… or at least, the State of New York's water, since most of our waterways flow from the north.

"Did they often drive out on private property?" the other officer asked.

"They loved to explore the woods," was all I could say.

This brought up the question of when exactly they had left the house on that Thursday evening, and the officers again asked Laura and Theo (Theo, of course, doing most of the talking) about the last time they had seen Mom and Dad, which was around five-thirty p.m., after dinner, when Mom and Dad left and said they were going on a walk, as they often did. Both having early workdays the next morning, Laura and Theo went to bed around nine and thought nothing of it until Theo got up the next morning and there was no trace of Mom or Dad, no answer on their phones.

So it was an accident. That was it: a simple, stupid accident that could happen to anybody. Except it didn't happen to anybody; it happened to my parents. All their lives, they had explored the vast network of roads and trails through the forests that carpet our Allegheny mountains. All their lives, they had driven through gravel and dirt and snow and ice, navigated inclement weather and wild terrain. They had walked through wilderness, spending hours away from another soul, knowing how to survive and keep warm and outwit a bear. They had done all this and come out unscathed, just like anyone else who grew up here would. But just once, there was a slip of a steering wheel, or a skid of a tire, or a swerve around a wild animal, and they were gone, just like that.

It was all so stupid, so ridiculously fucking stupid. I wanted to yell at the police, even that dreamy Officer Landers who I had fantasized about marrying once, a long time ago. I wanted to kick and scream and curse and say, "You're wrong. This would never happen to them. Never." But I knew it was no use. The police had checked out that landowner who found them, just to be sure he wasn't responsible in any way. He didn't know Mom and Dad from Adam and Eve. He didn't even recognize Dad's car, even though Dad had innocently trespassed on the man's land several times. So somehow, for some reason, it was simply an accident. But it couldn't be. But it was. So I detached myself, observing the situation and choosing not to feel anything. I pretended like it was a dream and all I had to do was wait it out before I inevitably woke up.

Later that day, I went with Theo to identify the bodies. Someone had to. Laura wouldn't. I was so sure that when we got to the morgue the two people lying on the stretchers, blank and pale and modest under white sheets, would be two random idiots who had gotten drunk and foolishly driven into the woods. Not my parents. My real parents would be out on an adventure somewhere, having fun, camping in the National Forest, or kayaking down the river, as they loved to do. Or they'd be taking a long nap in their bed, cozy and safe. Not dead, only sleeping, as Jesus once said.

But when Theo and I got there, we weren't led into a refrigerated room last decorated in 1972 and smelling of disinfectant as I thought we'd be. Instead, we sat in a terrifyingly pleasant waiting room on a blue corduroy couch surrounded by cream-colored embossed wallpaper, the light strains of soft muzak coming in from somewhere. Photograph prints were placed, face-down, on an IKEA coffee table, and we were left alone to look at them as we wanted. I turned the photos over quickly, like I was ripping off a band-aid, and the two faces I saw, blank and pale and modest, were not two random idiots. They were two forty-eight-year-old Irish Americans, one with a freckled face and auburn hair, and one with silvery brown curls and a worry line between his eyebrows. The gashes and cuts and bruising had all been cleaned as much as possible, and so I couldn't even say

14

they were unrecognizable, that there was a sliver of a chance it wasn't them.

Fuck you, Jesus; they are dead. And I never called her back to hear her sunny voice one more time. And I never told him how much I admired him for trespassing on private property to look at waterfalls.

So, this is why I am Judas.

I catch myself staring at the funeral home carpet, a green geometric pattern, wondering what year it's from. Either 1988 or 1992, in my estimation. The sound of someone laughing startles me, and I look up, perturbed. It's a collection of Mom's Catholic cousins remembering something she did once as a child.

Nanna Mae, Mom's mother, to my right, is still deep in conversation with Cousin Frank, her silvery-red head bowed under the light of the Victorian chandelier. On the other side of Laura and Theo, Grandma Nancy and Grandad George—Dad's parents—speak to an older man I assume is a member of the Presbyterian church where Grandad is the pastor. Our aunts, Maeve and Sophie, Dad's sisters, both stare at the floor, their dark brown heads glossy in the white light from the windows, their fair skin even paler against their black dresses. I wonder if they've figured out what year the carpet is from yet.

Next to me, Laura and Theo have been talking, but they pause. They hear the laughter too, and by the looks on their faces, I can tell I'm not the only one who finds it irritating.

"I wish they'd quiet down," I say, trying to drum up conversation.

Laura nods faintly. "Uh-huh," she says. Laura is naturally mellow, low-energy, but since Friday she's been like a deflated balloon, like someone emptied her skin of everything substantial and propped her up with a broomstick. Her voice has always been soft and quiet, but the soul of it is gone. It's nothing more than a breath, the suggestion of a voice. A breeze could come and carry it away.

15

"They're just trying to cope the best they can," Theo says. And I know he's right, damn it. He always is. He rubs Laura's shoulders gently. I turn back to the carpet. 1988, I've decided.

"I don't feel well," Laura says, and suddenly there's a flurry of activity next to me, and Laura is crumpled into a ball, sobbing loudly, and the sobs echo off the vaulted ceiling of this old ballroom or whatever it is, and everyone rushes to her and pats her back, and I feel too close to everything, yet too far. I lean out stiffly and awkwardly, while the murmurs of comforting words join her sobs in the ceiling, and sorrow rings through the room like a chime. I expect the glass windows to break. I want them to. I want all the attention of the dozens of people here to get diffused. I want them to look at the chunks of stained glass, and the shards of clear white, shimmering like soap bubbles. I want them to ooh and ahh and point and stare and cower.

I should hug my sister, hold her. Tell her I understand, because I do. But instead, I let everyone else do that, and I stare at the urns on the other side of the room. They are etched with names. *Margaret Elizabeth Flynn Reilly. Peter Alexander Reilly.*

I wish this were a real, proper rural Pennsylvania funeral, with a viewing where open caskets contain the bodies of the deceased, and you can see them and touch them if you want to. Because it doesn't feel real enough. It doesn't feel final enough. There's no way in hell those pots are holding my parents.

Chapter Two

I grew up thinking it was normal to play in ghost towns.

There was one just ten minutes from our house, deep in the woods. Mom and Dad used to take me and Laura out on drives. We'd leave the streets of Haven behind and plunge into the dark thickness of the forest, up hills and down valleys. Soon we rolled into Black Gold Cross, the defunct oil boomtown, with its overgrown streets and rows of spindly buildings.

The only part left of the town was—and still is—a train station along the tracks that lead to Haven in the South and Cainesville in the North; a grid of overgrown brick streets through the forest; and one last corner where there are still buildings: where Main Street and Petroleum Avenue make a sideways T. Main Street, the stem of the T, is lined with red brick buildings that all attach to each other: some storefronts have their windows boarded, while the windows of other are cracked and holey, like swiss cheese. Petroleum Avenue, the arm of the T, runs along the creek and looks more primitive, with houses and an old Post Office and a few brothels made of brittle wood boards that are lichened, sagging, and rotted altogether. At the corner where these two streets meet, the old bank building stands three stories tall, red brick and three chimneys and empty holes that used to be covered with stained glass.

When we visited Black Gold Cross as a family, Mom and Dad walked up and down the dirt streets while Laura and I played in that old bank building. It was our favorite, because it had a giant granite stoop in front that was perfect for jumping off and pretending, for a split second, to fly. We hid behind the old teller line, its little windows covered with spindly wood cages, or in the vault that had no door. We liked to play bank, taking turns being the Teller and Customer, or even better, Teller and Bank Robber. Once, we brought an old broom and swept the place clean of a hundred and fifty years of dust and debris.

18

We used leaves as money: long squiggly oak leaves made great 20s, coarse jagged-edged birch leaves stood in for 5s, and the smooth round aspen leaves were silver dollars

Little by little, the Teller and Customer amassed a tidy sum that sat in the vault until the Bank Robber (me) stole it all away, running gleefully out of the bank with silver dollars tumbling onto the floor. I hurried down Main Street, past the houses and post office, the three churches and ten brothels, all in varying stages of decay and overgrowth, to the nice couple walking up and down the street: the curly-headed man and the woman with the long auburn hair.

I, The Bank Robber, begged them not to tell the Sheriff (Laura) that they'd seen me. But it was all in vain, because soon the Sheriff came running, accosted the Bank Robber, and pulled me to the jailhouse where justice was to be served. And here is where the scenario always ended, because the jailhouse's roof had fallen in, and there was evidence that porcupines lived in it, and Mom wouldn't let us go inside.

Black Gold Cross was our creepy, deranged form of Disney World. Exactly the sort of Disney World the Rust Belt of Western Pennsylvania would have. A Disney World with real cemeteries where real people who fought in the Civil War and then came here to make their fortune in oil were buried. Instead of Mickey Mouse, we had rats: huge river rats that lived in the creeks which once ran black with sludge.

The best times exploring Black Gold Cross, however, were when Mom wasn't there. Despite all her efforts to be a "fun mom," Mom was still a mom, and all moms have a line where the fun things you want to do cross over into danger. Dads have no such line, and our dad's heart and soul was Black Gold Cross. So naturally, we enjoyed our outings with him alone even more. Sometimes he took us up into the wooded hills where there used to be farms and homesteads but now there were only hiking trails. If we looked hard enough, we saw the battered foundations of farmhouses through the brush, rusted plows overturned under moss, clusters of gnarled apple trees that used to be orchards. Dad taught us how to look for grandfather trees, which were always bigger and thicker than the others in the forest, their branches widely spread because when they were young, they weren't growing in a forest; they were growing on their own and had the room to stretch. People planted trees in rows, along streets and roads, next to houses or picket fences. When we found the grandfather trees, we mapped out what the rest of the land used to look like, mentally removing everything around them and looking back in time.

Soon I was so used to looking for grandfather trees and imagining what the land used to be, that I saw without even trying. When we went to the ghost town, it wasn't just playing anymore. I saw the bank exactly as it used to be; I saw the streets covered with feet of mud and oil sludge; the oil wells bleeding the earth dry; the jailhouse with its roof fully intact and housing no porcupines; the river covered with so much oil it could catch fire (and did multiple times); the three churches and ten brothels freshly painted and full of people, albeit for different reasons; and the quiet farms growing the grandfather trees.

Dad always told us that seeing things in this way was like remembering stories everyone else had long forgotten. He told us that sometimes, he could even see people: not ghosts, as he put it, but the memory of that person left behind, like a footprint in mud. "If you look hard enough," he said, "the past is still alive, all around you. You just have to be looking for it. You have to listen, then you notice what's going on, and then you can remember what used to be." I was always fascinated by that, and tried so hard to be looking, all the time, for the imprints of people in the past.

One time, Aunt Maeve, the oldest of Dad's siblings, came to visit from North Carolina. We took her on one of our family walks. Aunt Maeve grew up in Haven, like Mom and Dad, but something about living far away and then coming back had changed her. When we got home, she cornered Mom and Dad in our tiny green and white kitchen and scolded them.

"You can't let the girls just run around there like that. You can't tell them to look for the spirits of dead people. Have you ever thought about how weird it is?"

"It's history," said Dad. Dad was a History professor at Catawba University, our local college the next town over. "It's history" was his reason for everything. "And we're not looking for spirits. We're Christian people, after all. It's the *memories*—"

"The memories like the footprints in mud; yes, I know," Aunt Maeve scoffed. "But this is *a ghost town* we're talking about. And Haven isn't far behind, you know that? Everything is dying. Nobody has jobs. Every year a new factory or industry pulls out, and there's another family put on welfare, another twenty-something OD-ing on heroin or meth, another drug ring exposed. Life is so much better literally *everywhere* else. You can't even imagine how *freeing* it is to live in a place where you don't have to worry about that kind of stuff; it's a whole load off your mind. You could be thriving somewhere else. You can't raise your children in a rusty town left over from the Civil War."

"Before the Civil War," said Dad. "1859."

"Come on, Peter!" said Aunt Maeve. "This is serious!"

I remember hearing that conversation and being so angry with Aunt Maeve. I loved walking in the woods, through the ghost towns, under the grandfather trees. And suddenly she blew in from somewhere else and claimed that the life I had was worth nothing, that the things I loved weren't good enough, that they were flawed somehow. I was too young to really understand her. I was too young to know that she was right.

Haven *is* a ghost town. It's not a pile of bricks and toothpicks in the woods like Black Gold Cross, but it's more like a mouthful of old teeth: something that used to be whole and perfect, but now has missing places, and each year another tooth falls out.

I know the tale well. Long after the Erie, Seneca, and Iroquoian people were driven out, after small groups of Quaker, Irish, and German settlers had moved in, and only a year before the Civil War, someone found oil in the Allegheny foothills of Western Pennsylvania. Soon the area swarmed with fortune seekers, businessmen, and families looking to get rich quick. A constellation of towns sprung up. Oil wells were built. Barrels of black gold were shipped down the

Allegheny River to Pittsburgh. Some people became immensely rich, and they are still the most famous oil barons in the world. They built huge mansions and grand avenues. They built pleasure houses, casinos, parks and theatres. Then, soon, survival of the fittest took shape. Little boomtowns, like Black Gold Cross and others, ebbed away. Black Gold Cross has been abandoned for over a century now. But some towns, like Haven, or Cainesville, where Catawba University is, remained and stayed strong. They hummed with factories and refineries for decades, and while their industry of choice changed a little with each generation, they were threaded together with the common identity of being oil towns.

Then, in the seventies and eighties, when Mom and Dad were growing up, the industries pulled out one by one as places like Texas, the Middle East, and the Gulf of Mexico became the new oil hubs. The glass factories and machine yards followed suit. The towns shrunk, still sporting magnificent Victorian mansions and tree-lined streets. One by one, the shops downtown flickered out like dying stars, until whole blocks were empty, some of them torn down when the buildings became too derelict. An ever-revolving door of businesses and industries came in and out every few years now, hiring and then laying off swaths of people before the next big opportunity emerged. There are about three large companies now—a power plant, a glass factory, and a machinery company—that employ pretty much everyone, unless you're a doctor or a teacher or clergy, or you work at the dying mall or the only Walmart for thirty miles. Generations of families subsist on welfare, battling abuse and addiction. These are the people Mom, in her job as a social worker, tried tirelessly to help: people with so little hope that they couldn't even imagine a better life, and so couldn't even begin to move toward one.

This world was where my parents stayed and built a life. This was where Laura and I grew up. This is what Aunt Maeve wanted to save us from.

Mom and Dad's funeral service is held in the church Laura and I grew up in. It's a nondenominational church, unaffiliated with any umbrella or organization. It's the kind of church where you ask, "What do you believe?" and they answer, "The Bible."

The sanctuary is a simple hall with clean lines and soft, neutral colors. There's no art, stained glass, or candles; the only decoration is a mural on the stage at the front of the room, an abstract of richly-colored geometric patterns in the shape of a cross. It's new, and I've never seen it before; when I was growing up, a tapestry was there. One of the old church ladies had sewn shiny silk and velvet into the image of a white dove on a cloud with an olive branch in its mouth. The Holy Spirit. This lady had used the leftover scraps of silk and velvet to make little flags, which the kids waved during worship. I don't know what the purpose of it was, but I remember it being really fun. I waved the little flag back and forth and the fabric rippled softly, waves of tiny folds bending and stretching. The light from the plain, undressed windows caught the polyester threads and made tiny crackles of light and color. It seemed this fabric was sacred somehow because it had been used to make the tapestry. Each flag was like a little scrap of God and I decided then that God must be very beautiful.

I went to this church at least once a week, sometimes two or three times, from when Laura and I were infants until just a few years ago. Mom and Dad started attending before they were married; this was the first big nondenominational church in town and they left Mom's Catholic and Dad's Mainline Presbyterian upbringings, wanting something fresh and new. Their wedding was here, surrounded by the odd collection of ex-Baptists, Catholic refugees, and Jesus Movement hippies that all made up the community I knew and loved.

Faith seemed so simple, so black-and-white. Everything apart from God was lost, evil, destined to blow away like dust. But God was love. Everything in him was light, and joy, and belonging. Our church services were more like family reunions than regimented, liturgical meetings. We came together around ten in the morning—give or take —sang songs, and prayed out loud with abandon. Some people waved flags or danced in the aisles. When Pastor Jeff preached, it was either a planned-out sermon with points and subpoints, or it was a random collection of things he felt God was saying to him in the moment. Our theology ranged from rigid, literal readings of what the Bible said, to more spiritual, metaphysical, emotional interpretations. People like the Christian hippies fell more into the latter camp, while the ex-Baptists and Catholic refugees held more traditional understandings. But the way we saw it, this was a testament to our balance, our diversity, to how you can disagree but still be bound in love.

When I was seven, I asked Jesus into my heart so I would go to heaven when I died. The alternative, I had been taught by sermons and Sunday school and the culture around me, was hell. Mom and Dad were a little more ambiguous on this; Dad's love of perusing historic texts meant that he wasn't sure about hell being a literal place, but his Presbyterian and Mom's Catholic upbringing made the idea of hell hard for both of them to let go. So they kept their nuanced and complicated understandings of the doctrine to themselves, and the end result was that I had the vague idea that we should become Christians primarily because we loved God and God loved us, but also because we might be damned for all eternity, although if we admit that that is the reason, we have ulterior motives, and it doesn't really count, and we'll still be damned for all eternity. So I had a strange mingling of fascinated love for the God as beautiful as a scrap of polyester silk, and also a mortal terror of damnation, in my young brain when I asked Jesus into my heart, and this same weird combination of emotions stuck with me every day afterward, when I asked Jesus into my heart again and again, just in case I hadn't done it right the first time.

When word got out that little Amy Reilly had dedicated her life to the Lord, everyone at church commended me for the big decision I had made. When I was baptized by Pastor Jeff in the Allegheny River, at the shallow spot on the river's edge where there is a park and a marina named after an oil baron, I was dunked under the water and pulled up again, and Pastor Jeff said, "I baptize you in the name of the Father, and of the Son, and of the Holy Spirit," and everyone cheered and cried, and told me I was so brave and mature. I didn't feel either of those things; in fact, I felt late to the party, because Laura had made this commitment, with the same ensuing fanfare, a year earlier, when we were six.

What I did feel, when I came out of the cold, slightly fishy river water into the hot, humid summer air, was new: bright and fresh and reborn, all the things they say one should feel when one is baptized. I felt so incredibly good and pure, and ready to feel that way for the rest of my life.

Then, each day thereafter, I wondered if maybe the baptism hadn't caught on well. I still had a temper; I still squabbled with my sister; I still stole cookies from the cookie jar; I still stayed awake past my 9 p.m. bedtime. More concerning: I eventually stopped feeling perpetually bright and fresh and reborn; I returned to my stale, muddled, human state. So every night before bed, every morning before even being awake, every moment that my brain wasn't actively thinking or saying something, I was unconsciously asking Jesus into my heart again, trying to pray away my own damnation, hoping that perhaps at least once I would hit upon the right collection or intonation of words that would unscramble the cosmic locker combination and satisfy God into letting me into heaven, and perhaps, hopefully, stave off my perpetual anxiety.

I never told anyone about this anxiety, of course. I didn't have the words at the time, and it felt selfish, foolish, to worry about my salvation when everyone around me seemed so happy, so assured. Even Mom, with her fiery passion for justice and refusal to suffer fools; and Dad, with his quiet contemplation of the mysteries of the universe, still seemed solid and unshakeable in their faith. I was inspired by this, but I was intimidated too. I figured that I needn't bother them with my doubts or worries, that I would eventually grow up and become more like the people I admired.

Today, on this cold and white October afternoon, the sanctuary only has seats for about two hundred people, and the rows are bursting. Laura and I sit up front with Theo and the aunts and grandparents, so thankfully I can't catch anyone's sympathetic eye. But I sense everyone behind us, watching. Their sorrow is like hot breath down my neck.

I haven't been here in so long. I remember it smelling different. I look down and see new carpet. That must be why; the last time I was here, it was green and geometric-like at the funeral home. (Must've been a good year for carpet, 1988.) Now, it's a rich brown color, perfect for hiding the coffee stains of sleepy churchgoers. The paint is all new. Blond wooden blinds cover the windows. And of course, the mural. It draws you in, the one brilliant, colorful aspect of the room, pulling your eyes and attention to the stage. *Eyes front, Christian soldier.* The sanctuary feels less scrappy than it was when I was a child. It's more solid, more established, and matured.

I *really* haven't been here in so long. Maybe in a year. No, it was two years ago. They had just painted the walls, but not the mural. It was during my senior year of college, the day after Laura and Theo's wedding. Mom and I had gone to church alone because Dad had come down with a sudden cold, and Laura and Theo were on their honeymoon. I remember standing with everyone while the earnest group of musicians played worship music and I realized, with an odd mixture of fear and unsurprise, that I felt nothing. I looked at the empty spot where the old tapestry had been, where there was no mural yet, and it made me so empty and lost without that image of the dove. The flags, of course, had been put away or thrown away long ago. The congregation had slowly evolved past flag-waving. But I missed it. I missed holding my own piece of God.

God is within you, my heart said. *That's the whole point of your faith. The Holy Spirit isn't a dove; it's a part of God in you. Like a little flag. Like a breath. Like a scrap of light and color. He's not as far away as it feels. The Lord your God will be with you wherever you go.*

I knew that was the truth, but the truth felt flat and bland like it was just sitting out on a table, and I neither wanted to take it nor throw it away. I just wanted to leave it there and look at it. I wanted to wait, to see if I would maybe believe it again someday. But I didn't want to be forced to believe it or doubt it right now.

After church, Mom and I walked out the heavy, red-lacquered wood front doors—a holdover from when the church was a Victorian-era dance hall—and Mom chatted wildly, as she always did the moment church ended as if keeping silent and hearing new information at the same time made her burst with things to say. "We're commissioning a local artist to paint a mural," she said. "Something simple, but beautiful. Something that draws you in. That's why the new paint and carpet are so plain. We want the artwork to be the main attraction."

Stepping off the last stone step out of the building, I sensed that I would never go back to church there again. The fact was inescapable but neither bad nor good. Like that truth about God being with me. It was on the table, bland and neutral. The two truths sat next to each other, fine with each other and fine with me. I wondered if I was losing my faith or becoming an atheist. In my upbringing, there was no worse fate. I realized that maybe the fears I had had as a child were true; my baptism must not have stuck, because if it had, I wouldn't be having these kinds of doubts in the first place.

That was two years ago. I didn't become an agnostic, or an atheist, or really anything. I guess that's what's so weird about it; I didn't become anything. But in the past two years, everything I knew to be true plopped onto that table and coexisted with every other thing, until nothing was left in me anymore. There were no beliefs left in my head or heart, or wherever beliefs are stored.

Then my parents died, and everything's still on the table. The thought hits me that I believe nothing, and I disbelieve nothing, and I meant to sort it all out, but this terrible, terrible tragedy that you need some kind of belief system to handle happened, and I was still sorting everything out. But now I don't know if I can.

Aunt Maeve sits at the end of the row. She catches my eye and offers a sad smile. She must feel a bit like me, coming back home. She looks polished in her sleek black dress and boots, deep red lipstick, shiny brown hair falling in soft waves over her back. She has never looked her age, Aunt Maeve. She was always one to spend money on the newest face creams and nicest clothes.

27

I realize, suddenly, that I don't know what Aunt Maeve does for a living. In my head, it's always just been, "makes money and dresses well." Whatever it is, it's not something she could do in Haven. She left for college in Philly, then moved down South, and only comes back for holidays. I wonder if maybe, twenty years down the road, that'll be me. Doing exciting things in the world, making money and dressing well, coming back for holidays, weddings, funerals. Popping in for the highlights and then bustling away. I wonder how stressful it must be to do that: come home and see people you haven't seen in twenty years, catch them up on huge chunks of yourself, deal with people who don't approve of who you are now and who always hold up a mental picture of who you used to be. I guess I have been doing that already, but I've only been gone six years, not twenty-plus. When you only move away to go to college, people don't take it seriously. It wasn't until last summer, right after graduation, when I got an apartment with two roommates in the city, and got my first job as a lowly fact-checker at a little publishing house, that everyone—Mom and Dad included—realized I wasn't planning to come back.

Pastor Jeff walks to the front of the room and stands at the sleek black podium on the stage. Behind him, surrounding the mural on the wall, are flowers upon flowers. A table among all the flowers holds the urns, unassuming and plain. I can't get over how utterly plain they look. Dull gray. I remember that this choice was in Mom and Dad's will. When we made the funeral arrangements, which feels like a distant memory or a dream, but was actually only two days ago, the will said to buy the cheapest, plainest urns. They wanted money to go to their favorite charities, and to me and Laura and Theo instead.

But now, as I look at these ridiculous, shitty urns, I think we should have refused to listen to the will. I think we should have at least gotten something painted or stenciled for Mom; Dad liked old things anyway, so he'd appreciate a plain gray urn. It would remind him of finding clay pots in Black Gold Cross. It was like him: close to the earth, blunt, pithy, fascinated with the simplest, ugliest stuff. But Mom's breaks my heart. It's impossible that something so crude holds the body that carried my sister and me for nine months, that hugged us and

28

fed us and danced around the living room to The Beatles and once punched a man on the street for saying something inappropriate and walked down the aisle with Laura and threw back shots of Irish whiskey on our twenty-first birthday and cried when I waved my college diploma in the air.

"Today we gather to celebrate the lives of Peter and Maggie Reilly," says Pastor Jeff. His voice catches, pauses, and scratches multiple times, like a sweater getting snagged on furniture as you walk through the house. He and his wife Julie were some of my parents' closest friends. They met before Mom and Dad got married, when Jeff was a newly-minted pastor. Their first day at church was his first day at the pulpit. They were all nervous kids, playacting at adulthood and trying desperately not to show it. When people are young and terrified, they band together. So that's why Pastor Jeff's voice snags on every word while he conducts the funeral.

I'm sure he says lovely and comforting things, but I don't understand any of it. My mind is so tangled in knots, I can't make sense of my own language. I might as well be attending a funeral in German. All I hear is the voice itself, and its anguish, and it comforts me.

I've been to a family funeral before, when Laura and I were ten and Mom's dad, Papa Jim, passed away. It was different. It was better. Not because I didn't love Papa Jim; he was a wonderful grandfather. It was better, because his death was the end of a long illness, so it was a relief, an exhale. Perhaps I shouldn't say that, but it's true. I was glad when he died because he was ready. Even at ten, I knew that. But this time, death is an inhale: a bucketful of questions, not a resolution.

Suddenly, the service is over. Suddenly, we file out of the church, and people I haven't seen in years—or ever—hug Laura and Theo and me and shake my grandparents' hands and ask to be introduced to my aunts. Aunt Sophie, the youngest of dad's siblings, has never left the area, but she goes to the Unitarian church in Cainesville, so she might as well have. Everyone, of course, knows Theo and Laura well, because they were married in this church and they've come here ever since.

"We miss you," the church people say to me. Fluffy-haired old ladies and wry elderly gentlemen, middle-aged husbands and their peppy wives, young hipster mothers I grew up with, teenagers I used to babysit, little children I've never seen. Maybe they're just trying to be nice, but in every "we miss you," I feel a tinge of accusation. *We miss you. Why did it take this for you to come back? We miss you. You shouldn't have left. We miss you. Shame on you. Shame. Shame.*

I mentally apologize again, over and over, like I did on the Terrible Friday. Only a few days ago. *I'm sorry I'm sorry I'm sorry.* Perhaps they aren't the ones shaming me. Perhaps it's myself. I take a sharp breath and insist, to myself, that I have nothing to be ashamed about. I owe these people, this place, nothing. And yet, my parents *are* dead, and I could've spent more time with them. I did owe them that. I just didn't realize it.

Suddenly, we're in the car. Suddenly, we're at the family restaurant whose owner grew up with Mom's parents. Like all friends on my Mom's side of the family, this restaurateur is Catholic, and has supplied us with an open bar, which horrifies all the friends of my Dad's side of the family, who are conservative Presbyterians, and also most of the people from our church, who are liberal in finer points of theology only, and little else. Grandad George, Dad's dad, however, although a Presbyterian pastor, is also a surreptitious boozer, so when I go to the bar to get something—anything—he's there, squeezed against the wall at the end of the bar, quietly nursing a drink.

"What is it?" I ask him.

"Whiskey," he mumbles.

"I didn't know ministers drank whiskey at funerals," I say.

"Depends on the kind of minister you are," he answers. "I'm the kind who does. But if anyone asks, it's apple juice."

"Ashamed?"

"No." His look is one that used to be mischievous, but his skin is dull, his white fluffy hair lank and thin, blue eyes covered with a screen of sadness. His usually wry mouth is surrounded by lines I've never seen before. His whole face, in fact, usually youthful despite his age of seventy-five, has sunk and deflated, like all of Laura. "No," he says again. "Not ashamed. Just... trying to be sensitive. There are a lot of people from my congregation here."

I look around the restaurant, crammed with various family and friends, all clad in black and sorrow, flocking around tables and booths like hungry, sad, elegant crows. Laura sits at a table with Theo and the aunts and Grandma Nancy, who never joins Grandad George at the bar, but forgives him when he heads for it. People, endless people, surround them. Everyone cries or stares at the damn carpet. I haven't gotten a chance to study it in this room yet.

"I'll have a gin and tonic," I say to the bartender. "Mm... just gin. With ice."

I take a sip. It's sharp and cool and dry, like drinking a Christmas tree. I haven't eaten much the past few days, so this is ill-advised. But it tastes like the best thing I've ever ingested in my life. I take another sip.

"How are you?" asks Grandad George. He's been the strongest of all our grandparents since the Terrible Friday when everyone came over and we grieved and planned a funeral.

Nanna Mae, the origin of Mom's chatter and fire, plunged into the kind of desperate, quiet sorrow that frightened me with how unlike herself she was. Grandma Nancy tried to care for everyone, but she couldn't stop crying, and worse, she insisted she didn't need to rest or anything, so she just kept crying in front of us. Aunt Maeve was polite and pragmatic, Aunt Sophie spaced out. In short, we're handling our emotions as well as can be expected: terribly.

But Grandad George has been brilliant. He's said all the right things, kept quiet at all the right times, ordered pizza when we forgot to eat, started praying when it got dark and despair crept over us like a chill. So instead of answering his question, I ask him one.

"How are you?" I say.

"Hm." He takes a look around. I swear, there are a ton of people here. Now they circle around the buffet like turkey buzzards. A bunch of Mom's Catholic cousins are at the bar a few feet away from us, gathered in a cluster and sharing a few beers. Grandad turns back to me.

He lowers his voice. "I wish I weren't a pastor," he says.

"So you could have another whiskey?"

"So I could lose my temper at the funeral of my children and people would forgive me."

I press my lips together and pick up my glass of gin. "I'd forgive you."

He smiles sadly and hands his empty glass to the bartender. "Just a coffee, please, this time," he says. Then he turns to me. "Now. How are you?"

I smile despite myself, despite everything. My face feels like it's cracking. But his face is serious and it doesn't break. There's a panic at the pit of my stomach, where I've kept all the shit I feel. I've been found out and the fear threatens to bring everything up again. I can't risk that.

"I'm doing good." I drink my gin in one gulp, slam the glass down on the bar, and go to the buffet.

Later that night I shut myself into my old room with its orange walls the color of young pumpkins, floral-patterned curtains, and an orange and white-striped bedspread like a Halloween candy cane. In the next room, Theo and Laura are quiet. I figure they must have gone to sleep. It's only seven o'clock, but already dark. I open the window, smelling the damp earth and decaying leaves. I wish it were still light and foggy out so I could lie on my old bed and look up at the white marble sky and black tree branch fingertips and imagine the whole world being so pale and weightless.

I observe myself in the mirror. Golden-brown curls like wispy corkscrews, dark eyes. Shadows under them. The black dress Aunt Maeve bought me because I had no funeral clothes. It fits perfectly, just a little big in the shoulders. I unzip it and peel it off, feeling fresh and tender and new, like a snake shedding its skin. I put on an old, oversized tee-shirt, black with PITTSBURGH PENGUINS STANLEY CUP CHAMPIONS emblazoned across the front in faded yellow letters. The shirt is so big I can wrap the sides around my body like a cardigan.

I curl up into the bed. I've slept on it for three nights already but it still seems foreign, a memory I forgot about and have to get used to again. I feel a pang of homesickness for my little bed in Pittsburgh, which is white and gray and soft. I sniff the striped pillow. It smells like my hair, and Mom's favorite detergent, and this house. This house smells like them, like me, like us. Our home.

I think about Grandad George wanting to lose his temper and have people still forgive him. I'll never become a pastor. I want the freedom to lose my temper.

You'll never become a pastor, says a voice in my head, *because you still don't know what you believe.*

Ah, yes. I never sorted that out. Maybe that's why I feel so numb, so bland, floating through everything and thinking too much and not enough and saying too little and too much.

Maybe that's why I keep apologizing for everything in my head. Maybe that's why I can't cry.

You can't cry if you have no reason and there's no reason for anything if you don't know what you believe.

I smell my pillow again, breathing deep.

Your parents are dead. Your parents. Isn't that weird? Isn't that the most bizarre thing you've ever heard?

The dread and anger and utter sorrow I've kept in my stomach rise little by little until they hit my heart, and I sit up quickly, feeling a blind panic overtake me. It's like I'm being engulfed in a wave, or buried under dirt, or falling, falling, so fast I can't even reach out to grab something.

"Oh, fuck," I say out loud. "Damn it, damn it." My voice seems too loud, but I know from the pain in my throat that I'm barely whispering. "Mom and Dad," I say. "Mom and Dad. They're dead." I say it over and over, hoping it will feel real. But it doesn't. It isn't. I'm swallowed by a great darkness. I remember each memory of them, each touch and word. I remember how they smelled and how they laughed, how the light looked when it hit their eyes. I remember every joke and song, even every moment of lost temper, and it all comes together and adds to the tremendous weight on my chest.

And soon the pain is too much. And I cry because I know I will feel this pain for the rest of my life.

Chapter Three

I wake up to the dawn blasting through my east-facing window and setting all the orange of my room on fire. I remember Mom coming in here on such mornings to wake me up for school. She was the biggest jagoff about it, always bursting in and throwing open the curtains and yelling "It's morning!" as if I didn't already know. The obnoxiously bright sun reflected off the orange walls, which reflected off her coppery hair, which always tended towards dishevelment, and she looked like Anne of Green Gables or Pippi Longstocking. She sang a few bars of whatever song happened to be in her head and then clipped off cheerfully to Laura's room to give her the same treatment. Except Laura's room has only a north-facing window, and her walls are blue, so it never had the same effect.

This morning, I close my eyes and pretend that I'm sixteen, that if I stay in bed long enough, Mom will charge in to tell me I'm running late. I wait and wait. But she doesn't come. Then it all sinks in and that weight settles on my chest again until I can't breathe. The funeral, that sham of a party, is gone now, and normal life is here again. Except it's a normal I've never known before, never asked for, never wanted. It's a terrible new world, just similar enough to the old world to feel familiar, just different enough to feel alien. Like a bad dream where the sky is green and the grass is blue, and you know it's not quite right, but you can't scream, because you have no voice, because there's a weight on your chest. I get up quickly, hoping to dull the pain. I throw off the covers, put on my pajama pants, and trudge downstairs to the kitchen.

Theo has made coffee.

I've never lived in the house with Laura and Theo. They got married when I was still at school. Of course, when I came home for holidays they were here, but I considered those times more like visits than coming back home. I did wonder about how it worked to be married, very young, and in Laura's case, still in college, and to live with parents. I don't think I would really feel married living with my parents; I'd need a clean break. Also, I always wondered if it was weird, you know, having sex, with your parents in the next room, or if Laura and Theo timed it for when Mom and Dad were gone.

I've never asked Laura about this. In the past, I would have. In the past, we talked about every weird and awkward thing girls have to talk about. And girls have lots of weird and awkward things to talk about. But after she married Theo, I stopped asking her such personal things. It's not that I didn't want to know. It's not that I'm prudish or anything. It's just that we became different people. She now knew someone else so well and to try to be included in it felt too intrusive.

Okay, if I'm honest, it's because I judged her a little bit. Not for choosing Theo; I love Theo Carlin from the bottom of my heart. We've known him all our lives. His mom, Stacy, was best friends with our mom back in the early 90s, when Mom and Dad first moved into our house. Growing up, Theo was like our big brother, our best friend. We were all there for him and his dad, David, when Stacy betrayed them and the rest of us, meeting some guy on the internet and leaving for Seattle out of the blue and never coming back. We were there when David got really sick just before Theo graduated from high school and died soon after. There was never a line where our business ended and Theo's began; he was always just there, always a part of us, us a part of him.

When Theo started liking Laura as more than a friend, I was the first one he admitted it to and I was thrilled. It seemed like the perfect way to keep our little group together. Even when they started dating, back when Laura and I were in high school and Theo was just starting college at Catawba, it was never awkward or weird. I never felt like the third wheel. I was excited to see them get married and for us all to go off and conquer the world and do exciting things.

Then Laura decided to go to college at Catawba, with him. Here. And to be a teacher. Here. And they got engaged and married when we were twenty-one. And they moved in with Mom and Dad. Here. And I was bursting forth into the world, or at least Pittsburgh, which is the next best thing, and I was going somewhere and being someone and doing something, and I was doing all of it alone. Because they had suddenly decided that it was better here.

I know I'm being unfair because, except for the past few days, they're extremely happy with their life. I'm being unfair, because they never promised me that we'd all get out of Haven and make something of ourselves. I know this. Everything has turned out exactly as they planned. They wanted to work and save and buy a house of their own in cash next summer.

Maybe I'm not upset with how everything turned out for them. Maybe I'm just upset that they are content with it.

Whatever beef I have with Theo's life choices, his coffee is amazing. I pour myself a cup and rustle through the fridge for some cream to tinge it with. I wonder what containers of food were cooked and packed by Mom, what item of produce was the last thing Dad put in a shopping cart. The cream is the only safe thing because Theo is the only one who uses it. Theo and me.

"Morning," Theo says, coming into the kitchen from the mudroom. We're in the back of the house, which faces east like my room, but there's only a tiny window in the mudroom, and it cuts down the dawn into something more manageable. He looks rested, with only a slight glassiness suggesting exhaustion in his gray eyes. His thick dark hair is just a little too long on the top, combed neatly to one side. There's a shadow of stubble on his face, making his thick eyebrows even more pronounced and his eye sockets seem shadowed.

"Morning," I answer.

"Breakfast? I'm making eggs." His voice is as solid, cheerful, good-natured as ever.

"Please."

He goes over to the stove and gets out a frying pan, gathers the butter and egg carton, fishes a spatula from the drawer. "Did you sleep well?"

"Really well. Oddly enough." I leave out the part about the massive weight in my chest, the blind panic that is only currently being staved off with coffee and this conversation.

"Me too."

"Is Laura still asleep?"

"Yeah." He lets the butter melt in the pan, spreading it around with the tip of the spatula.

The room fills with a warm, salty smell. "She was really tired. Not feeling well. She'll probably stay in bed most of the day."

"Should we let her do that?"

"What else is there to do?"

He has a point. She can't go back to work for at least a few weeks, not with the way she's been taking it all. Haven Elementary School can't exactly have a Kindergarten teacher breaking down in the middle of snack time. But to get up and get dressed and eat, all to sit in your parents' house and think about how said parents died a few days ago in a freak accident, before brushing your teeth and putting on your pajamas and going to sleep again; it all seems so pointless. Suddenly, my day looks very bleak.

There's the panic again.

"I... don't believe it," I say to Theo. My nose fills with the smell of frying eggs. That terrible dread grips my chest and stomach and it won't let go.

He nods. "I know. I know." He turns the eggs, a little crisp on the outside, onto two plates, and hands me one. We eat silently for a few moments.

"How are you?" he asks. "You've been quiet the past few days."

"Would you like me to recite a poem?"

"No. I just think... I know you've been trying to help Laura out and I'm trying to help you out."

"Who's helping *you* out?" I ask.

"How are you?" he says again.

My heart pounds, and with each beat, a crescendo of fear beats against my body. I keep eating, but the food makes me feel sick. I am about to answer him with something dismissive, but then my gaze is drawn to the other end of the table, where the two urns sit, casually, as if in a conference with one another.

"What the hell," I say, "are those doing in the *kitchen*?"

Theo gasps sharply. "I don't know. Aunt Maeve must have put them there last night."

Last night is a fog in my head. I don't remember the journey home from the funeral at all. Aunt Maeve must have taken us home from the funeral. "Did we have them in the car with us?"

"We must have."

I know it's silly. The urns aren't corpses. But suddenly I feel so sick I can't look at food anymore. I push back my plate and set a napkin over it, turning my head away from Theo so I don't have to watch him eat.

"Do you want me to put them in the dining room?" he asks.

"Yes, please." This is stupid. I stared at the urns all yesterday at the funeral home and at the church. They're just pots. I know this. But I can't let go of the thought that this is the first time the ashes made of cells and skin and DNA have been in the house since Thursday night, and then they were all put together, breathing and thinking and being.

Theo gets up and gathers the urns, holding one in each of his large hands. I close my eyes as he passes by me into the dining room. He comes back into the kitchen and washes his hands before sitting back down.

"Thanks," I muster.

"No problem."

"It's stupid of me."

"No, it's not."

There's a sudden sound of Laura walking around in the bedroom above us. Her footsteps come out of the bedroom and go into the bathroom, and after a few minutes of running water, her footsteps come back out of the bathroom and begin to descend the stairs. Once she gets to the bottom, she turns to come down the hall into the kitchen.

"Morning," she says. She looks awful. She looks how I feel. Her long, reddish-brown waves are pulled up in a messy bun, and there are purplish half-moons under her green eyes. Her already fair Irish skin looks dull and pale.

"Morning," I answer. "How are you?"

She looks at us curiously as she sits. "What's going on?" she asks as Theo rises to get her

a plate.

"What do you mean?" I ask.

"You both look upset. What's up?"

"Well." That's a loaded question.

"Fine. Never mind."

"Sleep well?" I ask.

"Pretty well." She takes a plate of toast from Theo. "You should've woken me up," she says to him. "I wouldn't have slept so long."

"I wanted to let you rest." He sits down again.

I've had many breakfasts in this room, at this table, staring at the kelly-green subway tiles on the walls for over two decades. The ones Dad always wanted to replace because they were dated, to which Mom said, "But they're green for our Irish heritage! And I thought you liked old things!" They had this exchange about every two weeks or so. One time, Dad came back from Home Depot with tile samples in various shades of gray and taupe, paint chips in muted gray-greens.

"See," he said. "We can still have a green kitchen. Just updated."

"But I thought you liked old, ugly things!" Mom said again. Round and round they went. I never remember my parents really fighting about anything serious, which is incredibly lucky. They did, however, get in heated debates about stupid things. What time, exactly, did the sun set that day, who had eaten the last piece of cake, what kitchen color scheme better reflected a love for Ireland *and* antiquity. But their fights weren't really fights; they were just banter. We all knew that Mom would never let Dad update the kitchen and that Dad would never stop trying. We all knew that they fought over stupid things because there was nothing serious to fight about. Because they were best friends, and best friends fight about trivial things, because they agree on all the important stuff.

All those stories we have of them. A person's life has so many stories, five ones we don't know for each one we can tell. Until one day, one night, all the stories end. "I miss them," I say suddenly. My voice surprises me.

Theo and Laura pause. Theo nods sympathetically. Laura finishes her last bite of toast.

"Do you," she says.

I look at her, incredulous. "Of course I do."

"You haven't cried once."

"What?"

"You've shown no remorse whatsoever."

"*What?*"

"Throughout the whole funeral, you were a cardboard cutout who went to the bar the first chance you got."

My mouth hangs open.

"Honey," Theo says. His voice is gentle, sorrowful. But there's grit to it, the kind of edge he uses when people don't know what they're talking about.

I shake my head. "You think I'm not sad my parents are dead?" My voice gathers steam.

"What the hell? How can you say that?"

"I'm sure you are sad. But you could at least try to be helpful."

"How haven't I been helpful?"

Laura pushes her plate aside. "You were never here, Amy. You left us. You acted like this big shot, big city woman, going off and making it in the world, forgetting all about us in our piddly little town."

"I didn't forget you! I—"

"And then you come back and act all cavalier, chatting with people and partying it up at the reception."

I laugh, utterly shocked at how idiotic this sounds. "I was trying to keep everything together! Which is more than you can say for yourself!"

"You made us look bad! In front of everyone at church."

"*I* made us look bad?"

"I can't believe how you treated them."

"Who, the church people? I don't give a flying fuck."

"Mom and Dad! For months, they tried to include you, to do stuff with you, but you didn't give them the time of day!"

"I was *busy*!"

"Oh, oh right. *So* busy. Like I said, big shot city woman."

"I'm living my life, Laura! I'm sorry that it makes you feel bad, but it doesn't mean I didn't love my parents!"

Theo covers his face with his hands. "Honey," he says again.

"You didn't call her back," Laura says.

"What?"

"Last week. They wanted to meet with you. You didn't call them back."

"Are you saying this is all *my* fault? Are you really saying that?"

"I'm saying that maybe if you had just called her back—"

"What? If I had called Mom back, they would have rearranged their plans and not gone out on a drive? They'd have let the car rest, saved up some gas money? Bullshit. This isn't my fault; don't put this on me!"

"You're so selfish! And you've always been so selfish!"

And just like that, the wave of guilt—yes, guilt, Laura, that thing you don't think I have—hits me, and I am crumpled like a wad of tinfoil. "You lived with them, Laura! You lived with them, and you didn't tell them to stay in that night, tell them to watch a movie with you, or whatever shit you think I should have done. Tell me again how selfish I am!"

I walk upstairs to the sound of my sister sobbing and Theo whispering. The voice in my head perpetually chants *I'm sorry I'm sorry I'm sorry*, and another voice says: *You're a piece of shit.*

In my room, I find my duffle bag on the floor under my black funeral dress. I never considered myself a messy person, but during the past few days, my mind has been scattered, and so has everything I own. Everything I do. Everything I say.

I knew coming back here would make me like this. I knew I'd feel cramped and convoluted and not myself. I want to get in my car and drive and drive and drive, to a place where every single tree isn't familiar, where I can look at a house and not know who lives there. I want to go where there aren't so many hills that strangle and suffocate, where I can see more than a mile in any given direction. Maybe I'll forego Pittsburgh altogether. Maybe I'll just keep driving into Ohio, into Indiana, into Illinois.

I pack the wrinkled black dress and my smattering of clothes. I make the bed and put on jeans and my favorite flannel shirt, the white and blue striped plaid that feels like a blanket. My hair is a mess, so I put some oil on my hands and smooth it over before throwing my curls up in a ponytail. In the mirror, I stare into my own eyes: Dad's dark brown tinged with Mom's bronze-green, which I was always so proud of as the perfect mixing of them, the perfect half-and-half. Her feist, his humor. Her fire, his earth. Now, looking into my own eyes makes me so ashamed.

Yes, Laura's assumption that I'm not really sad about Mom and Dad is crazy, but some of the stuff she said is true. I really have been acting like a big-city career woman, something no fact-checker at a Pittsburgh publishing house should ever do. I'm just a random, unknown soul in a random, unknown apartment in a maze of a city, a speck of dust in one of many layers of strata. I didn't want to visit; she's right. But it was because I didn't want to come back to Haven, not because I didn't want to come back to my family. I like the anonymity of a city; the very thing everyone derides cities for. I like being able to invent a new self, to be in a place where people don't know me or my parents or my grandparents or great-grandparents, where I can tell someone I'm Irish and Scottish, or that I have a twin, or that I'm actually kinda/sorta/was a Christian, and this information is brand new information, a fresh, never-before-seen identity that fascinates people. I can fascinate my roommates, acquaintances, coworkers. I can't fascinate anyone in Haven. So there it is: I'm just a huge narcissist. Great.

I go to the bathroom and brush my teeth, wash my face, brush on some mascara and powder. I dump my toiletries in the duffle bag. Then I stand at the top of the stairs and take a deep breath. All the unclaimed beliefs in my head jumble together, and there's a sudden, quiet assurance of one of them peeling off the table, presenting itself to me. I accept it and take it in.

God is real.

So there, one new thing I've decided to believe. Hooray. God help me. You could have picked a better time for this, you know. I swing the duffle bag over my shoulder, turn the corner at the bottom of the stairs, and head down the hall to the kitchen. I pause in the doorway, and see Theo and Laura still at the table. Laura's bent over the table, her head in her arms. Theo rubs her back. He looks up at me and raises an eyebrow, draws his mouth in a tight line. It's an expression of his I know well. He understands me, but he also thinks I'm an idiot.

I clear my throat. "I'm... leaving. I know you think I'm selfish, and maybe you're right. But I didn't mean to miss her call. God, if I could go back and answer it again, I would. I've thought a lot about that, even if you don't think so." Neither of them says anything. She keeps crying, more softly now. I want to tell her exactly how I feel: that I have the weight of a thousand tons on my chest, wave after wave of dread hitting me every second. I want to tell her that I still don't believe it's really happened, that I still feel them here, just around every corner, their breath in every breeze. I want to tell her that this fucked-up town is playing with us all, and with each moment we're getting absorbed into it, further and further, and if we don't leave now, we won't make it out alive.

"Well... goodbye." I turn and walk back down the hall. I slip on my boots and put on my hat and coat and open the front door, emerald green-painted wood surrounding an oval of beveled glass that casts tiny rainbows on my skin.

"Wait!" Laura's voice calls from the kitchen, and there's a clatter of chairs on tile and the smacking of her feet against the floor. She stands in the doorway, where I'm sure the floor is still warm from my feet.

We look at each other across the length of the hall. I stand in the door, black boots on my feet, knit hat on my head, my duffle bag slung over one shoulder, and I notice how eerily light the bag is, almost useless.

45

"Please don't go," Laura says. "Not yet."

She looks up at me. I think it's the first time I've seen her whole face, turned toward me or really anyone else since I got here. It's not bent down toward the earth, hidden under the shadow of her hair, covered with a veneer of tears, or awninged by the hood of a raincoat. No, her face is up and out, with her small, pointed chin, nose full of freckles, the green eyes that change shade ten times a minute, the soft dark brows that seem perpetually raised just a touch, as if always asking me to explain myself, to defend myself, and the wry pink mouth that tells me no matter what I say, I am forgiven, if not a little laughed at. For a moment I see my sister again. I see a little sliver of who she was, of who I was with her. I want to be that person again.

"Okay," I say. Before I can say anything else.

Hannah Allman Kennedy

Chapter Four

I don't know what happens to me in the days that follow the funeral, but something disconnects. I can't remember any of my responsibilities: my job and apartment in the city, student loan payments, bills. They all fall out of my head, and in their place is an emptiness which is impregnable, and cannot—will not—be filled with anything. Because of this empty space, whole periods of time are disembodied from each other, until I can't tell what I'm currently doing, or what I was doing just before that. I find myself in bed each night wondering what I did that day. I see myself each morning in the bathroom mirror, brushing my teeth, and don't remember waking up. I find myself eating (or at least trying to eat) breakfast, wondering how I got down to the kitchen. I sit in front of the TV with Laura and watch shows, and even though they're in English with actors I recognize, I can't remember their names or even understand their lines.

I'm alive, but I have no cognizance of living.

I know our grandparents are here every day, hovering around like a group of sad hummingbirds. At some point, Aunt Maeve goes back home for work and tells us she'll call, but I don't remember if she ever does call. I know Aunt Sophie comes over every few days and brings takeout Chinese and McDonald's, but I don't remember eating these meals; I just see the leftovers in the fridge and wonder how they got there. When Grandad George, Grandma Nancy, and Nanna Mae come to visit, they walk through the house back and forth, getting us things we don't need and whipping up food we don't eat. I wonder if they're trying to absorb the essence of Mom and Dad before it fades away: touching each wall, hoping their fingerprints overlap with Mom's or Dad's from weeks ago; breathing in the scent of the house deeply, ingesting the last molecules of skin cells or pheromones. I think we all do this. It's a kind of communion.

Of course, there's always the simple explanation that our grandparents hang around because they want us to be okay. This would certainly explain why they suddenly spring back to life a week after the funeral, like pictures in a pop-up book, unnaturally colorful and exciting and overwhelming. Nanna Mae, Mom's mom, after becoming so quiet and brooding at the funeral, is back to her normal practice of coming over with a roast or meatloaf and handing us new prayer cards and rosaries every time we see her. Dad's parents are similarly affected: When Grandma Nancy isn't at our house, she takes day trips to Erie and comes back with a lot of gifts from TJ Maxx. Grandad George has remained steady, checking in and asking caring questions and suspiciously inquiring about all the new prayer cards and rosaries. He's always suspected Nanna Mae of trying to convert us to Catholicism.

Of course, none of us have had any heart-to-hearts or talked about our feelings. We don't have the energy for that. But there's an unspoken hope that if we just take care of the practical needs, just bide our time, the terrible hole torn into our lives will knit back together, stitch by stitch. But I see the cracks, in the little scraps of vision I remember before they fade away into the black hole in my brain. I see the twitches of sobs around Nanna Mae's mouth, and the little checks of regret on Grandma Nancy's face because she put yet another shopping trip on the credit card, and the dullness in Grandad George's eyes, which are usually crackling with blue electricity. I feel guilty that they can be so busy, so productive, in the midst of their grief, while I can barely get out of bed to sit on the couch and get off the couch to go to bed. I can't even be productive internally; I don't know what I believe or who I am, and I can't sort out all the shit that's happened, because there aren't any boxes in my mind for them. There's just one, flat, bland table, and one measly belief that God is real, with little more to hang onto. I can't even pray.

Then, of course, there's Laura, who isn't herself at all. Theo is the only person who's actually somewhat normal: no false cheerfulness, no crippling grief, no shopaholism or excessive religious gestures. He's steady as always: saying what needs to be said, doing what needs to be done, letting people feel what they need to feel. He goes to get food when we've run out, he pays the bills, he eventually returns to work. I'm glad, in these moments, that Laura married him, even if I wasn't always glad of it. In our family portrait of *The Last Supper,* he is Jesus indeed.

For as empty as my brain is during this time, the pressure on my chest is ever-present, and I feel constantly nauseated by it, wave after wave of blind panic. It makes it difficult for me to sleep, to wake up, and impossible for me to eat. The few clothes I brought have become loose on me, and I've started revisiting some clothes from high school still left in my closet.

One night I go into their room. No one's been in there since the Terrible Friday. On that day, the day Laura spent huddled on the couch while the police asked us questions and our grandparents filtered in and out to cry and make funeral arrangements, there was one moment when I went upstairs to put my duffle bag on my bed. I got up the stairs and turned the corner, swinging unconsciously from the smooth top column of the banister, and I realized how difficult it would be to get to my room. Because on one end of the hall was the bathroom and Theo and Laura's room, and on the other end of the hall was my room, and in between those two poles was the door to Mom and Dad's room.

I didn't go in. I reached over the threshold and pulled the door shut. There was the little suction sound that always happened when shutting the door to their room, the combination of wood brushing over carpet, and the airflow of the room being disturbed. I shut that door, and none of us opened it again. Ever since, Laura and Theo and I have gone back and forth past that door, all knowing why we aren't opening it. Because as long as the door is shut, the room still belongs to Mom and Dad, and we can keep pretending that they are there, inside the room that was just as they left it. Not dead, only sleeping.

But one night, I don't know exactly which day, sometime after Laura and Theo have gone to bed, I can't stand it anymore. I have to go into Mom and Dad's room. I keep feeling that they are there, keep hearing the faintest footsteps in between each of my breaths as I lie in bed. I sneak down the hall and carefully, quietly, open the door and flick on the lights.

The bed is made. There's a little pile of Dad's dirty laundry in front of the closet as usual, the ever-present pile of note papers on Mom's nightstand, the windows open just a crack to let in fresh air, the gauzy white curtains floating up and down with the breeze, making the room cold, probably racking up our heating bill. The last lipstick that touched Mom's lips, her favorite combination of bright red and spicy orange, is on the vanity, the last shoes Dad took off thrown under the bed. Their room is just as they left it, days ago, weeks ago. It seems so normal, like I always remembered, like it used to be when I was small and came in here to take naps because their bed was always so comfy.

I tiptoe across the room cautiously, feeling like I did when I was eight and snuck in here to try on Mom's jewelry, only for her to somehow discover me each time. I walk over to the bed now, and sniff the pillows, breathing in the scent of Mom's lavender lotion and hairspray, Dad's minty shampoo and Polo cologne. And it all comes flooding back so vividly, and I remember every time I kissed her cheek, and every time I hugged him, and these memories compress into such intense, physical pain, that I double over and collapse onto the bed, convulsing into such sobbing that I feel I might be torn apart. I take their pillows and hug them desperately, breathing into them and crying and crying. Somewhere in the back of my mind is the knowledge that by doing this, I am ruining Laura's chance to smell these pillows too, to see the room the way they left it too, but I don't care enough to stop.

I fall asleep at some point and wake up because of the cold. The night is late, and even with the lights on, I feel eerie. Once when I was young, an older lady at church, one of the uber-spiritual Christian hippies who believed that everything bad that happened to you was caused by a demon, told me that the spiritual realm is most alive at 2 a.m. I don't know why she would tell a child this, and when it caused me a slew of nightmares which Mom and Dad had to deal with, they laughed it off and told me not to listen to this particular titan of the faith (and, I suspect, politely told this particular titan of the faith to go suck an egg). But that thought stuck with me, all through college when I was up late partying or studying, every time I was driving home at night, every time I couldn't get to sleep. Whenever I was awake for 2 a.m., I became paranoid about what might happen, about what I might see: a ghost, or demon, or angel, or some combination of the three. Even after letting go of the faith I grew up with, even after deciding I didn't know if I believed in a spiritual realm anymore, I couldn't, can't, let go of that idea. It's a habit now. 2 a.m. I begin to shiver uncontrollably, but I don't dare get under the covers, because I can't stay in this room anymore. It's giving me the creeps.

I get up and go to the window next to Mom's nightstand. I reach up and pull the windowpane down, shutting out the night, shutting out the cold. One last whoosh of air blows inward, scattering the papers on the nightstand. I bend down and gather them up. They're a bunch of notes from one of Mom's note pads, which she was always scribbling reminders and lists on, trying to organize the fleeting thoughts running through her head. Once I've composed the papers into a pile and set them on the nightstand again, I turn to leave, and out of the corner of my eye, in the split second it takes to turn around, I see the shadow of a person in front of Mom's vanity mirror, a sudden glint of brownish-red. My heart is in my mouth before I can make sense of what I see, and the thing is gone before I can let out a gasp.

I feel cold from the crown of my head to my toes. The bedside clock ticks away, too loud and too faint at the same time. 2:15 a.m. I was just seeing things. I'm tired. I'm paranoid. I hurry out of the room as quietly as possible, shutting the door behind me almost all the way before sticking my arm inside and switching off the lights, cursing that old church lady, who I think is dead now.

Days pass. My mind is sucked into that black hole, all my obligations and responsibilities faded away and forgotten. I don't remember to check into work but have a vague sense of guilt that I should do something. I don't keep in touch with my friends or roommates. I've deleted all the apps off my phone, but don't remember doing that either. I get lots of calls, but I send them all to voicemail, and then delete the voicemails. There's a string of texts from my best friend from college, Joy, who couldn't come to the funeral because she was tied up with grad school in California.

Thinking of you.

How are you feeling?

Praying for you. Love you.

Let me know if you want to talk.

It's okay not to be okay.

One day, she calls me, and I'm so startled by the sound of the phone that I answer.

"How are you?" She asks. "I'm so sorry I couldn't come."

"It's okay. You didn't need to."

"What do you need? How can I help?" Her voice is full of care, but everything feels off. I can't read her tone; I can't make sense of anything.

"I'm fine. Just getting through it."

"I'm going to come visit the moment I can."

"You don't have to."

"I'll come for Thanksgiving and Christmas."

"Don't bother." I hang up on her, without really knowing why. Everything is too much, too loud and bright and confusing.

I met Joy in school when we randomly became roommates, and we hit it off immediately. She was a dance major: unique, independent, and quirky; the perfect manic-pixie hipster artist girl. A part of me, I think, was in love with her. She grew up in Pittsburgh and was also the daughter of Christian parents, but her upbringing was a little different; her church and community not as black-and-white, not as sheltered, as mine. When I began emptying everything out on the table, when I grew angry, when I neither believed nor disbelieved anything, her faith stayed calm and unbothered. She was still my friend through it all, and the relationship flourished even when my relationships with everything else died away.

I know she wants to help me. I know she's the safest person in my life right now, someone I could tell everything to. I know California isn't so far away; that if I asked her, today, to drop everything and come, she would. But something keeps me from doing that. Joy knows what she believes. She knows if she prays, someone cares enough to listen. Right now, there are too many people in my life who are certain of that, so I don't really want to talk to another one. All I know is that if I pray, there's someone there who could potentially listen, but I don't know if that someone cares enough to act, or is even able to act, and this enrages me.

At some point, I turn off my phone and put it in the underwear drawer of my childhood dresser, under a pile of bras that haven't fit me since high school. I block out the noise of all the things I should do, all the people I should respond to. I am both keyed-up with anxiety, and numb, dull to any sense of action. I don't remember what it's like to not feel that panic in my chest, which dissolves every thought and feeling into a single, pressing weight.

One morning, after Theo has gone to work and I've barely swallowed down another breakfast alone while waiting for Laura to wake up, I can't take it anymore. I feel so sick with panic that I have to do something. I leave the house and get in my Subaru, which I parked haphazardly in front of the house on that Terrible Friday, and which hasn't been touched since.

I almost forget how to drive, but true to my mental state in the past few days, I soon find myself driving through downtown Haven automatically, with no memory of any of the streets I took to get here. It's a rainy, overcast day, saturated with chill and moisture, as if the air is quietly weeping. I find myself taking the road out of town, south, which winds its way up sloping hills to a plateau of smooth farmland, the only semblance of flatness we get up here in the Alleghenies. After a few miles, I hit the intersection of 322 and Frasier Church Road, where there's an unexpected explosion of civilization: a grocery store, a Sheetz, our dying mall put in by some 1980s developers who intended to bring a little culture to the Haven area, and who succeeded until about ten years ago. There's only a fabric store and a Chinese restaurant in the mall now; the rest of the store spaces are occupied by an ever-changing roster of pop-up flea markets and seasonal gift shops. At Christmastime, Santa greets children in the abandoned Sears.

I go on through the intersection, and the area turns rural again quickly; soon I am out in the middle of nowhere, the road curving through forests and sharp hills, ancient farmhouses, and rickety, overgrown mobile homes. I follow the road past all its intersections, as it gets narrower and narrower. About a mile after I pass the eponymous Frasier Church—a weathered white, one-room building leaning slightly to the side, but still hosting a regular congregation each week, planted by the first group of Methodists who came here in the 1870s— the road turns from pavement, then to gravel, then to dirt. The last leg of the road has a sign, cautioning me that I am now on private property. I pass a giant wooden barn that hasn't been occupied in years, the foundations of a brick house next to it. I keep going. The trees get thicker, thousands of fall colors punctuated by dark evergreens. The road curves down to the left, suddenly and sharply, and I know I'm here. Just before the turn, I pull off to the right as much as possible, avoiding the deeply rutted ditches on each side.

I get out of my car quickly. The past hour of my memory has come in short bursts, but now I feel terribly present, terribly calm, and conscious. There's the expectant feeling in the air, halfway between an inhale and an exhale. It's cold. I pull my red wool coat tight and tie the belt around my waist. I don't even remember grabbing my coat, but I'm glad I did. It takes the edge off the cold and matches the maple leaves that pave the earth, wet with the misting rain. All the leaves are brilliant, the yellows and reds and oranges and browns all mouthwateringly rich, even under the overcast sky.

I cross the dirt road to the edge, which is rutted from the heavy machinery they used to pull the car up. I steady myself against a tree and look down. The earth falls away below my feet, carpeted with a heavy layer of multicolored leaves, save for one deep, dark rut carved into the hillside. At the bottom, many yards down, there's a big patch of disturbed earth, crushed trees, a chunk taken out of an oak. I follow the road down on foot, barely able to keep my balance on the steep grade, going from tree to tree for stability. Finally, at the bottom, the road goes on through the forest, toward the waterfall, which I can't see, but can hear. I make my way through the brush, which is usually thick, but is bare and spindly now. I stand in front of the patch of earth, where the car came to its final resting place. The police combed this area thoroughly, I know. But there wasn't much for them to find: just two people in an SUV that didn't make the turn.

I expect this place to make me emotional. I expect to break down crying, as I wonder which tree was the last thing Mom saw, or which rock happened to catch Dad's eye as the car went down. But I don't break down; I don't cry. I just see. I just am. Breathe in. The breeze blowing through the brush, the rustle of leaves. Breathe out. The cold, pale sky, the warm, bright colors of the woods. Breathe in. The deep ruts in the mud, the splinters of trees, a young pine bent in two. Breathe out. The beating of wings, the cooing of an owl. Breathe in.

"Can I help you?" someone asks. I whirl around and find a man behind me, in his sixties, balding and lean, a weathered look to his face. He's dressed in equally weathered jeans, a flannel jacket, orange baseball cap, heavy boots. His face is folded into a suspicious expression. I notice a pickup truck parked behind him, on the bank of the creek, and I wonder why I didn't see it before.

"Oh, hi. No," I stammer, backing up a few paces. "I just… I'm, I'm the daughter." I gesture to the flattened patch of brush, the thick track cut into the hillside. "Well, one of the daughters, I mean."

"This is private property," he says, crossing his arms.

"I know. I'm sorry. I just…" Before I know it, I'm sobbing, and on the third contraction of my lungs, I become so weak in the knees I drop to the wet, muddy ground. The man watches me for a moment, which is embarrassing. I clear my throat violently, trying to get it together. I was trying to figure everything out. I was trying to find a clue, a sign, that this was all part of some fantastical story, that if they had to be dead, there was a good reason. But I was so foolishly wrong: there's nothing to figure out. There's no great conspiracy, no great mystery. They weren't special. They were just two ordinary people, who are dead now, and the world won't remember them. They will never be as important to the world as they were to me.

"Listen," the man has walked toward me a few paces and touches my shoulder lightly. "Listen, I'm sorry. I really am. But you shouldn't be here. No one should be. If people hadn't started coming here..." He mercifully cuts off, but I know what he was going to say: if Mom and Dad hadn't been where they weren't supposed to be, they would still be alive.

"They loved the waterfall," I say, trying to explain it to him, trying to defend them, trying to justify everything to myself. I gesture past him, toward the hushed roar that echoes through this little valley.

"Lots of people do," says the man. I know he's a Frasier, the owner of this land, the descendant of post-Civil War Methodists, but I forget his first name. "But I can't be letting everyone in. I just can't. Sometimes people fish, and I used to have no problem with that. But there were troublemakers, too. People doing drugs. Drinking. Poachers. I just can't let everyone in anymore."

I get up, feeling terribly childish. I look him in the eye, and as much as I want to, I can't fault him. "I'm sorry," I say.

"I'm sorry," he echoes. Despite his gruff demeanor, I know he means it.

I turn and walk back up the steep hill to my car, a sharp pain in my diaphragm. Before I know it, I'm in the car again, backing slowly up the hill, turning around in the driveway that used to belong to the farmhouse.

When I return to the house, Theo is still gone and Laura is still asleep, my absence making no ripple whatsoever in their life. As the days pass, I don't tell them that I left or where I went. I feel the keen pain of embarrassment and disappointment, as well as the defiance of being unnoticed. And so on it goes: the fog, the grief, the unaccounted-for time.

Chapter Five

I'm driving my Subaru through downtown Haven. It's nighttime, and all the buildings are dark. The vast network of stars overhead mirrors the warm glow of the streetlights. I stop at an intersection, right at the corner where the empty old bank building, the tallest structure in Haven, sits across from a park that used to be a city block. I look over to the next lane to my left, and there's a bright blue SUV, playing loud music, Mom and Dad in the front seats.

Frantically, I roll down my window. "Hey!" I scream. "Wait!" They can't hear me, don't even look at me. The light turns green, and they speed on ahead, through town, due south, towards the mall, the wilderness, the waterfall. I hit the gas pedal, but my car won't accelerate. I hit the horn and keep screaming, "Wait!" I watch them disappear from view, across the bridge over the Allegheny, winding through the streets of Haven until the car is just a blue speck on the edge of the uneven Pennsylvania horizon.

Finally, the gas works. I speed through town, the route I think they would take. But I can't find them. There are no other cars, no other people, in the entire town. I'm completely alone. I drive out into the countryside, up the hills to the wide plateau, and it grows terribly dark. One by one the stars burn out. The land, miles upon miles of flattened farm fields, is black and silent as the sky above it until I can't tell which is the earth and which is the sky, and I am caught between them. They press me together like a vise, tightening and tightening.

Then I wake up. *I'm sorry I'm sorry I'm sorry.*

The panic in my chest throbs, because I don't know what day it is, or what year it is, or how old I am. I don't know how long I've been sleeping in my old bed every night. I don't remember the last time I looked at a calendar. I bound out of bed and dig through the underwear drawer with the old bras. I turn on my phone, but it flashes the dead battery signal, so then I search my purse, my duffle bag, the few possessions I have scattered around, until I find the charger. I plug it in and tremble while waiting for the phone to boot up. Eight a.m., October 27th. A Saturday. Three weeks and a day after the Terrible Friday. My phone has dozens of missed calls, and just as many unread texts, and hundreds of unopened emails. My mind scrambles. Should I be working today? Have I paid my cell phone bill? When is rent due? How much money do I have in my bank account? Did I use my credit card? Did I miss a deadline on a student loan payment?

I toss my phone onto the carpet. It bounces and lands a few feet away, undamaged. I pull off my pajamas and circle around the room naked, feeling the chilly air of an autumn morning in an old house lap up my skin. I make the bed, straightening the blankets and fluffing the pillows. I get dressed. My clothing choices are sparse: jeans I think are relatively clean, a gray tee shirt I know is not. I need to go to Pittsburgh and grab more clothes. I need to reemerge into the world, to move. I pick up my phone again and see that the texts are mostly from Joy and a few other friends. There are a handful from my two roommates, Abbie and Becca; several from my boss, Chelsea. I scroll quickly through the voicemails. All from the same people, with a few spam calls threatening to cancel my vehicle's registration or discontinue my social security number. Hell, maybe they're not spam. I don't know anymore.

Downstairs, Theo and Laura are having a quiet breakfast. Laura seems fragile, as usual, and looks as if she can barely hold her fork.

"I'm heading to Pittsburgh," I say. "To get my clothes."

She looks up at me. Her eyes are suspicious. "Are you okay?"

I shift from foot to foot. I feel so antsy. I need to move. "Yeah, I just have a million things to do. I have to look at my finances, pay rent, see how much money's in my checking account. I need to check-in at work."

"You haven't checked in to work at all?" Theo asks.

I stare at him silently, a wave of panic engulfing me. He's right. Damn it, he's right.

What have I been doing? Where is my brain? What's wrong with me?

59

"Hey, don't worry about anything," he says, calmly and evenly. "We can help out. Just let us know what you need."

"I don't know. I need… I need to go to Pittsburgh and sort everything out."

"Are you staying there for good?" Laura asks.

I avoid her gaze. "You asked me to be here for a while. I'm just getting more clothes." I don't want to explain more; I want her to know how I feel and what I mean. I don't want to have to hold her hand through every painful exchange of information. I need to go.

"Why don't you check in with work and your roommates, and let us know what you decide?" Theo asks, good-naturedly. He always pretends a tense moment isn't tense at all. It's infuriating, but also very nice. "You're, of course, welcome for as long as you want. If that works."

I don't know if that works, if I want it to work. I don't know anything but that I need to go, to get out of this three-week-long fog and get back into the world, at least for a day, at least to clear my head. "Yeah, of course. That sounds good."

"Why don't I come with you?" Laura asks. "I can help you pack up some clothes. I can help drive."

I'm taken aback by this. "It's fine. I can go alone."

"You shouldn't make a big drive like that yourself."

I don't know if she's trying to be nice, or if she's trying to make sure I come back, by effectively letting herself be kidnapped if I don't. As much as I want to resist, the idea of making that drive alone does, I have to admit, give me anxiety.

"Okay, if you'd like to go, I'm leaving in a few minutes."

"Do you want me to come too?" Theo asks.

"No," we say together, without meaning to. Theo laughs, feigning a look of hurt, and the house seems startled by the laugh; it hasn't heard one in such a long time.

We leave Haven and set off, first west and then south, west some more, and then hit I-79 and shoot down the length of Western Pennsylvania. My car passes hills and farms and forests, all mirroring the area around Haven. Everything here looks the same, and yet different enough to be somewhat interesting. I've traveled this route many times throughout my childhood and college years, but my heart still swells with the beauty of the Pennsylvania countryside: the contrast of buttery yellow leaves and dark brown tree trunks, the myriad shades of brown grass, the rich red barns and autumn berries, the familiar abandoned farmhouse leaning to one side in a perfect rhombus, the dozens of tiny junkyards filled with forgotten cars hollowed out and riddled with rust. I am calmer now; assured that the world isn't just Haven in its river valley, our street, our house, my room. The panic in my chest softens. I breathe full breaths for the first time all day, maybe the first time in three weeks.

"So," I venture to Laura, who's been mostly silent so far. "How are you?"

She looks at me.

I try another question. "How did you sleep last night?"

"Fine, I guess."

"Do you have trouble falling asleep? Or staying asleep? Or do you have nightmares?" I don't know why I'm chattering so much.

She waves her hand at me like one might wave to a fly or stray dog or irritating child. "Shh. Please, I have a headache."

"Are you hungover?"

She glares at me with a ferocity I'm surprised to see, on account of the headache. "I'm never hungover."

"You've been drunk before, though, right?"

"Nope."

"Do you drink?"

She rolls her eyes and fiddles with the inside panel of the car door. "Yes, I do occasionally. I'm just not an idiot about it. You know this."

"I just wasn't sure if you'd started the Pastor Jeff program for non-alcoholic consumption."

"Alcoholism runs in Pastor Jeff's family. That's why he doesn't drink."

"Yes, I know."

"It's not because he judges people who drink; he just doesn't do it himself."

"I know."

"Then why are you asking me such asinine questions?" She glares at me again.

"You didn't have to come with me."

"I know. I wanted to."

"Do you still want to?"

She sighs. "Well, it's too late to worry about that now." She fiddles with the radio, hooking up her phone to the Bluetooth. "How did *you* sleep?" she asks, once the sound system has started playing the intricate notes of the first Fleet Foxes album. I forgot we had the same taste in music.

"Fine." I can't even remember how I slept last night. I can't even remember which night last night was.

"Good."

The music, the soft ringing sound of the car speeding down the highway, the feel of the road in the steering wheel, my pulse pounding. "Can I ask you something?" I say.

"What?" She takes a sip of the water bottle she brought.

"What was it like... that night?"

She looks at me. Outside, the wind kicks up, and the trees on either side of the highway whip from side to side, wildly. I pass a slow-moving semi-truck. It's started to rain. "That Thursday night?" she asks.

"Yeah." My voice cuts out, a whisper.

She clears her throat a few times. "I don't want to talk about it."

"Please. I wasn't there." I grip the steering wheel, painfully familiar in my hands.

She gives me a look that I can feel, more than see. "Whose fault is that?" she asks. Before I can tell her off, and I almost do, she goes on: "It was just like any other night."

I exhale, letting out the energy of my aborted tirade. "Really?"

"Yes, really. Which is why it sucks so much."

"Tell me about it."

"I worked, Theo worked; we both got home around four." She talks fast, as if trying to build up momentum. "Mom was home already, making dinner. Lasagna. Dad got home right at five, and we ate. It was the same as any night. Dad joked around, Mom complained about a stupid thing one of her coworkers said. Just… normal."

My eyes are burning. I blink.

"And then, they said they were going out on a walk, to catch the sunset. They said not to wait up. I didn't even give them hugs because it was so normal. I wouldn't even remember that night, you know, if I didn't have to. But that was it. That was the last time I saw them." Her eyes are glassy, tears tracking down her face one by one. She grabs a few napkins from my glove box. She knows I always keep some there.

I feel small, and wish I was smaller, wish I could dissolve into the wind and rain and not exist anymore, not feel anything anymore.

Laura finishes: "They left before six, I think, and Theo and I hung out for the evening and then went to bed early. We didn't wake up until the next morning, and Theo noticed they hadn't come home, and then the police were there."

"I'm sorry," I say.

"For what?"

"That you had to be there. That you were there for all of it."

"It's okay."

"I'm sorry I wasn't there."

She rolls her eyes again, sheepishly this time. "It's fine. It wasn't your fault." She crumples up the wet napkin and tucks it into the door pocket. "I'm sorry you didn't get to have lasagna."

I reach across and touch the top of her arm, ever so lightly. "Thanks."

I feel energized from this moment with her, this one almost-normal moment that, while it began in a fight, didn't end in one. This bubble of calm bursts quickly, from the buzzing of my phone in the cupholder between us. I have catching up to do, so I answer without recognizing the number.

"Hello?"

"Amy." I'm taken aback; it's my boss, Chelsea, and she usually calls people by their last names, like a hardboiled reporter from the 1940s. "Amy, how are you? Is everything all right?"

Chelsea is in her thirties, and she's commanding and statuesque and doesn't take shit from anyone. I admire her, and I'm terrified of her. Except now, when she's acting very kind, which makes me more terrified. I last texted her that Terrible Friday, on my way up north. *I have to go home. Familu emergeny. My parents passed awat. I'm sorrt.* I texted very fast, hence the misspellings. That's the last she's heard from me.

"Yeah, yeah I'm okay. I'm just… well, my parents… passed away."

"I'm so sorry; I saw in the papers. We sent flowers; did you get them?"

I don't remember at all. "Yes, they were so nice. Thank you."

"We've been trying to get ahold of you."

"Yeah, I'm just… I've been home, you know. With my sister." Laura looks at me briefly, then stares out the window at the scenery.

"I understand, of course." I'm not used to her being so nice and I don't like it.

"I'm going to stay a little longer, but I wondered… I could do some work online." My computer is still at my apartment in Pittsburgh.

"Amy, I'm sorry, but we were short-staffed. There was that Watkins manuscript we were working on. We needed someone to help out. We hired someone else."

"Oh, oh, that's fine. I could still do—"

"Amy, I'm sorry, but we need to let you go."

My heart constricts. "Well, you can't though—"

"We'll give you severance, of course. I'm so sorry. We just couldn't get ahold of you, and we needed the manpower. You dropped off the face of the earth. Which of course, I understand."

I'm too stunned to say anything.

"Amy? Spend all the time you need with your family. Maybe in the spring we'll be hiring again."

All the momentum that's been stored up in my body since this morning explodes and I start shaking, but she can't see that. "You know what, Chelsea? Damn you. You have some nerve to treat me like this, you bitch!"

There's a short silence. Very short. "You know what, Amy? I've been nothing but nice about this. But to give us no word, for weeks? And then to insult *me*? This is a workplace, not a charity. You are not welcome back in the spring, or ever. I hope you get the help you need." Her voice cuts out at the very end, as she hangs up on me.

I grip the steering wheel and stare at the blurry road.

"What's wrong?" Laura asks. "What happened?" Her voice sounds like it's underwater.

I don't answer her. I drive silently for a while, my mind scrambling. So I don't have a job. I had paltry life savings before, which now must go to pay for my apartment for a month. An apartment I won't be living in. Whatever severance those idiots will give me—if they'll still give it to me—will just cover it. Maybe I can do odd jobs in Haven in the meantime. Maybe Theo will let me shine his shoes or something. Maybe all the inheritance stuff from Mom and Dad will process unusually quickly.

Soon, the pockets of wilderness outside get smaller and farther between. Soon, I am joined by more cars as the exits get more numerous and the highway gets wider. The road cuts into valleys and swerves around hills covered with trees and townhouses, sleepy culs-de-sac and steep streets. The road tunnels under wide bridges that hum with cars and busses. One bridge, made of blue steel, is very high, spanning a wide valley like a gate. Downtown Pittsburgh is close now; the hazy tops of skyscrapers sit within the hills like a ring in a cushion. There's the brown Steel Building like an anvil, the Highmark Tower that has always reminded me of the Sword in the Stone, and PPG Place, which looks like a castle made out of glass. As we move in closer, I get glimpses of the many yellow bridges that staple the city together. The horizon is framed by tall brown hills checkered with colorful houses. I breathe in sharply and sigh, feeling suddenly more relaxed, even in the face of my lost job. This sight always takes my breath away. This is my city. This is home.

I stay on the highway and plunge through downtown, weaving through the skyscrapers of the Golden Triangle. The layers of the city: old, new, stone, concrete, water, glass, and steel, envelop me. Soon I'm through it, taking the Birmingham Bridge to the South Side. Carson Street is busy as always, with boutique shoppers and brunchers, and pub-goers lining the sidewalks. I take a side street and drive up the familiar hill to my apartment building, an old three-story brick house that's perched on the South Side Slopes and looks out over the Flats to the Monongahela River at the bottom of the valley. It's so weird to be here: so familiar, yet I am a completely different person than I was last time I saw it.

I park by the trash cans in front of the house. We're not supposed to do that, but someone is in my usual spot. I turn off the car and gather up my purse, phone, and keys.

"I got fired," I say to Laura. My voice breaks right at the end. "She fired me."

She bites her lip sympathetically. Obviously, this isn't a surprise to her; I'm sure she figured out what the phone call meant. "I'm sorry," she says.

I nod and get out. I lead her up the steep cracked sidewalk, up the rickety front steps to the front porch, where three doors mark three separate apartments. We enter the middle door, which opens into a little hall barely big enough to turn around and close the door behind us. Then we start up the steep, narrow stairs, where at the top another door brings me into the apartment.

"Here it is," I say to Laura. "Home sweet home." She's never been here before, and to be honest I don't think I ever expected that she would be. There's no one in the living area—small, gray, and with a single fluorescent light—nor in the neighboring kitchen. I turn to the left, to the hallway where there are three bedrooms and the bathroom, a lovely lemon-yellow number from 1973. The room in the farthest left corner, facing the front of the house, is mine. I open the door.

There's a girl on my bed. Her head jerks up, her blue eyes hardening in fright as she sees me, her fine brow furrowing and shadowing. Her lanky frame, at first folded and relaxed, tightens as she backs away from me.

"Hi?" I say.

"Can I help you?" she asks.

"Um. That's my bed." But it's not my bed; my soft gray and white blankets and pillows aren't there. Instead, the bed is covered with a garish purple and green pattern that looks like someone found it in a box in the attic marked, *Ski Clothes, 1996.* I steal a glance around the room. Nothing is the way I left it. Panic rises in my chest.

"Oh," she says. "Oh I'm sorry. You're Amy."

"Yeah." I clear my throat. "Yes, and you're—"

"Charlotte." She leans forward a bit and extends her hand. I step forward awkwardly to shake it. "Your stuff is in the living room."

"What?"

"Abbie and Becca said you'd be over."

I turn around, dazed, and walk back down the hall to the living room where I left Laura and where all my worldly possessions (which admittedly aren't that numerous) are piled against the wall to one side of the TV. Laura is inspecting the boxes, having recognized some of the things as mine. I hadn't noticed them before. What else haven't I noticed?

"Amy?" One of the bedroom doors creaks open. Abbie. Tall, skinny, strawberry blond, perfect, blue-eyed Abbie. "Hey, how are you?"

"What's going on?" I squeak. The panic is like an anvil on my chest.

"We've been trying to call you." She flashes a glance toward Laura, who has come up next to me, arms crossed.

"You're renting out my room to someone else? What the actual hell?"

"You didn't answer any of our calls. Rent's due soon. We needed the money."

"You couldn't cover me for one month? My parents died!"

"I know, I'm really sorry." She looks down. "Honestly, I wanted to stick up for you, but Becca knew Charlotte was looking for a place, and…"

"Where is Becca?"

"At work."

I shake my head, trembling again. "I can't—I wasn't *moving* back home. I'm just back to get clothes. I was going to handle rent. I have the money; I just need to write a check. I don't know where my checks are. You messed with my stuff! Damn it. Damn it." I turn around and rush past Laura, and begin to tear through the mishmash of boxes. It's all a mess. Suddenly I'm on the floor, hands and knees, sobbing, and I don't remember how I got down here.

"Okay, calm down," Abbie says. "I know you're upset, but just calm down."

"Calm down, Abbie?" I scream. "Calm down? My parents are dead and I have to go live in their shit town, and I lost my job, and you two idiot bitches can't even be decent human beings for three weeks!" My voice has an unnatural quality to it, a gagging, gasping sound after every three words. Every exhale is interrupted by a spasm from my diaphragm. It doesn't sound like me at all.

Laura still stands between me and Abbie, arms crossed, surveying this whole scene with an intense look of mingled confusion and horror. Abbie stares at the floorboards, the ugly chipped brown paint. "I'm sorry," she says. I hear the soft padding of Charlotte in the next room, my room, pushing the door shut the rest of the way with a *click*. Her weight leans against the door as she listens to this show. My nostrils flare, my eyes leak tears. I never knew Abbie and Becca well. But I thought I knew them well enough, that we were friends.

I have nowhere to go. I have no one. Just Haven. Just my sister, who hates me. Just Theo, who ignores discomfort like it's his job. I don't have a job. I'm lost. After everything I've tried to do to grow up and make it in the world, I'm still lost. I'm an idiot. A child. A failure.

The voice that usually tells me I'm a piece of shit keeps talking, telling me I'm a piece of shit in eloquent sentences. My skin is cold. I'm still on my hands and knees, but can't feel the floor. I can't feel anything. I dig my fingernails into the wood, scraping up the brown paint and getting splinters in my fingertips. I can't feel that either. All I feel is sick. My eyes open and close, but everything is blurry like I'm underwater. Drowning, falling, lost, and hidden in the cleft of a dark forest ravine.

I first moved in here a year and a half ago. Abbie's college roommate had moved out, and she placed an ad on Facebook. There were red flags from the get-go; Becca was the only one on the lease, and I paid her to pay the rent. I trusted that she wouldn't do something like this, and I gambled wrong. Joy told me it was a bad idea, to live with people I didn't know. She told me to move to California with her, or wait until she was done with grad school, and then we'd go adventuring together and see the world, live in a flat in Berlin or Helsinki. I should have listened to her. I shouldn't have hung up on her. I should have returned her texts. I should have told her everything I was really thinking, because now I'm going to die on this ugly floor, and she'll never know.

I've been pushed out, and the only place I can go, for good, forever, is Haven. Damn it damn it damn it. I'm going to die. All I can do is keep half-breathing and sobbing and gagging.

Abbie still stands awkwardly in front of me and I realize these girls don't care that I'm having a panic attack on the floor. They don't care that I was gone for three weeks. They don't care that my parents died. I can't breathe. I can't feel anything.

Then, I do feel something. Cool, small hands smoothing back my hair, resting on my shoulders, putting me back together like someone compacting playdough into a ball.

"Come on," Laura says. "It'll be okay. I'll help you."

There's an empty space in my mind, a blank span of time. Then, little by little, I come back to my body, and my brain puts itself back together. No, I'm not going to die. I'm having a panic attack on the floor. Lots of people have panic attacks on floors. I'm not alone in that, at least. I rock backward off my hands and sit on my heels, exerting a monumental effort just to move. My knees stretch, the joints pop, and I feel the pain of my thigh muscles folding over my calf muscles, like the sky and the earth pressing together in my dream. I am material, physical, solid. Laura bends over me, smoothing my hair one last time before straightening up. The apartment is very quiet. Someone snores in the apartment downstairs.

"I'm sorry," Abbie says again.

Laura stands to her full height. A voice emanates from her, one I've never heard before, stern and solid, and used to taking charge. "You'll help us carry all this stuff down," she says to Abbie.

It's not a question.

Chapter Six

The next hour is a blur. Before I know it, we're back in my car, which is now filled with my belongings, driving back north on 79, passing the same scenes we just saw. Laura is driving, and I'm in the passenger's seat. The car is so weighted down it moves sluggishly.

I feel so stupid. Not just because I lost all semblances of adulthood in a short few hours (or, rather, a terrible few weeks), but more because everything made me so upset, that I had a complete meltdown in front of one of the world's dumbest people, (and my sister, and a complete stranger,) on the world's ugliest floor. I wonder, with a jolt of terror, if I'm going crazy, and can't control myself anymore. My whole life, the one thing I could always control was myself: my opinions, my body, my mind. But now my mind is going in a million directions, and my body keeps pumping itself with adrenaline and then crashing, and my opinions… well, I still don't know what I believe.

"Thank you," I say to Laura.

"Of course," she says. There's a pause, a heavy space of silence. Then she fills it again: "I actually like driving in Pittsburgh."

Three weeks and a day. Three weeks and a day ago, I was driving this same exact route, and I saw that tree and this house and that exit. I saw that restaurant, and I started crying and pounding the steering wheel and screaming the worst words I knew.

I'm sorry I'm sorry I'm sorry.

It didn't feel real then. I was still in that state of denial, like when you have a nightmare in which there's a volcano erupting, or a tsunami coming to engulf your house, or a white van pulling up and snatching your sister, and while you're terrified, there's a little part of you that stays calm. "This is only a dream," it says. "Just wait a few minutes; you'll wake up." That's what this drive felt like, three weeks and a day ago. And then it took all that time, and a drive down to Pittsburgh and a drive back, for the truth to dawn: this isn't a dream, and we aren't going to wake up. They're dead.

It seems like a thousand years since the Terrible Friday, and also like a few minutes. I can't trust my perception of time either; I can't trust myself at all. The utter terror of this builds, swelling with the constant panic in my chest. I begin to cry again, softly. I'm so tired of feeling this way, and so terrified that I'll feel this way forever.

"What's wrong?" Laura asks.

What isn't wrong? "Nothing," I say. "Just... everything."

She clears her throat "You know," she says, "I've been thinking."

"Of what?" I swat my tears away with the back of my hand.

"I think we should go to therapy."

I laugh out loud.

She glares at me. "I'm serious."

"I don't need therapy."

"You just had a panic attack."

"Lots of people have panic attacks."

"Yeah, and it's usually a sign that they need therapy."

"Well, I don't."

"Our parents just died."

"I'm aware."

She sighs. "Well, *I'm* going to therapy."

"Good. I hope it works out for you and you get the help you need." This comes out more pointed than I mean for it to, but it's too late to fix it once the words have left my mouth. She shakes her head and rolls her eyes, and the bristling, fragile demeanor she had this morning is suddenly back.

"Never mind," she says. "Fine."

I had had a fleeting thought, in the fog of my episode at the apartment, that maybe things between me and Laura weren't so bad after all, that maybe some time together would fix everything. But that was a foolish thought.

It shouldn't be this way. I wish that grief would bring my sister and I closer together like it does in all the sitcoms. Instead, it makes us more awkward around each other, more painfully aware of how we've grown apart. We used to be best friends. That cliché of twins being inseparable was true for us. We did everything together in school: volleyball and choir and band and spring theater. We ran lemonade stands in the summers. We stayed up late every night, talking. Then it changed: slowly, and then swiftly.

It started in little ways. When we graduated high school, I wanted to go to college in Pittsburgh. I had grand visions of us going together, sharing a dorm, making friends, and having fantastic fun. But she wanted to attend Catawba University, where Dad taught, and take advantage of the discount she'd get for being his daughter. Fine, I thought. Pittsburgh's not that far away; we'd still be together as a family on weekends and holidays.

Then I started not knowing what I believed. For the first time in my life, I realized how sheltered I had been, growing up a little Christian girl in a little rural town. I was suddenly surrounded by diversity, by the untidiness in the world, and I had to examine myself. I started taking pieces of my ideals out of my head and putting them on the table and letting them mean nothing to me anymore until I decided what did mean something to me. I let go of the fear that had kept me asking Jesus into my heart every night as a child. I started questioning everything and doubting everything. At first, I tried to talk to Laura about these things, in texts or on the phone when we chatted.

"I knew college would do this to you," she said. "People go to college and don't have support systems, and then lose their beliefs. And you haven't visited a church at all since you moved to Pittsburgh. What do you expect?"

"I'm not losing my beliefs," I protested. "I'm just not taking everything at face value. I'm not blindly believing everything I've been taught."

"You're giving in to the temptations of the world," she said. And the conversation always ended here, because it always went there, and I was tired of hearing it.

A part of me thinks that if she hadn't been so abrupt, so insistent that I had fallen away before I really meant to fall away, maybe I'd still believe some things. But her fear of my questioning or doubting anything made me wonder if God was big enough to handle my doubts and questions, or if all of Christianity just collapsed because I wasn't sure about it. I decided that that was too much pressure, so I took out all the beliefs in my head and threw them on the table, and decided to leave them for a while. This made Laura even angrier, and she argued with me about theology, or judged me for not going to church on the weekends when I visited home, or reacted to my stories about partying with my classmates and sleeping around with disdain.

The funny thing was, Mom and Dad never judged me for these things. I knew they didn't approve of them, especially the time I confided in Mom when I finally lost my virginity, not because I really liked the guy, but because I wanted to be done with it. Mom asked, "Why is it so important for you to get it over with?" and I had no answer except, "Because everyone makes a big deal about it," which was admittedly a rather dumb reason, one I wasn't even satisfied with. I knew where my parents stood on these things: they had conservative sexual ethics. They believed that drinking was okay, but not partying. The new words I introduced into my vocabulary made them raise their eyebrows. But while they might have disagreed with some of my new habits, they didn't fly off the handle about them either. Their faith, like Joy's, was calm. They took things in stride. They asked me questions and didn't assume what my answers would be, didn't try to have any answers at all. Their God was big enough to handle my doubts.

All this time, of course, all through the end of high school and the beginning of college, Laura and Theo were dating. They were the perfect Christian couple: no sex, no partying, and dates which consisted of Bible studies and strolls in the park (I assume). It all made me snicker, but it also made me jealous. Here I was, being so liberated and questioning everything and wondering if all religious people weren't just big, fat repressed hypocrites, and my sister, who had the kind of chaste relationship most people would laugh at, was deeply in love and thriving. I loved her and Theo together; truly, I did. Theo had

75

been in our lives forever, and it was so good to see him happy after his young life had already been so riddled with sadness.

I was Theo's partner in crime when he first asked Laura out, helped him orchestrate their date to the nice Italian restaurant in Cainesville, when we were seventeen and he was twenty-one. Even then, we all knew they belonged together. It was good to see my sister happy, too.

Laura and Theo got engaged on a hot night in May when the air was thick and soupy. I was home from school for the summer, just before our senior year of college. This was when things between Laura and I started changing swiftly.

The two of them had gone out again to the nice Italian restaurant in Cainesville. After dinner, they walked to the park that has a fountain in the middle. They sat on a bench and watched the water make tiny prisms of the sunset. Then at dusk, Theo dropped to one knee and asked her to marry him. She said yes.

When they left for that date, I knew what was going to happen. Theo had confided in me around the same time he asked Mom and Dad for their blessing. They of course said yes, because they'd known Theo since he was four years old, and they also knew that Laura loved Theo a lot. But when Theo told me, asking for my blessing as it were, when he showed me the beautiful big pearl—Laura's and my birthstone—flanked by tiny little diamond starbursts on either side, the only thing I could say was, "The ring is beautiful."

Unfazed, he smiled. "Thanks," he said. "I got it custom-made." He showed me the swirling vine pattern engraved in the white gold band.

"It's very nice."

"I thought of giving her the family ring, but... I think it should skip a generation. Bad memories."

"Yes." I remembered the day when Laura and I were six, when Theo's dad David brought him over and told Mom and Dad that Stacy was gone. She had met some guy on the internet, sealed a note and her rings in an envelope, and left. Theo was ten.

"It's a beautiful ring," I said.

He grinned. "Do you think she'll like it?"

"Of course."

Eventually, he realized I was less than enthused. "What's wrong?"

"Nothing."

"Are you mad?"

"Why would I be? You guys love each other. I'm excited for you."
My words lay flat upon the air.

"Are you sure you're okay with this?"

I really didn't want to ruin his moment. It wasn't that I was mad at
him. I just felt as if I had made a life to-do list, and Theo was trying to
do one of the things out of order. In my mind, it was: *Reilly sisters go
to college. Reilly sisters finish college. Amy gets a dream job (or at
least the entry-level version of one) at some cool, faraway city. Laura
and Theo move to the cool, faraway city with her. Laura gets a job as a
teacher at a cool school in the cool, faraway city. Laura and Theo get
married somewhere exotic that is not Haven. Maybe a Bahama.*

So I did want them to get married. I loved them together. But I
didn't want them to get married yet. It didn't feel right. "I'm just...I'm
just surprised this is happening already," I said.

Dear Theo, sweet, stupid Theo, got a giddy look on his face. "I
can't believe it either," he said.

Then I realized that Laura's life, which had for so long been linked
closely with mine, was no longer any of my business. Every milestone
of her life was hers to choose, and I was deluding myself, really, to
think I could force her into what I thought would make her happy. I
knew it was stupid of me. But still, it stung. For the first time in our
relationship, I felt left out, as if she'd outgrown me.

So they got engaged and planned a wedding in five months, which
made me even madder, but I kept it under the surface because I knew I
didn't have the right to be mad. Then came the day I was standing at
the front of the church next to Laura, in my burnt orange bridesmaid
dress holding her creamy white flowers. Pastor Jeff read some
scriptures about marriage, the ones people always quote. "And a man
shall leave his father and his mother and cling to his wife, and they
shall become one flesh," Pastor Jeff said.

A light snicker came up from the crowd. Everyone pretty much
knew that Laura and Theo were planning to stay with Mom and Dad

for a while until they saved up for a house. Not only was Laura not leaving her father and mother; she wasn't even leaving her childhood bedroom. I'll give it to everyone; that is humorous. Quirky. Rom-com-esque. *Congrats, Pastor Jeff; you're fucking hilarious.*

I spent the rest of the wedding, the lovely reception decorated with brilliant fall leaves and copper wire and ivory lace, sulking. I faked my way through the maid of honor speech. I pasted on a smile and tried to look happy. Everyone was fooled. At the end of the day, when the party wound down, we sent Laura and Theo off to their wedding night at the Cainesville Inn, before their weekend honeymoon trip to New York. By then, my anger and sadness, and shame had mingled with the tiredness of a long-ass day, and I knew it was all showing up on my face, as all my feelings eventually do.

"Everything okay?" asked Mom. We were stacking chairs and taking down decorations because this is rural Pennsylvania and we have to do everything ourselves.

"I'm fine," I said. But everyone knows it's a lost cause to lie to your mother.

"It's been a long day," she said. "A lot of emotions."

She hugged me suddenly and I breathed in her characteristic scent of lavender lotion and hairspray.

"I'm going to miss her," was all I could say. Maybe that was it. Maybe that was all of it.

"I know."

"I know I'll see her. It's stupid. But I wanted..." All the things I wanted, all the things on my list, flashed behind my eyes in violent burnt orange light.

Mom knew what I wanted. We had had many talks about how frustrated I was with Haven, how I thought everything was so out of touch, so backward, so insular; how the people were too content to not live in the world, too short-sighted and devoid of vision; how I wanted to be in a place that hadn't lost itself. She knew I wanted that for Laura too.

"She's on a different path than you, Amy. But it'll be okay."

I started to cry, and I buried my face in her shoulder, which was covered with burnt orange sequins, because Mom never did anything by halves, especially dressing up for her daughter's wedding.

A week later, Laura and Theo returned from New York. She was still in school at that point and had used her fall break to get married. I had gone back to Pittsburgh. Mom, who was always full of joy and understanding and who sometimes—somewhat naively—expected other people to be as well, told Laura upon her return that I was missing her, and might be having a hard time adjusting to this new arrangement, and that Laura should check in with me. I know Mom meant the best by trying to get us to talk. But I wish she hadn't done anything.

I got a call from Laura when I was coming out of my last class that Friday afternoon: American Literature. I was hopped up on Flannery O'Connor and Southern culture and Catholic symbolism and a lot of gore. Getting a random call from Laura was, then, not unusual at all. I answered, all chipper.

"Hey!" I said. "How are you?"

"I'm fine," she said, in the way that means one is not fine. I brushed it aside, because like I said, I was hopped up on Flannery O'Connor and Southern culture and Catholic symbolism and a lot of gore. Also, I was genuinely happy to hear from her.

"How was the honeymoon?" I asked. "How was New York?"

"It was good," she said.

"Tell me about it."

There was a pause, her making space in the conversation to think. I waited, each second telling me that something wasn't right.

"Mom says you're...upset," she said.

"Upset?"

"I think you're mad I got married."

I let out a sigh, swift and sharp. "No. I'm not mad you got married. Did Mom say that?"

"Mom said, 'I think Amy is having a hard time adjusting to the idea of you being married. Make sure she knows you'll still be there for her'."

"Okay. 'Hard time adjusting.' That doesn't mean mad."

"But you are."

"I'm not! I don't think Mom meant to say—"

"She didn't. She said you were having a hard time adjusting."

"Well!?"

"If it was just that, you would've told me. But you didn't, so that means you're mad."

She was right. The intense, precise truth of her conclusion was like an ice pick boring into my skull. It took my breath away.

She spoke again, each word louder and faster. "You know, you have no right to be gone all the time only to come home and judge me! That's all you've done for years. You judged me for the school I went to. You judged me because I wanted to be a teacher. You judge me for where I live. And now you're judging me for marrying Theo."

"I'm not—" I struggled for words, for thoughts, for something. "I love Theo!" I meant this purely platonically, of course, which she understood. I've always loved Theo. If my sister was to marry anyone, I'd want it to be Theo. I was just upset that she got married *now*, and that she was living in Haven, and that she wasn't filling the shoes I believed she could fill, the potential I thought she could reach. Most of all, of course, I was upset that I felt shut out. Not because of anything she had done, but because when someone gets married, everyone else is automatically shut out. I had once known Laura better than anyone else, and now I didn't. Now, my opinion meant nothing, except when it was the wrong opinion.

"You've always judged me," she said.

"That's *not* true."

"It is! I've always been your sweet little sister, who's weak and delicate, who you have to boss around and protect, and now I've done something you don't like, and you can't stand it!"

She was right here, too; damn it. She knew me well. She knew me better than anyone, but wouldn't let me return the favor.

"I don't think you're weak." My voice was as taut as guitar strings.

"Do you think I'm stupid? I know that's what's going on." There was a pause. I heard my blood pumping through my veins. Then her voice came back again, and it was low, calm, deadpan. "Amy," she said. "I always know what you're thinking. Please don't try to be polite.

Please don't try to hide it. Just be honest. You're mad at me, right?"

At the end of the day, at the end of every day, I can't hide anything from her. I swallowed. "Yeah, Laura," I said. "I'm sorry. But I am. I shouldn't be. But I am."

She exhaled into the phone, a *whoosh* of soft static. "Alright," she said and hung up. And my sister and I never had a really honest, heart-to-heart conversation again.

I should've been angry with Theo for taking my sister away from me. But when I imagined calling Theo, and yelling at him, I stalled out. There was nothing to yell at Theo for. He was just a man with a rather shitty life who fell in love with a girl. He's the good guy in every young adult novel.

I should've been angry at Mom, too, for meddling. But when I imagined calling Mom and yelling at her to "Mind your own business!" I stalled out there, too. Because Mom was our mom, and when your kids hurt each other, it *is* your business.

I thought I was angry at Laura. I imagined calling her back and screaming, "I just miss you, you idiot!" But at the end of the day, the end of every day, I wasn't nearly as angry with her as I was with myself. For being so stupidly upset when I should have been happy, for crying on Mom's burnt-orange-sequined shoulder, for letting this be the thing that broke the two of us apart. But it was too late now. I'd treated a precious thing too carelessly and now it was gone. I lost it. I shattered it. *I'm sorry I'm sorry I'm sorry.*

Christmas that year was awkward as hell. What do you do when your former best friend, who's also your sister, who also shared a womb with you, won't speak to you until you apologize for something that's not exactly something you *did* as much as something you *feel*? I couldn't unfeel the fact that I didn't want her to get married yet. I could apologize that I'd hurt her, but a feeling is ongoing; it's not one event to repent of. I couldn't unfeel the sense that I had once been a part of a wonderful, beautiful relationship unlike any other that I was now cut out of. It was as if she had broken up with me, then was angry when I didn't keep sending her flowers. Though it was worse because fighting with your twin sister isn't like breaking up with someone you love. It's like having a piece of you cut out and attached to someone else.

So what do you do?

Here's what you do: you sit awkwardly around a Christmas tree and hand each other presents and politely say, "Thank you, and Merry Christmas to you, good sir." And when your dad, theoretically, says something like, "Man, is it just me or is it chilly in here?" and your mom, theoretically, gives him a look with enough heat to burn the house down, you just stare at the Christmas tree and hope next year is better.

But it wasn't. There was still the awkward stepping around each other, giving Christmas presents because you can't not, the bad feelings piling on each other one by one until you can't even remember what the original problem was, or how to fix it.

Chapter Seven

When we arrive home, it's halfway through the afternoon and the house is empty; Theo still has a few hours of work. The prospect of being in the house alone with Laura is only slightly better than being in the car alone with her for a sum total of four hours, so I busy myself with lugging my stuff into the house and disengaging with my thoughts so I don't burst into tears.

"Do you want help?" she asks.

"No, I'm fine."

"Of course," she mutters. And usually, I would retort, ask her what she really means, poke her passive aggression like one pokes a sleeping bear, as I've always done. But today I'm just too tired.

When I've finally finished getting everything out of the car and into the house when the kitchen and dining room are strewn with all my worldly possessions, I find her sleeping on one of the couches in the living room, and for once she looks so peaceful, so innocent, and everything seems simple again. I wish we could just forget, pick up where we left off once long ago.

I lug each box up the stairs, one by one, walking warily past Mom and Dad's room each time, as I've done since that night at 2:15. I've carefully avoided it ever since, running past it in the hallway at night, skittering by casually, and pretending not to look at the door, as if acknowledging my fear might either flatter the room too much or hurt its feelings; I can't decide which.

Once I've gotten everything upstairs, I'm *incredibly* tired, and I lie on my bed for a quick nap, which soon turns into a deep, dark sleep. When I wake up, it's night, and the house is silent. I want to get up—I'm terribly thirsty—but my body feels so weighted down I can't move. I doze off again, and the sleep is deep and dark and full of dreams I can't remember a second later. When I dip out of sleep again, I panic. I don't know what time it is or where I am or who I am; I only know that I'm thirsty. But again, I can't move. So again, I doze off, and the sleep is deep and cozy except for the underlying, terrifying, pressing thought that I have to get out of here, I have to move, or I'll never wake up. I'm being buried alive. When I dip out again, as close to consciousness as I can muster, I throw myself out of bed and onto the floor, with a nasty headache and a nauseated stomach and a throat drier than the Sonoran Desert in July.

I rush to the bathroom and turn on the sink, drinking water from the tap like I used to get in trouble for doing when I was young. I splash cold water on my face and hair, and brush my teeth, trying to trick my body into thinking it's morning, even though the sun has gone down. Downstairs, Laura is knocking about in the kitchen, emptying the dishwasher. I squint my eyes in the blaze of the overhead lights.

"You look like you had a good nap," she says.

"You too." I feel ill.

"Theo's picking up some salads from the grocery store," she says. "He's getting you a Caesar."

My stomach turns at the thought. "Yum."

She sits at the kitchen table, a steaming mug of tea in hand, flipping through a magazine that came in the mail. I sit down across from her, feeling woozy, my muscles sore from all the heavy lifting I've done today.

"So," she says. "Would you… like to stay here a little longer, then?"

By the tone of her voice, it's an invitation. But we both know I have no other option, at least for the time being. "Yes, I guess so," I say. "Until I find a job somewhere else."

She takes a sip of tea. "You know, Haven is a pretty fine place to live."

"I don't want to live here."

"I'm just saying… until you get back on your feet."

"I'm on my feet, see?" I stand up. It's ridiculous, but she makes me ridiculous. "I'm up. I'm standing. I'm fine."

"Okay." She flips another page of the magazine. "I'm just trying to help."

I roll my eyes, but she doesn't see it. Maybe she thinks she's trying to help. But that's just the way people are here. Their world is so small, and the only way they can think to help is to give you exactly what you don't need.

"What do you need, then?" she asks as if she's read my thoughts. "What would be helpful to you?"

Her question catches me off guard. Because the truth is, I don't really know.

"Why are you asking?" I say.

"Because I'm honestly trying to help. You had a really bad day, and I'm trying to help."

It's all so infuriating. I *want* to tell her what I need. I *want* to be helped. But I don't know where to start. I just want things to be better, *now*. I want her to sit inside my brain and see all I think and feel, even the things I'm not aware of myself. She only seems to be able to read some of the things in there, and it's all the wrong things, which give her a wrong impression.

"Remember that time," I say, "right after you got married, and you called me because Mom had told you I had a hard time adjusting to you being married?"

She grimaces a little, as if the memory makes her brain short out. "Yes."

"You said I judged you for all your life decisions."

She sets her chin. "Yes."

"Maybe you were right. But I think it's the other way around, too. You judge me for *everything*."

"I don't—"

"Yes, you do."

"I just think you have so much potential..."

"And what? I'm not living up to my potential? Should I have a Nobel Peace Prize by now or something?"

She glares at me. "Obviously not."

I nearly laugh, despite myself. "Then what? What should I be doing?"

She sighs. "I don't know. What should *I* be doing?"

I blink. "I don't know."

She nods. "Sounds about right, then."

Before I can retort, or explain, or even cry, the backdoor opens and Theo comes in, with a bag full of groceries on his arm. "Hey!" he greets us. "Dinner is served!" And I want to scream at him and hit him and also thank him from the bottom of my heart for coming home at just this moment. Laura gets up to set out the plates.

"I'm sorry to hear about Pittsburgh, Amy," Theo says as he takes off his coat. "Laura told me. Your roommates really are a lovely bunch."

I smile faintly. I wonder what else she told him, what else he knows or thinks of me but won't say. I wonder why it's so easy for him to pretend to be kind to me. "Yeah, it sucks," I say.

Theo gives Laura a hug and a little kiss before they join me at the table. She sets a plateful of salad before me. Theo pats my shoulder. "You are welcome to stay here as long as you need to," he says. "Anything we can do to help. Just let us know."

I don't know why, but in spite of everything, I believe him more than I believe her.

The night sky looks like a Japanese beetle: black, with an iridescent film on it, clouds obscuring the stars. I stand at the top of our hill, in the middle of the cemetery, watching the chiclet houses dark and asleep, while the twin spires of the Catholic church glow with light and shoot two beams up to the muddy sky. It's windy and warm, like those first warm nights in the spring when you feel stupidly giddy and the world feels impossibly wonderful and wide. I'm not afraid of being in the middle of a cemetery, alone in the dark. I'm not afraid of the dark at all.

"You're it!" a voice echoes across the summit of the hill and falls down the grave-covered slope to the street below, the street below that, all the way down to the foot of the mountain. A blur of a person runs past me, hurrying down the hill as if trying to catch the echo and bring it back. The form is dark and shapeless, but it has a mane of long, reddish-brown hair, not curly or straight, not messy or neat, but a bundle of contradictions. I cry out, part anguish, part glee, and I tear off in hot pursuit.

We run down the hill. Gravity pulls at my bones and makes my heart somersault. I nearly catch up to her. I reach out to grasp her hair, so bright and colorful in this beetle-black night. Then, suddenly, a sharp pain at my knees. I fall down, rolling forward. The sting of granite on skin, hard earth on joints. I've tripped over a gravestone.

"Come back!" I cry. "I'm hurt!" Blood blossoms upon my clothes, growing brighter and brighter red. "Please help me. Please help me. I'm hurt."

She disappears down the hill.

I wake up. My room is dark, black as a Japanese beetle. It presses on my chest and neck and head, eyes, and ears. I switch on the light and take gulps of breath. My throat is sore and tight. When I try to relax the muscles, they unravel into sobs, and I cry into my pillow, crouched under the covers of my bed like a child. Dear God, I can still feel the pain in my legs. I sit back and inspect my ankles, my shins, my knees, sucking in sobs all the while. No blood anywhere.

Good as new. The pain ebbs away.

I sit for a while, rocking back and forth. Each pause, after coming forward and after going back, is a moment of panic, but the motion of rocking, the journey between the two poles, is soothing. I've had so many nightmares in this room. I used to have one nearly every night as a child. It was the deciding factor in Laura getting her own room when we were eight because I kept waking her up, and she didn't want to share a room with me anymore. (In retrospect, this was rather shitty of her.) Before Dad installed the folding door over the closet, there was only the gaping hole of it in the dark, and I was sure some monster or ghost or demon lived there, waiting for me to be caught off guard so it could come out. I would dry my eyes out staring at that closet before I went to sleep, and if I did drift off, I dreamt I was still awake, still looking at it, while the clothes on their hangers twisted into ghouls and grim reapers, my flowing dresses wafting into the room and howling at a pitch that froze my bones.

I would wake up and lie perfectly still, trying to trick the terrors into thinking I was still asleep, into leaving me alone, into going down the hall where my cruel and unusual sister lay perfectly alone in her own room. Then, when I could barely breathe for trying to stay still, when I was dripping with sweat from the fear and heavy blankets (my only protection, of course), I threw caution to the wind and screamed, "Dad! I need you!"

Panicked mumbles from Mom and Dad's room, the bumping of feet into dressers, the swinging of their door and then mine, and Dad throwing on the lights, wearing a white tee, plaid boxers, and tube socks. "Whaswrongyouokay!"

"I had a bad dream." Finally, the spell was broken. I could move; I could throw the blankets off. I could cry. "I had a bad dream. I'm scared."

He came over and knelt at the side of the bed, put his head next to mine on the pillow, held my hands, and told me not to be scared.

"I can't help it. The closet is scary."

"I'll put a door on it."

"You said that last time."

"Nothing can hurt you. There are no monsters."

"What about demons?"

"Well you know Jesus, so demons can't hurt you."

"What about ghosts?"

"Ghosts aren't bad at all."

"So there are ghosts?"

"Not 'ghosts.'" Yawn. "The leftover memories of people from the past. A print in mud. Stone tapes. But no; they aren't bad at all."

He was usually half asleep by then, and so was I. The next time I woke up, it was morning, and he was gone.

But now it's still dark, and he's still gone. I cry and cry, thoroughly soggying my pillow. They're gone. The people who used to comfort my nightmares have become them.

God is real, my single belief says. And I realize that if this is true, if I believe it, I am even angrier now. I sit up again and glare at the ceiling, as if glaring hard enough will make God materialize, emerge from where he hovers in the upper corner of my room.

"Fuck you," I breathe, a sharp, rasping whisper. "Fuck you. If you are real. If you are there. Fuck you for letting them drive out in the middle of nowhere. Fuck you for that single moment that changed everything, for that moment where their drive turned into an accident. Fuck. You." I begin to shout in my whisper. "All my life, all those people who said you cared, that if we prayed, you'd protect us, keep us safe, make good things happen. That you were in control. Bullshit! Where were you, then, that Thursday night? You don't have to protect me; I don't care. I haven't been faithful in any way at all, so it's fine, I don't deserve it. But they deserved it. They loved you more than anything. Church three times a week, giving money, giving time, loving people. Loving everyone. They did all that, and you still didn't have the decency to keep them safe on a drive in the country! Fuck you for that. If you insist on being real, I insist on being fucking furious with you." I take a breath, winded and sore in the throat. I wait for some kind of answer, some kind of miraculous sign. But none comes.

When I was a kid, the Sunday school teachers always said God was like a father. That's how we prayed to him, *Father God.* Some of the uber hippie Christians took it a step further, starting prayers out with "Daddy God" (weird, but they meant well). I was taught to always think of God as a father, the ideal father with the purest of love and the best of intentions. At the time it seemed like a profound idea, but now the thought sours. My real father, the one who's dead, comforted me from my nightmares. My purported heavenly father refuses to. He wants me to believe he's real, but won't come down from the nebulous place between my bedroom wall and ceiling, and sit down with me and let me yell at him.

I lie down and turn off the light. I stare at the ceiling and cry myself into a kind of stupor that will have to do for sleep.

Chapter Eight

I get in the habit of taking long walks. It's properly brown season now, at the end of October when the fall colors are gone and all that remain are the crackling brown oak leaves that hang on when everything else has fallen away. The air is damp every day; the sky is overcast. The moisture in the air makes the earth musty, the tree trunks black, and my hair frizzy.

Taking a long walk in Haven is a strenuous feat in itself. Everywhere you go, there's a hill. Even walking to the end of our street is walking to the bottom of a hill, a hill that keeps going into another street, and then another, and before you know it, you're at the foot of a mountain, looking up at rows of spindly trees and houses, and you have to walk back up it to get home. No taxis here, either. My ridesharing apps are useless.

Sometimes I walk in the cemetery that tops our hill like a cap, going up and down the rambling driveways that tattoo the summit of the hill, reading the names of the graves, which are all so familiar that they are burned into my memory and flash in my vision when I close my eyes. We used to walk here as a family, too. Dad knew all the names of all the people buried in this cemetery. He knew their sisters and mothers and cousins and uncles, how each person connected to another, like stitches in a row of knitting.

When I come to the top of the hill, I stand among the dead and look down into the valley where people live, where each house is a tiny, colorful chiclet. The blue twin spires of the Catholic church Mom went to as a child rise above the brown and reflect off the patches of sky that show through the cloud cover. Far down at the bottom of the valley, which is a pavé of houses, brick buildings, and grassy patches; two bridges link each side of Haven across the Allegheny.

I walk this area, too, and soon the bridges become my favorite place to walk, though I don't admit it to myself. At first, I rationalize it, telling myself I need to go to the bank or get a coffee at the little café where Laura used to work in high school. I tell myself I have to check out a library book, or that I'm looking for Help Wanted posters in the windows of the five businesses we have. All of these errands are on the side of town across the river, and taking a bridge is the only way to get there. But after multiple trips in which I haven't visited the bank, or gotten a coffee, or checked out a library book, or inquired about a job, I realize that I'm fooling myself. I'm walking across a bridge because I want to, because I relish the pause I take in the very middle, the way I grip the railing, the bow of my head as I peep over the edge into the water, which is much deeper now with all the rain. I watch the water glide over the river rocks, turning each dull stone into a kaleidoscope of color that changes minutely with each millisecond, and I'm so mesmerized that I understand why some people jump this bridge sometimes, why some people sacrifice their lives to it. I understand the appeal to be a part of something so living, so deep, so beautiful.

One afternoon, I'm halfway up Alice Street, the steepest road in Haven, which runs from the bottom of our hill to the top at what is nearly a forty-five-degree angle, when I get honked at by a car passing by. The car slows and pulls over, four-ways flashing. A Toyota 4Runner, gray, 2003. It's Theo. The car creaks as the brakes hold on for dear life, gravity trying its hardest to pull the car down the hill. Good thing it's not cold enough for ice today.

"What are you doing here?" Theo asks, rolling down the window. "Get in!" I obey, too tired and dazed to be smart about it.

"What, were you taking a stroll or something?" he asks, pulling back into the street.

"I've *been* taking strolls."

"All the way down here?"

"Everywhere."

"Why? You have a car."

"There's nothing else to do. Besides, there's no gym here. I have to stay in shape somehow."

He harrumphs. "You need a job."

"From your lips to God's ear, most excellent Theophilus."

"Don't call me that."

"I like it. Super biblical."

"I don't."

Theo's car is much what you would expect a guy's 2003 4Runner to be on the inside: dusty, with a peppermint air freshener hanging from the rearview mirror and a bunch of used coffee mugs clinking around in the back.

"You know, there is a part-time thing open at the paper." His voice sounds resigned to the fact. "Just a receptionist job. Really small. Really cheap. Not even full-time. I didn't want to insult you by bringing it up, but you called me Theophilus."

"Thank you, but I'm okay." I make a smiley face in the fog on the window, and another in the dust on the dashboard.

"Aren't you looking for a job?"

"Not here."

He nods. "Okay. Just wanted to help."

I smile at him. He's sweet and uncomplicated. I wish everyone in the world could be. "Thank you. I appreciate it."

"Just don't call me Theophilus again."

"No promises."

"Why were you really downtown?"

"I told you. I was taking a walk."

"Is Laura at home?"

"Yes, as far as I know."

"And she lets you just leave?"

"I'm twenty-four years old. I'm not a baby. Also, when I left, she was taking a nap. I was bored. Was she supposed to lock me in my room?"

He shakes his head and mutters something.

"Is it really a crime to take a walk? Damn it, Theo. I'm a grown woman."

"I know. I just feel like we should stick together."

"You go to work all day. Laura is probably starting work again soon. How's that sticking together? What do you even mean?"

He shakes his head again and clears his throat. "I'm sorry. I'm just worried about you both and I want to make sure you're okay."

"By keeping us shut in the house all day so you know where we are."

"I realize it's stupid. I'm sorry."

"I understand. But, yes, it is stupid."

We pull into the driveway and he takes his time putting the car into Park, turning off the heater, switching out the lights.

I get a sudden wave of nausea; he's a fast driver, and it's just caught up to me. Of course, the ever-present heaviness in my chest doesn't help. I take a deep breath.

"You okay?" he asks.

I nod, trying to wait for the moment to pass. I feel myself on the verge of another panic attack, an overwhelming feeling of fear, urgency, sickness. I grip the door of the car, trying to talk through it. "Theo, can I ask you something?"

"What?" He looks nervous as if he might make a run for it.

"When your Mom left. I know you don't like to talk about it." I close my eyes and try to concentrate. "When your Mom left... were you angry?"

He relaxes a little bit, presses his lips together, stares out the windshield at the alley behind our house, where lines of garbage cans await trash collection tomorrow morning. "Of course I was angry. I was a ten-year-old boy whose mother left."

"How long were you angry?"

"I was low-level angry for years, and then it got pretty bad after my dad died. She didn't come to his funeral, didn't call, didn't even send a card. But I don't know; as I got older, it got easier to move on."

This is oddly calming me down. I grip the door handle tighter, feeling the fine pebbly grain of the vinyl under my fingertips. "Were you angry with God?" I ask. "*Are* you angry with God?"

"No," he says simply, quickly, definitely; the tone of someone who's decided on their answer long ago.

"How?"

"It's not worth it," he says. "It's not worth it to be angry. Why should I let someone else decide how I live the rest of my life?"

It's a noble thought, and I admire him for thinking it. But it's not enough for me. "But I mean, how can't you be angry at God? If you believe God could change or fix everything at will, and he doesn't, won't? How can't you be angry at that?"

He looks down at the steering wheel.

I realize what I'm doing: asking him to explain himself so I feel better, so I can figure out my own shit. "I'm sorry." Cold air creeps into the car little by little.

"It's okay," he says. "It's a good question. To be honest, I still don't know the answer. Some days I am angry with God, especially lately." He gives me a knowing look. *We're all in this together,* it says. He goes on. "But I just can't shake the idea, the feeling, that everything will be okay. That there's an answer to my questions, and I don't have to know it to be okay."

"You're a better one than I." I release my grip on the door, finally calm, if a little dazed and fragile.

"Hundreds of dollars on therapy as a kid wasn't spent for nothing." He gives a wry laugh. "You know, I think of her—my mom—as dead. For all intents and purposes. The person who was my mother doesn't exist anymore. Maggie became that person for me. Peter too. They were there, unchanging, until the end."

My eyes burn. I blink very fast. "Yeah."

"You know, Laura's just trying to help," he says.

I grumble a bit, pull my gaze outdoors. "Yes, of course."

"I know she's clumsy at it sometimes."

I break into an involuntary smile. I *tsk.* "You shouldn't talk about your wife that way!"

He rolls his eyes. "I love her, and she loves me, but we each have our weaknesses. I have mine, and I'm sure she tells you about them."

"When she's not busy telling me about my own."

"She really is trying to help. She's dealing with her own stuff, too. Apart from… all of this."

"Like what?"

"You'll have to ask her yourself. I refuse to talk about my wife that way." He lifts his palms and gives me a plaintive look, lightening the mood as always, and again I'm so grateful for him.

In the weeks that follow, we get into a routine that grows both familiar and bizarre. I become the unduly elected errand girl: grocery shopping, going to the bank, making dinner. I have always liked to cook. I throw away everything in the fridge, even the soy sauce packets, and buy everything new. I make cozy meals: potato soup and rolls, butternut squash, roast chicken. Theo works and comes home. We talk. We watch TV. We go to sleep and start it all again.

People from church bring over food for us, too. The freezer is full of casseroles and baked goods made by church ladies. People call the house phone and leave messages or mail us cards and letters of sympathy. Pastor Jeff and his wife Julie visit a few times, and when they do, I shut myself away in my room or head to the shower or run out to my car, pretending I have pressing things to do, errands to run, letting Laura and Theo be comforted by these people, feeling too muddled to let myself be comforted. I'm still, after all, furious with God. Laura and Theo probably assume I avoid the church people because I'm a bona fide heathen, but the truth is that everything is still on that damned table, and it feels too raw, too personal, to share with a whole community. I want to know what *I* think about everything, before I go sharing it, or before it's shared with me.

Sometimes our grandparents come over for dinner, or we go over to their houses. Nanna Mae lives all alone, in the small brick rowhouse Mom grew up in. The house has paneled walls and shag carpet and is crammed with family photos, most of them of Mom, since she was an only child. "I talk to her every night," Nanna Mae says to us. "I pray to all the saints and tell your mother to take good care of you."

I want to ask a few questions: 1. Why doesn't Nanna Mae also pray to Dad? And 2. Where the hell are the saints, and what exactly are they supposed to do? And 3. Why haven't they been doing it? But I don't ask her these things, because I know that Nanna Mae is still sensitive about the fact that Mom, so carefully raised to be a dutiful Catholic, left it all to be a Protestant heretic with Dad. I know that Nanna Mae had visions of me and Laura going to Saint Joan's School in the blue and green plaid uniforms, and mourns the fact that we never had infant baptisms or first communions or confirmations. I also know that she prays to the saints and to anyone else who might listen because she's terrified for Mom's soul. Dad's soul, of course, is already damned, but Mom has a chance.

Laura and Theo thank her politely for her prayers; they've never been ones to appreciate praying to saints or dead people. Neither of these activities is encouraged in the evangelical circles we grew up in. We pray to God the Father usually, sometimes Jesus. The Holy Spirit is sort of hovering in the background, aware of everything, but we don't really pray to him. Some of the Christian hippies we knew did pray to the Holy Spirit. They were also the ones in church who waved the polyester silk flags and danced in the aisles and shook tambourines like it was Mardi Gras, and sometimes spoke in languages that sounded like Portuguese. They were the ones who taught us how praying in another language made your prayers extra potent somehow. Mom never liked that brand of theology, but Dad did.

When we go to Grandad George and Grandma Nancy's house, the experience is different. Grandad is more cerebral, less metaphysical. He doesn't pray to saints, especially not to his dead son and daughter-in-law. He believes everything that happens is God's will, and our job is to try to wrap our minds around it, to figure out the equation that strikes the perfect balance between "This sucks," and "But God isn't a dick, really." He asks us how we are, what we've been up to, if we saw the maples turning red or the purple sunset yesterday. Grandma Nancy gives us more gifts from her most recent trip to Erie.

At some point, Laura goes back to work, rising early and dressing nicely and spending each day teaching kindergartners; somehow, I assume, not breaking down into tears for the entirety of a day. Then the house seems even more empty and I feel even more alone. I peruse the internet, applying to jobs I can work from here—or even better, jobs which will take me away from here—and I come up empty each day. I move the two urns gingerly, from the computer desk where Theo left them, to the dining room table which is covered with papers and junk mail, to the mantel of the nonworking fireplace at one end of the room, which Mom restored when she was pregnant with us. The mantel is where the urns remain, and day by day the sting of their gaze lessens, until I forget they are there at all.

What I don't forget, what I can't shake, is the feeling that even when I am alone in the house, I'm not. In between each breath, I swear I can hear something: footsteps above my head, a stray word or laugh, the brush of clothing. I roam around the house following these sounds, certain I can hear them and also certain they are figments of my imagination. Laura's words ring in my head: *That's usually a sign someone needs therapy.*

"I don't need therapy," I say aloud, to myself, to whoever's listening. Maybe to God. "I don't need therapy. And fuck you."

Even with Theo explaining how he can go through life and not be angry, even after knowing Laura means well, and that most likely everyone else means well too, I'm still furious at God. No other beliefs have peeled themselves off the table yet; I only have the one. *God is real.* God is real, so where is he? God is real, so what is he up to? God is real, so why the hell are my parents dead? The belief offers no answers, only a bucketful of questions.

One day it's time to grocery shop again, so I drive down into town to the store. Theo has given me his credit card. I pull into the parking lot of Tom's Riverside Mart, where we do most of our week-to-week shopping. Tom's is a great bastion of the American Dream, meaning it's the only store in Haven to not close in forty years. It's your stereotypical supermarket: cinderblock walls, rows of fluorescent lights, floor tiles the color of Bermudan waters. To its credit, it does have everything. I push the cart up and down the aisles, throwing in anything that looks good. After picking out a bag of everything bagels and a loaf of bread, I turn the corner from the bread aisle to the canned foods aisle, and nearly run into a woman about my age, pushing a cart of her own with a baby buckled into the front.

"I'm so sorry!" I shout out reflexively, backing away.

"Amy, hi!" she says, and it takes me a moment to register: Emma. Emma McHale, now Richardson, I think. One of Laura's and my best friends growing up.

"Oh my gosh, hi Emma," I say, smiling wide. It is good to see her. Well, not good, exactly. But not bad. I give her a hug.

"Who's this little guy?" I greet the baby, who looks about a year old.

"This is Samuel," Emma says. "Sam."

"Hello Sam, how are you?" I say, patting his head gently. I never know how exactly to talk to children, and I end up being too formal and polite. The baby stares at me with his round blue eyes, which he got from his mother.

"He's so sweet," I say to Emma. She nods and looks at him tenderly, smoothing his fine white-blond hair while tucking back a strand of her own.

"How have you been?" she asks. Her voice is full of worry and care, and I feel compelled to convince her I'm okay.

"Oh, you know. Getting through it."

"It was such a lovely service. Pastor Jeff did a great job."

"Oh, yes. Absolutely."

"I've really missed seeing you all at church."

This is why seeing her isn't exactly good: Emma was our best friend growing up… in church. Her family was more conservative than ours, and Emma didn't go to public school like we did. Instead, she spent several stints at the local Christian school, the majority of her time homeschooled. Her parents were always strict about movies and music and dress codes, fastidious about academics and social graces. This isn't to be mean: she's a sweet girl, and always has been, but there's a veneer of something I've never been able to identify over every interaction with her, a *This is how you ought to live: separate from the world; don't let the evil in; if you just try this way hard enough, you will have the best kind of life. You will be the right kind of person.*

I'm sure she and Laura still keep in touch, although Laura is a working woman, and Emma doesn't believe in being a working woman. Laura hasn't ever told me about how Emma's been, although in Laura's defense, I never asked.

"Thank you," I say. "I've missed... everyone too." I feel guilty for lying, which makes me feel better about it. "How have you been?" I ask. "I heard you got married a few years ago."

"Our fourth anniversary next month, yes," Emma beams. Four years. She was nineteen. Laura was in the wedding. I, the prodigal daughter, was too busy with school to go. "You've met Daniel, right? My husband?"

"I think so?" Never in my life. "Congrats on your anniversary!"

"Thanks," she beams, dimples on her fair cheeks. "It's been great. This little guy just had his first birthday in August, and his big sister will be four next year!"

I'd forgotten; she has two children. Rachel was born nine months after the wedding. "How fun!" I say, inadvertently addressing the baby.

"You know, you should really come over for dinner sometime, and catch up," she says. She rocks the cart gently back and forth, as Sam grips the shopping cart bar and makes gleeful noises. "It's been ages since we've seen you."

The feeling of dread churns up my stomach. "Oh, yes, of course."

"I know what Laura and Theo have been up to, of course, but I want to hear about you!"

Maybe she thinks she does, but I don't think she does. I swallow. "Yes. That would be so fun. Just let me know."

She smiles and prepares to move down the aisle. "It was great running into you!"

I nod and say something automatically polite, and busy myself looking at canned soup as she goes.

I get home later than intended and begin putting away the groceries as the shadows outside lengthen. The unintentional meeting with Emma runs through my head. She's my age and married. Two kids, which is a feat even Laura hasn't accomplished. For as much as I mourn the fact that Laura settled down here in Haven so young, it could be worse. I feel a twinge of guilt. Emma seems happy. Who am I to say what should make people happy? Another twinge, equally powerful, of anger. No. Getting married so young, your whole life spent raising children; it's such a waste. I'm right about that. I know I am. I'm doing things the right way; the way you're supposed to. Education, career, independence. A third twinge, guilt again. Everyone thinks their way is the best way. Who's to say who's right?

It grows darker, and I busy myself around the kitchen, begin to make dinner. Something warm and cozy, I think. Meatballs and gravy, mashed potatoes. Laura and Theo should be home soon; Laura is usually home by now. I really don't like being alone when the night comes. I think of my dreams, of the night in Mom and Dad's room, of the thing I saw. I've since convinced myself it was nothing: tiredness, sleep paralysis. Maybe I wasn't really awake but thought I was. It's easier to believe these things I tell myself when it's not dark outside.

I hear a car park in the driveway behind the house, and crisp, light footsteps down the walkway to the porch. Laura's footsteps. My heart beats a little faster. I dread being alone with her too, but it beats being by myself. Ever since the day we went to Pittsburgh, things have been frosty again, punctuated by moments of strange politeness and bursts of anger, words saying too much or not enough. Theo's attempts to smooth things over have helped a little bit, but not completely, though that's not his fault.

The back door opens and Laura bursts in, looking more put together than I have in weeks. Her face is still tired, but her hair is brushed and styled and she wears makeup.

"Hi," she says.

"Hi."

"How was your day?" she asks.

"Oh, fine. I looked up some jobs on the computer. Cleaned the house a bit. Shopped."

"Nice." She takes off her coat and shoes. She's wearing elegant black pants and a gray blouse with tiny white polka dots on it, a necklace of purple glass beads that glimmer in the warm light of the kitchen.

"How was yours?" I venture.

"Today we learned about shapes," she says. She goes into the dining room and sets her bookbag on the computer desk, emptying it out.

"Fun."

"They thought so."

"How are the kids? How many do you have?"

"Twelve. They're good. So sweet. One of the moms baked me cookies," she produces a container from the bookbag. I take it from her and pause my dinner preparations to put some of the cookies on a plate. I take a bite from one. Chocolate chip, the perfect texture: chewy and soft without falling apart.

"Oh," I say as she comes back into the kitchen. "I ran into Emma McHale today. Richardson, I mean."

"How is she?"

"Good. I saw her son."

"Sam. He's cute." Laura inspects her fingernails, goes to the sink, and washes her hands.

"She misses... you at church," I say.

"We're planning to go back this week. I'll have to catch up with her."

"You are?"

She dries her hands. "Of course. We weren't going to stop."

"It just seems soon."

"It's been six weeks."

That long. Dear lord, it's almost Thanksgiving. I need to find a job.

Laura goes on. "Honestly, I don't know why we haven't gone back sooner."

"I do."

She gives me a look. I start boiling water for the potatoes.

"Why, then? Why haven't we gone back sooner?" she asks.

I count out four big russets from the cupboard, go over to the sink to scrub them. I take a breath. "Because it all seems too overwhelming to face people after everything."

She looks at me keenly, and I can't avoid meeting her gaze for a split second. I expect her eyes to be a stormy, dark green, but they're cool, nearly gray. "You assume a lot about people, you know that?" she says.

"I'm not wrong, though, am I?"

She ignores my question, grabs another cutting board and knife, and helps me cut potatoes. "I started therapy today," she says.

That's why she was late. I'm both relieved and anxious over the change in subject. "How was it?"

"It was… really good. It was nice to talk to someone who isn't in the situation, you know?"

I don't know because I haven't talked to anyone. But I have a good imagination. "Mhm."

"My therapist is named Dr. Mueller. We went to school with his son."

"Charlie."

"Yes. So Dr. Mueller knows me. He knew Mom and Dad a little. It's nice; he's close enough to not be a total stranger, but removed enough to not be in the thick of it."

I'm not used to her talking to me like this: casual, vulnerable. There's a catch; I just know it. "Well, that's nice," I say. I drop the cut potatoes into the water one by one.

"Dr. Mueller said something about acceptance, about how we don't have control over anything but the present, and what we'll do in it. It was… comforting to me." She becomes quiet, as if she's said too much, and I feel a hefty pause of expectation, but I don't know what she's expecting.

"That's awesome," I remark. I'm glad something was comforting to her, truly.

"You know," she says, "if you're looking for someone to talk to, Dr. Mueller is great. I think he could really help. Especially since you're back home."

Back home. My eyes blaze red and the dread in my stomach grips tighter. Back home. Said of all the people who left, for a little while, only to come back, drawn like a moth to a flame, a fly to sticky paper. *Back home.* The people who didn't make it, who weren't strong enough to go out into the world, so they came back. Back to safety, back to familiarity, *back home.*

"Thanks," I say. "But I don't need a therapist. And I'm not 'back home.' I'm just back temporarily. Till I find a job."

"I know it's not for good," she says. Her voice rises in pitch. "I just meant—"

"Brrrrrr!" Theo comes in, suddenly, through the back door. "It's a cold one, isn't it?" His rubber-soled shoes echo against the linoleum as he stamps his feet.

I turn away from Laura and melt some butter in a skillet, beginning a roux for the gravy.

"Hi, honey," she says to him, her voice tired.

He kisses her. "Sorry I'm late," he says. "How are you guys?"

I turn back to them and lean against the sink. "We're great." I smile. "Laura taught a bunch of kids about shapes today."

"Awesome," he says. He doesn't see the tense look she gives me, or if he does, he chooses to ignore it, as he does all unpleasantness.

That night, my dreams are vivid and lucid, ridiculous and terrifying. Laura with a gaggle of babies, all the same age, with mouths of adult teeth. Mom and Dad trying to drive up the waterfall in Dad's SUV, which barrels through the forest like a monster truck. Theo as a hellfire-and-brimstone preacher, telling me that the spiritual realm is most alive at 2 a.m.

In the most detailed of these dreams, I do go to therapy and have a complete conversation with Dr. Mueller. However, because I don't know what Dr. Mueller looks like, my imagination conjures up a not-quite-right Grandad George with a Nietzsche mustache, Charlie Mueller's brown eyes behind round Freud glasses, and Emma Richardson's white-blond hair. This amalgamation opens the door to his comfortably furnished office and shakes my hand.

"Good afternoon, Amy," he says.

"Hi, how are you?" I reply.

"I'm doing well." He nods thoughtfully, then narrows his eyes and says, "How are you?"

I have no idea whether to answer this tritely, in the way you do, or to count it as the beginning of the session. Soon I find myself plopped down on the couch and talking and talking:

"Well Doc, my parents drove down a cliff. They're dead now. Obviously. It was a high cliff. We had a funeral. They wanted to be cremated, so we did that, and we put their urns on the mantel in the dining room. That sounds like something from *Clue*, doesn't it? Miss Scarlett with the urns in the dining room.

"My parents were really devout, loving, Christian people. Not in a sickly-sweet way, you know, but in that just genuine good way, like when you go to Europe and all the pastries actually have flavor to them, not like the baked goods in sugar-sodden America. I've been to Europe, by the way. I spent two weeks in Berlin one summer in college. So I know a thing or two.

"I used to be a Christian. Then everything kind of fell apart. Laura thinks it was because I went to a liberal college in the city, but that's not it. I think everything was falling apart already, that there were cracks in it, like the buildings in Black Gold Cross. Then a storm blew along, and it all came tumbling down.

"What was the storm? I don't know exactly. It wasn't a single event, a single cataclysmic tornado. It was more like a bunch of hurricanes after a long season. Leaving Haven, I think, was one of the storms. Seeing life go on every day, somewhere else, when all my life the world was just a single river valley in a forest. Seeing that Aunt Maeve was right: people could thrive somewhere else. Those were storms. Another one: having been taught that for every question, the

Bible had an answer, that life was black-and-white, simple. And then finding that that wasn't true; the Bible isn't a manual; life isn't simple. There are some questions with no answers, some people and situations and places that don't fit the dichotomy. Seeing how some people had been so hurt by people who said they were acting on behalf of God. Wondering how, if my religion could be wrong about these things, what others it was wrong about. Wondering how far the stitches would unravel if I pulled hard enough.

"But what I can't reconcile is that *they*, my parents, did thrive, here. *They* did thrive, knowing God. Loving God. They subscribed to all of what I think is narrow and sheltered and small, but to them, it was big and generous and all-encompassing. How is it, Doc, that two sets of people can believe and do and be all the same things, and to one set it's ignorance, while to the other it's enlightenment? How?"

I wake up to the light of an early morning, pale and gray like the day of the funeral. My own words, this entire conversation so plotted out in my unconscious brain, still ringing in my ears. I laugh a little bit, astonished at the vividness of it. Then that old dread emerges, gripping the space between my navel and collarbone. The thought of really releasing everything to another person, even a stranger, is too terrifying to even think of. I can't imagine what would even happen if I let out all my thoughts to someone else, spoke them into the atmosphere like flint sparks in a cloud of gasoline fumes. I think the world might explode.

Chapter Nine

I'm still not used to living in this town again. It's more normal, more familiar than before, yet not quite comfortable. This town, where all the stores close at 4 p.m., where parking is free because the meters are broken, where it's not out of the ordinary to see men in hunting gear, camo and orange, sharing lunch at one of the two restaurants in town before getting in their pickup trucks and heading back into the woods. I'm struck by the weird dichotomy of wilderness and civilization: in town, the rows of empty storefronts separated by a few bright bastions of entrepreneurship, there's a semblance of urbanization. But in a few minutes, the world changes drastically: drive out into the countryside, and there are wooded hills hiding remote cabins; farms with open, windswept fields; damp valleys where people have lived in the same ramshackle houses for fifty years, and you can tell how long it's been by the piles of rusted junk in the yards: the abandoned cars representing each era, the turn-of-the-century tractors, the rows of defunct refrigerators and washing machines.

The thing I'm most unused to is being *known*. When I go to the grocery store, the cashier babysat me as a child. When I stop in the post office, I run into someone from my parents' church. When I walk the streets, people driving by honk their horns, not because I'm very attractive and they're pigs, but because their mothers are my great aunts, or they went to high school with Dad, or they're the dental hygienist I've had since I was four. All of these interactions don't make me feel comforted or cared for or loved; they make me feel spread out on a petri dish and microscoped. *How's the grief coming along?* I hear them thinking. *We're so glad you came back from the dreaded big city to our fun little home here. Please, stay forever. Stay forever and be sad as long as you want. We'll all watch you.*

Emma finds me on Facebook, my profile which I so carefully crafted to be invisible to people from Haven, and invites me to dinner one night about a week before Thanksgiving. Unfortunately, the night she's invited me also happens to be Laura and Theo's first planned dinner date since everything happened and I don't want to be alone in the house after dark, so I can't really come up with a good reason to say no. Also, I have a morbid curiosity to see what her life is like. So I say yes.

The day before this social engagement, I drive to Cainesville, fifteen minutes away, to sort through Dad's stuff in his office at Catawba University. Laura offered to join me, but she just started work again, and anyway, I want to do it alone.

Catawba's University title is rather misleading: it conjures up images of musty halls of academia, where thinkers in tweed brush suede elbows and speak in couplets. In reality, the whole campus is three buildings: the administrative offices/student center in a building that looks like a transistor radio with a gym tacked onto the back; the Humanities Department of tall sandstone, with vines creeping over it; and a giant nursing building that sort of looks like a hospital, which also houses the Business/Accounting/Education departments. A fountain stands in the middle of this cluster of buildings, anchoring them with a kind of gravitas.

Dad's office is on the top floor of the Humanities building, which houses the History, Communication, Art, and English departments. Inside, the halls sport scratched wainscoting, old pendant lights, and creaky floorboards. The building is musty and slightly cold, but this makes it feel more like the image of academia I have in my head. In the basement is the library, which is small but well-stocked; and then there are three floors of classrooms, some of which have class in session right now, the sounds of professorial voices lilting on about important things in between the squeaks of chalk on board. I climb three flights of stairs (this building is not ADA compliant) to the third floor, which is quiet, carpeted with soft turquoise shag for some reason, and full of offices the size of big closets. I spent a lot of time here as a kid; sometimes Mom brought Laura and me here to visit Dad in between his classes. We ate lunch on a blanket on the floor, like a picnic.

The door to Dad's office is closed. The dormer window above shows gray darkness inside. The door itself has the little name card: *Dr. Peter Reilly*. Yeah, Dad was a *Dr.* He never harped on it; he hated people calling him "Dr. Reilly." He always said the reason he got his Ph.D. was not because of the accolades, but because he was a massive nerd and just wanted to study dead things until the end of time. Unfortunately for him, that comes with a certain level of prestige.

Usually, Dad's door was covered with posters for upcoming events, or doodles he made while he was working on lectures or a list of his office hours. But today, for the first time ever, his door is covered with little sticky notes of all colors, which flutter like the feathers of a giant paper wing. I move in closer. *We miss you,* says one. *We love you Dr. R*, says another. *Prayers for you. Thank you for everything. Good vibes. See you on the other side.*

I feel my throat again, sore and clogged up. I swallow and swallow. Why couldn't people make a door of notes for our house? I could do without the whole running into people business, the calls, the random hugs at the grocery store. Just come and leave a sticky note.

The door to the office is locked, but I came prepared with Dad's keychain, a nondescript collection of keys for the house, his car, Mom's car, and a few others I can't place, one labeled *Office! Don't lose!!!* Mom made him this after he left his office key in the pocket of one of his many jackets—subsequently losing it—too many times. She labeled the key and put it on his keychain ("Like a normal person!" she said), and added a giant red tassel from one of our old living room curtains, so he wouldn't lose it. The tassel got caught on something and fell off long ago, but there's still a knot of red thread tangled around the keychain.

Inside, the office is cold and dark. I assume it hasn't been disturbed at all since he last left it, because as usual, it's a terrible mess, and there's no way any average person could come through here without compulsively cleaning it up. There are piles of papers on the desk, all arranged in what I am sure was some kind of system. The walls that aren't covered with bookshelves are lined with his drawings, which he was always doodling on when adults aren't supposed to be doodling: meetings, movie nights, family conversations, church. They're minimalist, pen-and-paper sketches, all in black ink lines and shadowy smudges. They depict simple things: buckets, tools, trees, houses, rocks. I recognize some of them as sketches of Black Gold Cross and the other ghost towns. As usual, he didn't try to capture the big vistas, but the little details and shapes. One page is a sketch of a single corner of gingerbread trim on what I know is a crumbling pre-Civil War house in the middle of the woods; the drawing is nothing more than spidery lines and angles.

The tall, heavy, dark wood bookshelves are filled with tomes that have boring titles. *The History of North America. Penn's Woods: A Chronology. Europe.* The sight of these books is comforting; I remember him toting them around the house, reading them on weekday nights or over Saturday breakfast. What a wonderful nerd.

One whole bookshelf is filled with notebooks of various shapes, sizes, and colors. Probably all notes and drawings on his beloved ghost towns. The floor, covered with the same turquoise shag carpet in the hall, has stacks of books on it, making only a narrow path to the desk, which has chairs on either side of it, and a wall of windows behind letting in the only light. The tops of the bookshelves have artifacts on them, things he was especially interested in: some blue porcelain china he found in the woods and tried to gift to the historical society, but they didn't want; old framed photos of Haven and Cainesville; railroad spikes; hunks of coal shaped like other things; Iroquois arrowheads; colonial bullets. On the desk, the only artifact is our family photo from the year Laura and I turned fifteen. My hair is terrible, but we all look so happy.

Where to start organizing this? I know someone else took over his classes for the rest of the semester. What if there are students' papers here somewhere, and they want them back? Do I have to run all over campus and track students down? Should I give his books back to the University? Should I take them home? What would I do with them there? It's not as if Laura and I are itching to read *Penn's Woods: A Chronology.*

There's a soft knock on the open door. I turn and see Dr. Lynda Williams, the head of the English Department, who was Dad's colleague for as long as I can remember. Dr. Lynda is the kind of person you know is a poet just by looking at her. She wears a characteristic outfit of black jacquard pants, a blazer embroidered with glass beads, jewelry that looks like it belongs in the Met. Her eyes are piercing blue, her salt-and-pepper hair cut short and severe, her frame short and rail-thin. She seems intimidating but has the softest voice, and if you get her talking about philosophy or literature—or poetry— the beauty of her voice and her words and her ideas make you cry. This happened to Mom many times.

"Amy," she says. "How are you doing?"

A million people have asked me this, and a million times it has sounded like a simple question with a simple choice of answers, more to comfort others than myself. But with her, the question contains multitudes. "I'm getting by," I say.

She walks down the path between the books and gives me a hug. The top of her head comes just under my nose, but somehow, I feel cradled in her arms, small, mothered. I know I saw her at the funeral and we probably had this same exact exchange, but I can't remember.

"Thanks," I say.

"How's Laura?" she asks when we pull away from the hug.

"I think she's doing okay. She's started work."

"And you?"

"I'm... in between jobs. I lost my job in Pittsburgh."

"I'm so sorry."

"Yeah, so I'm just here... for now."

"I'm sure your family is glad to have you here."

I give a dry smile. "Yes."

"How are you coping with everything?"

I shrug. "I do my best. I take walks. Laura wants me to go to therapy, but I don't think it's for me."

"You might be surprised. Sometimes it's good just to let out the thoughts in your brain, the emotions in your gut." She speaks evenly, not trying to convince me one way or another, but merely stating the options as if considering the merits of iambic pentameter against free verse. "You take everything out, lay everything out, and see how they connect, see what you want to let go of, see what you want to keep."

The image of my table of beliefs flashes in my eyes. I blink. "Yeah. Yeah. You're right."

"This is a hard season. It's okay to move through it slowly."

I nod. "Thanks. Did you…" I look down at my shoes, speckled with drops of mud from the street. I wipe each toe off the backs of my ankles. "Did you see him?"

"I saw him that Thursday."

"How was he?"

There's a pause. The office is silent, muffled with the many layers of pages of books.

She takes a shaky breath. "He was… Peter. Just Peter. Messy and passionate and goofy and obsessed with the newest old and rusty thing."

I try to smile, but the expression sours. "I should have been here to see it." Judas. *I'm sorry I'm sorry I'm sorry.*

She looks at me, those piercing blue eyes like the winter sky on icicles. "You were exactly where you should have been," she says. "You have nothing to be ashamed about."

My eyes fill with tears despite myself.

She goes on, "Your parents knew you loved them. They were proud of you."

"Really." I blink, tears squeezing down my cheeks.

"So proud of you. Nearly every day, your dad bragged about you living in the city all by yourself. He was so excited for you."

Now I hug her. "Thank you."

"Do you want help?" she asks. "There's a lot to go through here."

"Thanks, but no. I'd prefer to do it alone."

"I understand." She squeezes my shoulder before she goes.

I start two piles of books: a pile for us to keep and a pile to donate to the University library. I don't know what would be the use of keeping some of them—I'm not a history nerd, and never will be—but there are books so familiar, which I saw him reading so often, that looking at them is like looking at his face again.

I get lost in the journals, which go back decades, to when he was about my age. While the majority of the books are filled with sketches and little notes he made on his many treks through the forest, some of them have large sections of written accounts of his day-to-day life. I've never really read Dad's writing before, not even the research papers he found so fascinating, but when I read the journals, I can hear his voice, excitedly introducing a new idea, making the past real to us. I read from one journal, dated 2002:

> *Pittstown was founded in 1863 and became a ghost town less than two years later. Once called the wickedest city east of the Mississippi. John Wilkes Booth acted in a few plays in its makeshift theater before he got his big break. Maggie and I took the girls there tonight. Amy was less than impressed.*

I remember this. Laura and I were about seven, and I had been under the impression that Pittstown had full blocks of buildings, like Black Gold Cross. I kept asking to see the ghost town, and when Dad said, "This is it! See the plaques? They tell us where buildings used to be!" I became irate and said the town was "a disappointment," a phrase I recently heard Mom use about politics, and which seemed apt for this situation. Mom and Dad laughed at me and I couldn't understand why. Now I do, and I laugh at myself too.

I force myself to stop reading, otherwise I'll be here all day. I continue to organize, finding some empty cardboard boxes in the utility closet of the shaggy hall, and carrying everything I'm keeping to my car, shutting them in the trunk.

A few hours later, I depart from campus, leaving everything that seems to belong to someone else with Dr. Lynda. "Please, please let me know if there's anything I can do," she says when I leave. "I know many people have said that to you, but I mean it." She gives me a sad, soft smile, and squeezes my shoulder with a warmth that travels down my body and loosens the fear at my core just a little bit.

As I drive back into Haven, my car is sluggish and weighed down, protesting under the weight of the many books. It hasn't had to work this hard since I lugged all my stuff up from Pittsburgh. The road is winding and surrounded by so much thick forest that even with all the leaves gone, it seems like it's nearly dusk, not two in the afternoon. Without the leaves, I see the rusted remnants of oil pipelines, squat corrugated steel sheds, and giant rotted wood barrels that used to mark this area as a place where things happened.

There's a brief break in the trees, where Seneca Creek runs through to downtown Haven from its origin somewhere in the hills. This is the creek they used to ship barrels of oil down, first through these woods, then into Haven to the Allegheny River, then down that into Pittsburgh. This was the creek that was once perpetually covered with a layer of oil, and as a result, caught fire multiple times. This is also the creek that runs through Black Gold Cross.

The sign for it shows up on my left, a brown sign with white letters. *Historic Black Gold Cross. 2 Mi.* This sign is the same exact one my parents drove past when they were my age; it was posted here in 1966, and it shows. Words and symbols have been graffitied over it and then scrubbed out, leaving faded patches. The edges are rusted from the rain and snow and blazing summer heat. But despite the decades of vandalism and weathering, the sign has not been replaced, because it's not really anyone's job to replace it. For years, Dad had been trying to get the place recognized as a national landmark, and eventually, hopefully, a state park, but to no avail. The land belongs to the township, but no one has the money or the will to either fix it or tear down the town and build something new. So it sits, waiting, gathering dust and decay and crime as time goes by.

The thought stabs me so much that I pull over just past the sign, then I put the car in reverse and turn onto the narrow, potholed road into Black Gold Cross. The road swerves sharply to the right, then the left, climbing up the bank of the creek. The way is paved, but there are hairpin turns and narrow parts, and some places where the edge of the road abruptly gives way to a hillside, betting on the aluminum guardrail catching you should you really need it. The forest here is even thicker, shutting out the pale light of the sun. There are no buildings along this stretch, just faint foundations in the brush telling me where houses used to be. And of course, this place is crawling with grandfather trees.

When I finally come down into the gentle slope and curve right before town, I take a sharp right into a little dirt parking lot. This is where we always used to stop. My car groans and skids as I hit the brakes. I can't remember the last time I was here; it had to have been before college. What used to be a family event a few nights a week turned into a Sunday stroll, and then eventually a holiday outing, and then only a memory. Just for me, of course. Mom and Dad walked here all the time, even when their children grew too old to play Teller and Bank Robber.

I lock up the car and head down the paved road, which slowly turns to broken-up chunks of asphalt, and then to stones, then to gravel, and finally to soft packed dirt. The road leads around a thicket of trees and across some train tracks, and suddenly, I'm in the ghost town, walking down Main Street. The old brick train station leans precariously away from the tracks, as if the very sight of trains revolts it. I walk down the abandoned main street, and suddenly I am a child again. There's the old bank that Laura and I used to play in, its marble front stoop glittering in the little scraps of light that come down through the trees. There's the Sheriff's office, which Mom never let us in, and for good reason, as it's now collapsed. There are houses and places where there used to be houses, a saloon or ten, a handful of brothels, a rickety, defiant church.

This place makes me so sad. I think of all the men who left their families or brought their families to come here and make their fortunes, all the women forced to sell their bodies or break their backs for a place to live, all the children growing up, thinking this place of four-foot deep mud and burnt trees and scarred earth was normal. I think of all the foolhardy church people who thought building a chapel

116

next to a whorehouse would do some good. I think of the hedonism, the lust for power, the visions of greatness, the trauma from the Civil War, and before that, the trauma of invasion and colonization. All to leave nothing behind but shells of places where a random girl can come for a walk, where animals shit, where teenagers get pregnant, where people sell drugs in the dead of night.

I breathe in slowly. You'd think it'd be creepy as hell to walk down the main street of a ghost town all alone on an overcast fall day. But right now, all I feel is overwhelming, painful longing. Because the last time I was here, I was at least seventeen, and there was no Pittsburgh, no lost home, no lost job. There were no awkward Christmas mornings, no brother-in-law, just Theo. Laura was my friend. And Mom and Dad were here, with me, seeing everything with me. My legs buckle under me, and I sink to my knees into the muddy earth of Main Street. I cry, letting the wind that whips the trees blow the tears off my face, washing and chapping my cheeks.

"I'm sorry! I'm sorry! I'm sorry!" The words come in their familiar rhythm, the ever-present chant like a heartbeat. *I'm sorry I haven't been here, fully, in seven years. I'm sorry I never came back here with you. I'm sorry I was gone for so many things, and I'm sorry you'll be gone for everything else. I'm sorry that the land you loved so much took you for itself, and left us all behind. I'm sorry that the way you had to go was so senseless, so random, so ridiculously, fucking stupid.*

When I come back to myself, my eyes are closed, my face is dry, and I'm cold, still kneeling in the middle of Main Street, surrounded by trees and abandoned buildings. I get a shiver up my spine and open my eyes. Without trying, I look for the grandfather trees. I mentally remove everything around them and look back in time. My eyes reassemble the fallen buildings, mend the shattered windows, and cut down the overgrowth. I see glass and curtains in each window, chipped paint smoothed again, rooves reassembled and on top of their buildings where they belong. There's a weight on my chest, that dread, that fear, but it morphs into something else. I feel surrounded by people, like in a crowded room, even though there's no one here but me. I sense the intense pressure of emotions and thoughts and memories that are not my own. Whispers of voices, like wind chimes, are carried by the wind. Inhaling sharply, I stand up, tottering on numb legs.

"Who's there?" My voice warbles. "Who's there?" I say again, louder, deeper. This is like that night in Mom and Dad's room. But now, it's not 2 a.m.

There's no answer. The whispering dies down, and little by little my view of the town dims and deconstructs, and soon I see it as it really is: only a shell, only a mouth full of missing teeth. I wait, daring it to transform again, but it doesn't. So I turn and walk back to my car, feeling vaguely chased away, forcing myself not to run. When I get in the car and turn it around, I punch the gas all the way back up that winding road.

Deep down, I know I've had that feeling before, that sensation of not being alone when I really was, of being surrounded by people who aren't there. But I don't know what exactly this feeling means. I only know that it is familiar, and on the fringes of my memory I know I felt it back then, too, the innumerable times I came here with Mom and Dad. But trying to remember if it was the same, so vivid and real, is like trying to remember a word on the tip of your tongue: the more I think about it, the more the memory recedes from me, like darkness running from the light as the earth turns on its axis.

I return to the house, still rattled by my time in the ghost town, from the emotional weight of cleaning out Dad's office, and the physical weight of carrying all the boxes. Laura has just returned from work and she helps me carry stuff from my car to the dining room, although I insist I don't need help. We pile the boxes in one corner of the dining room, between the fireplace and the table, and I realize how much the room has become a dumping ground for things we don't want to deal with.

"We should really organize," I say.

"Yeah, at some point," Laura replies, heading to the kitchen for some water. She looks both flushed and pale at the same time.

On my way out of the room, I notice Mom and Dad's phones on the dining table. They're dead, and look weathered, as always. "I didn't know these were here," I say, picking them up gingerly.

"They've been there," Laura takes a deep drink of water.

"Have you looked at them?"

She stares out the window. "No."

I rustle around the computer desk, looking for the extra chargers Dad always kept in the drawers. I find one, and plug Mom's phone in.

"Why are you doing that?" Laura asks. "What are you looking for?"

I realize I don't know. And then I realize I *do* know: I want to see if there's anything else they left behind: a last message, a last text, something to make me feel better about the times I forgot to answer back, the times I sent a call to voicemail. Something to rewrite the List of Lasts for me.

Soon Mom's phone boots up, and I type in the passcode Laura and I have always known because she was always forgetting it. *It's our birthday, Mom*, we'd remind her. *0610*.

The phone unlocks, and the home screen is a picture of the four of us on a hike long ago, the same picture Dad had in his office, the one in which my hair looks terrible but we're all so happy. I cradle the phone in my hand like it's a newborn kitten, breathless at this sight, this utterly commonplace piece of technology that held her gaze every day. I open the texts and find some everyday ones between her and Dad, her and Laura, some of her friends and family members. *Please pick up milk*, she asks Dad. *I'm on my way home,* she tells Laura. *You look gorgeous!* She says to her cousin, who sent a selfie in a new dress.

Sorry to miss you. Call back. Love!

My heart stops. The phone tells me that this text was read a moment after it was sent, but there's no reply. No reply, from an ungrateful Judas of a daughter.

I'm sorry. I'm sorry. I'm sorry.

119

Laura has crept up behind me and watches the screen from over my shoulder. I hurriedly close the texts and open the calls, scanning a long list of short calls to or from Dad, a long call from Nanna Mae, a missed call going to me. I swallow and move on to pictures. Little snapshots of random things, a few selfies, some pictures of her and Laura out for lunch. The envy is there again, the jealousy that Laura was here and I wasn't. The guilt, because that's my fault. I turn the phone off, my hands shaking.

"Here," Laura says gently. She takes the phone from me. I cover my face with my hands and bend over the cluttered computer desk. "What were you looking for?" she asks softly.

"I don't know," I say. "I should have called her back."

I expect Laura to harp on this. After all, it was apparently what made her so angry at me the morning after the funeral. But this time, she lays her hand gently on my shoulder and says, "You didn't know."

The big weight of dread in my body, the weight of panic and guilt, is weakened. A small tear forms in the tightly-knitted mesh.

Chapter Ten

The following evening, I dress in jeans and a nice blouse, throw on a sweater and some ankle boots, and drive through town, picking up a bouquet of cheap flowers at the gas station on my way to Emma's house. Emma lives out in the middle of nowhere. She shared her address in our Facebook message, but I know the place. It's one of those houses you pass all the time without knowing who lives there, until you do; one of the many homes dotting the countryside, connected by the narrow highway stretching toward Erie, the same road our family took each summer when we drove up to the Peninsula.

The house is a simple ranch, brick, with neat gardens—winterized now—in the back. I park in the gravel driveway behind a huge pickup truck with muddy wheels, which sits next to a little white car which I assume is Emma's. I take the walkway down to the front door, avoiding the frostbitten grass of the lawn, and ring the doorbell, fluffing out the bouquet of flowers while I wait. A few petals drop from one of the button mums.

"Welcome, welcome!" Emma greets me as she opens the door. A wave of warmth from inside hits me and it smells like lavender and vanilla, coffee and seasoned meat. Emma gives me a hug, which crushes the flowers. "I'm so glad you were able to make it," she whispers.

I want to laugh, inwardly, at her sincerity, but I can't. I want to assume she has an agenda, an evil plan to get me to swear loyalty to all five points of Calvinism, but I can't do it. She's too sweet, too earnest. She always has been.

"I'm just finishing up dinner," she says. "Oh, lovely flowers! Thank you." She takes them.

"Do you need help?" I ask, taking off my coat and shoes.

"Here, I'll grab a vase, and you can put these in water." She disappears down the hall to a closet. I hear the clink of glass. I wait for her in the living room, a simple and clean space with hardwood flooring that extends into the rest of the house, soft blue painted walls, a big stone fireplace with a family photo hung above it. Sam, the baby, was brand-spanking-new when this picture was taken and looks incredibly put out about it.

Speaking of Sam, there he is: in a little bouncing chair in one corner of the room, playing with some toys and staring at me while he slobbers on them. "Hi Sam," I say. His eyes crinkle, and he laughs. I must be damned hilarious.

Emma comes back with a vase and beckons me into the kitchen beyond, where the same wood flooring is paired with bright green walls the color of fresh avocados, and the stainless-steel appliances gleam under the light of a beautiful blown glass pendant lamp.

"Gorgeous kitchen," I say. This makes Mom and Dad's tile squabbles seem lame.

"Oh, thank you," Emma says. "We just got it redone a few months ago." She sets the table on the other side of the room.

I fill the vase at the sink. "Something smells good," I remark.

"Pot roast," she smiles. "Mashed potatoes and green beans."

"Sounds amazing."

"I was going to make chicken, but we're all having turkey next week, so I went for something a little different."

"Pot roast is perfect."

Heavy footsteps echo down the hall, accompanied by a pitter-patter of weightless ones. In comes Daniel, Emma's husband, followed by a small girl who must be Rachel. I almost do a double-take: Rachel is only three, but already has the precocious demeanor of an oldest sister, a commanding and mature air. What surprises me is how exactly she looks like Emma at that age, the image in my mind I still have when I think of Emma. Long, wispy curls of blond hair, bare feet—despite the cold weather—and a flowing knee-length dress over leggings. She twirls and dances a little bit as she comes into the kitchen.

"Hi, I'm Daniel," Emma's husband interrupts my thoughts. He holds out his hand to shake. "Nice to meet you!" He's very tall, nearly a foot taller than Emma and me. His hands are clean, but rough, and I remember that he's a contractor, probably responsible for this beautiful kitchen. I know he's only a few years older than me, but he already wears a look of assuredness of someone much older, which contrasts amusingly with the shock of very curly, blond hair at the top of his head. He smooths the hair down to the side absentmindedly.

"Nice to meet you," I answer.

"And this is Rachel." Emma comes over to us, finished with setting the table. "Rachel, remember your manners."

"Hi," she says shyly. Then, at a look from her mother, "Welcome to our home."

I almost burst out laughing, but hold my composure. "Thank you very much."

Dinner passes smoothly, and I am surprised to find how at ease I am, despite the ever-present dread in my stomach, and the ever-sneaking suspicion that Emma is trying to reconvert me. I hear about how Daniel's contracting business has been doing well, how Rachel will be starting home school next year, how Emma has begun a side business selling baked goods on Facebook. Sam isn't up to much, but I'm sure he'll turn out fine. They ask me about college, about Pittsburgh, seem genuinely excited for me, and genuinely hopeful that I'll find a job and home there again. If they are suspicious of my spirituality, or certain I'm a wolf in sheep's clothing, they don't say it. We laugh at some of the stories Daniel tells about work, I hold Sam while Emma washes the dishes, Rachel shows me her dollhouse, we have dessert and coffee. I leave just before they put the kids to bed, thanking Emma for the invitation.

"You're welcome any time," she says. "I think of you guys often. I'm so sorry for your loss, and I'll keep praying for you."

"Thank you," I stammer.

"They're in a better place." She rests her hand on my shoulder, ever so lightly. "This world was not their home. They're the lucky ones, you know. They get to see the Lord before we do."

Stunned, my reply is stuck in my throat. I nod instead.

She hugs me. "It's good to see you again. I'm glad you're back home."

Back home. I totter out to my car and start it. *Back home.* I drive down the worn highway, through the dark forested land that goes on and on and never ends, squeezing out breath, shutting out light. *Back home.*

Why the hell is Emma Richardson so happy? Why does she have all the things I don't want, that I think are problematic or ignorant or sheltered, but she's content, and safe, and satisfied? It doesn't make sense to me; I can't wrap my head around it.

I know she didn't mean to offend me when she told me my parents were lucky to be dead. I know what headspace she was—is—in, because I can easily put the memory of that mindset over my own head again, like a well-worn cap. She was trying to comfort me, trying to offer me hope of a great beyond Mom and Dad have now gone to, a world with no tears or suffering or pain. But it stings, so badly. *They're the lucky ones.*

I remember when Papa Jim died, when Laura and I were ten. While he was ready, and it was an exhale, because he was at peace, Mom was of course depressed about it for a long time. She was the only child of her parents and was close to both of them. Papa Jim was one of those kind, tender men who considered himself successful because he had all he needed: a little house, retirement from an honest job as an engineer at one of the old factories, a community, a family. He went to confession each Saturday night, and mass each Sunday morning. He was in charge of the raffles at the Catholic church festivals each summer, and at the fish fries each Lent. Although, of course, he and Mom got into spirited debates about why she wasn't Catholic anymore, or why she should send her children to Catholic school anyway, Papa Jim didn't let it bother him. He was faithful to the church he'd grown up in, however problematic it may have been through the decades. His old-time religion was good enough for him.

One Sunday a few weeks after his funeral, we were at church. Laura and I were milling around the building, waiting for Mom and Dad to be done visiting with people so we could go home. They were chatting with Pastor Jeff and his wife Julie, both longtime friends, and I remember catching just the tail end of something Mom said about

125

missing Papa Jim terribly, though she was glad he was in a better place.

At that moment, Mrs. Gladys Bolger, an older church lady, came up to them, finished with her rounds of setting the church in order after the service, and joined the conversation. Mrs. Gladys was one of the ex-Baptists, who never raised her hands during worship and couldn't be bothered to wave a colorful little flag like the Christian hippies did, but who could be compelled to clap a little if a song was lively. She had short, curly white hair, piercing blue eyes, an endless supply of colorful appliqued sweatshirts, a tarnished gold wedding band she wore faithfully even twenty years after her husband Ralph passed away.

Mrs. Gladys shook her head, and in a voice full of concern said, "I'm so sorry for your loss. It's… such a shame when our loved ones don't get a chance to reckon with the Lord before they pass." Mom, Dad, Pastor Jeff, and Julie all turned to her, taken aback.

"What?" Mom said quietly. An inexperienced person might have mistaken her low tone for meekness, but I, her most stubborn child, recognized it as the quiet before the storm. I stopped and hid behind a chair a few aisles away. Laura sat behind me. We peeked around the chairs to watch the action.

"Well," Mrs. Gladys went on glibly, in a nonchalant voice polished with a veneer of worry, "he was Catholic, wasn't he? I just hope he got to accept Jesus as his Lord and Savior. The Lord knows, of course, if he had a moment of clarity. But we don't know. We can only hope."

"Excuse me?" Mom said, giving her another chance.

Mrs. Gladys smiled sympathetically. "Were you with him when he passed? Did you get the chance to witness to him?"

"My father and I talked about God very often," Mom said.

"Did he ever make a confession of faith?" Mrs. Gladys asked.

Dad saw where this was going. So did Pastor Jeff and Julie. "Jim was a faithful man," said Dad, trying to smooth things over. "A loving man. We're all unfortunate that he's gone from the world."

"He spread the love of Christ everywhere he went," Pastor Jeff echoed.

Mrs. Gladys was unfazed. She went on in a conspiratorial, chummy tone of voice. "Well, you know, it's not enough just to be faithful to your church. The Catholic Church is idolatrous. It's possible for someone to go to church each week, and think they are worshipping God, and still go to hell when they die."

Mrs. Gladys wasn't trying, I don't think, to be cruel, but that's usually when people are cruelest. She thought she was preaching to the choir. She thought she was being, I guess, some kind of comfort. I don't know why she thought this, but she did.

Mom, of course, was not comforted. "Why would you say that to me?" she said.

Mrs. Gladys blinked. "Well—"

"Why would you think that that is something you could say to a person? Did you think that would make me feel better? Would it make me feel better for some random, ignorant person to tell me that my dad has gone to hell?"

Now Julie tried to smooth things over. She patted Mom on the back. "It's okay, Mags. I don't think anyone's trying to be unkind. You've had a hard few weeks. Emotions are high. It's all right."

"No," Mom pointed directly at Mrs. Gladys. "Don't tell me that my dad wasn't faithful enough, or that he didn't know God enough. You know nothing about this. It's none of your damn business."

"I-I'm sorry if you're offended…"

"Of course I'm offended. Wouldn't you be offended, if I told you Ralph might actually be in hell now too?"

"Well… Ralph wasn't Catholic," Mrs. Gladys stammered.

"It's possible to go to church all your life, and still go to hell when you die," said Mom. "Isn't that right?"

"Come on, Mags," Dad said. "Let's go home."

Somehow, we all got into the car for the most stressful drive of my life. Laura and I sat in the backseat, each staring out opposite windows, trying desperately not to cry even though we knew Mom wasn't mad at us, while Mom herself unleashed a tirade on Dad, and his face grew redder and redder, even though he knew she wasn't mad at him either.

"What is wrong with that damn woman?" Mom asked. "What the *hell* is wrong with her?"

"She's just ignorant," Dad said. "She meant well. There are lots of people who think—"

"I don't care what people think!" Mom said. "The *audacity* to come up to me, to tell me things about *my* father, to tell *me* what I should have said to him, to tell *me* how he should have lived his life!"

"She shouldn't have done it," said Dad. "You're right. She shouldn't have."

Then Mom began to cry, and that was worse than the yelling.

"It's okay, it's okay," said Dad.

"What if she's right?" Mom sobbed. "What if he is in hell?"

I heard sniffles beside me, and I jabbed Laura in the elbow. She jabbed me back. I felt tears welling up in my eyes and shut them tight, which made me get motion sickness as the car swerved around the sharp turns of the streets of Haven.

"She's wrong," Dad said. "She's wrong."

"Dad did the best he could," Mom said. "He wasn't perfect. He wasn't spiritual. He wasn't a theologian."

"I know, I know."

"I tried to talk to him about things. But we disagreed."

"Mags, it's okay."

"He followed God the best way he knew how."

"He did. God knows that."

The rest of the drive home was silent, and I couldn't wait until Dad pulled into the driveway, so I could eject myself from the car and run down through the backyard, letting all the too-heavy emotions evaporate off me into the air.

"Girls," Mom said when Dad parked, and I groaned silently.

"Yes?" Laura said, her voice squeaky.

"You know that when you give your heart to God, he has it for good, right?"

"Uh-huh," we said together.

"No, I'm serious," said Mom. Her voice sounded raw and a little ragged, but gathered strength with each word. "God doesn't let us go.

God doesn't leave us or forsake us. If you want to be with God, He will be with you. Even when we're confused, or scared, or flat-out don't know what's going on, God doesn't let us go. He's bigger than all of it. He can handle it. God," she paused, "is not a fucking wuss."

"*Honey*," Dad said. But he laughed, and Mom laughed back, and Laura and I giggled nervously, completely confused and knowing full well we'd get in trouble if we said something like that, but Mom had special privileges.

"I only use strong words when they are warranted," said Mom. "I'm teaching my children important spiritual truths, and that deserves strong words."

"So Papa Jim is okay then," Laura said.

"Papa Jim knew God," Mom answered. "I don't know what that means, but I don't have to know. It's none of our business to figure out what that means."

I remember that being one of the first days I felt a belief in my head. I had obviously believed many things by the tender age of ten. Most Christian kids do. We knew all about the history of the Israelites and all the gory detail of that; we knew that there is a hell and you are responsible to make sure you don't go there; we knew that God loved us so much that despite our putrid sin He murdered his own son to pay our fare to heaven, and if you ask that son to live in your heart, God sees Jesus when he looks at you. He doesn't even see *you* at all. We knew that you are responsible to pray and read your Bible and share Jesus with others and not think about sex too much (even if you're not quite sure what sex is); and that someday Jesus will come back to judge the living and the dead.

So I knew all that. But this was the first time I felt touched by something profound, the first time I felt a belief really stick itself to me. *God doesn't let go. He's not a fucking wuss.* And it kept sticking to me, until I eventually emptied out my head and put everything on the table.

I drive stormily through the wilderness until I come back into Haven, puttering down the streets slowly as the speed limit changes. I stop at a red light and realize I'm at the intersection in my dream: where the old bank building faces the park which used to be a city block. When the light turns green, I hit the gas sharply, and the car rears ahead. Out of the corner of my eye, I register that I'm passing Benny's Bar, a popular mainstay in town, one Laura and I were never allowed to go to, even when they introduced food to the menu and let under-21s in before nine at night. I slam on the brakes and park along the street.

I'm foggy, dull, numb. Like the whole world is blunt, covered in carpet, underwater. Little images register: the crack in the sidewalk, filled in with brown moss; the door of the bar, chrome handle faded from years of hands; the sharp smell of fried food and beer hitting me on the way in. The place is dingy and dark and kind of lame, far from the pit of hell everyone in church always talked about it being. What else was everyone at church wrong about? The music is loud, pounding in my ears and I head to the bar and order gin on ice.

"Amy?" a voice calls, misty, far away. I turn and find a familiar face. Katie Brown. Oh God, I'd forgotten about Katie. Another friend from church, long ago, before her parents divorced. Even before that, the church ladies whispered about her because she was wild and rebellious, wore too much eyeliner, and liked ripped jeans. Later, she was kicked out of the Christian school because her mother had a live-in boyfriend. Then there were rumors Katie was bisexual, and that was enough to completely scare the youth group girls from ever talking to her again. It never quite bothered me, but our paths never crossed for me to tell her that, and then we lost touch.

"Katie," I breathe. The gin has started to work its way to my fingertips and feet, and I turn unsteadily toward her. "How are you!" My voice is loud, but it too seems far away. I give her a sloppy hug. "I've missed you!"

She looks too old: her face pale and weathered, hair choppy and unevenly dyed. She's skinny as hell. "I never thought I'd see you in here!" she yells over the music.

I drain the glass of gin in one gulp and ask for another. "I'm different," I reply.

This thought seems to please her and she gives me a wry smile and invites me over to a booth in the corner, where a group of people I vaguely remember is gathered.

The hours pass in a flood of disjointed memories. I drink and drink, swallowing each thought that comes to my head as soon as it pops up. I live in the moment, letting the atmosphere surround me, embrace me, coddle me. The people at the booth are all familiar faces: old high school classmates, people I never really hung around with, because at the time I was a good Christian girl and they weren't. These were the people I couldn't be friends with, me upon my high road of spiritual purity. These were the people our youth group leaders had in mind when they told us how living the Christian life was like standing on a chair high above the rest of the world, how it was easier for someone on the floor to pull you down than for you to pull them up. *Do not be unequally yoked together with unbelievers.* I remember this, and I remember all the similar times a church lady or visiting pastor said something snarky about the secular people of the world. I also remember all the times Mom made friends with the homeless people who slept under the bridge, and all the times Dad asked people walking, laden with groceries, if they needed a ride home. *Why does Jesus eat with tax collectors and sinners?* And the contradiction of it all makes me sick with fury, and I keep drinking to drown the memories out.

At some point I'm in the bed of a pickup truck with Katie and a few others, driving through the woods in the frozen November night, shrieking, giddy, at the top of our lungs. The cold air combs through my hair and makes prickles on my scalp, and Katie grips me tight as the truck swerves around curves in the road and throws us from side to side.

Then we're in Black Gold Cross, and I stare up through the bare trees to the black sky, pricked with stars like shards of glass over velvet, as the others run down Main Street whooping and laughing. I feel suddenly cold, and all the noises die away, and I blink and blink and get that feeling again, of being surrounded by people I can't see.

And then, at once, I can *see* them: people walking up and down the street. Explorers and ruffians and farmers, all around me, brushing against me, taking no notice that I stand in the middle of the street. The stained-glass windows of the bank, the brothels humming with rowdy music, the church resounding with hymns. The creek on fire, the pinpricks of light from the quiet farms off in the distance, growing the grandfather trees. I'm doing what I always wanted to do, what Dad told me I could do if I really listened enough: I'm seeing the stories of the people of the past. But I don't want it. It's too much. It terrifies me.

I crumple to my knees again, like I did last time I was here, and scream, and close my eyes, trying desperately to shut it all out, as the others laugh and the swaths of ghostly figures surround us.

When I open my eyes again, I'm at home, on the living room couch. The morning sun has broken through the white-gray clouds, and everything outside is crystalized with moisture. Laura stands over me, her long hair tickling the edges of my face. There's a scent I can't place. It's familiar, pleasant, yet makes me sad.

"Are you okay?" she asks. Her eyes are grayer today, green-gray like a rough emerald.

I sit up, feeling woozy. "What time is it?" I fumble for my phone, but can't find it. I'm still wearing my jeans and blouse from last night. I wonder if everything was just a dream, if maybe I did drive straight home from Emma's house, only to fall asleep on the couch and conjure up the whole rest of the night in my sleep.

"It's eleven."

"Why aren't you at work?"

"It's Saturday."

I press my eyes together. The light is so painful; everything is too sharp, too pointed.

"You smell like beer," she says.

"Thanks." I lie back down, hands over my eyes. Maybe it wasn't all a dream after all.

"We were really worried. You were out so late and didn't call."

"I was fine."

"You drove home, you know."

I didn't know. I have no memory of it at all. "Well, I guess I shouldn't have done that." I hope my car is okay. I hope other people's cars are okay.

"No. Who were you with?"

The images flash before my mind and I don't know who I was with. All I can remember is Katie. Just Katie.

"Some friends."

"I doubt it was Emma and Daniel."

"No, it was after I left their house."

Laura nods, straightens up. "Okay."

"You disapprove, don't you? Just tell me. Tell me how terrible I am, how fucked-up you think I am."

She glares at me. "Stop it. You're drunk."

"I'm hungover. I'm a good little hungover Christian girl. Falling off chairs so you don't have to." I laugh and laugh. I'm about to say more, which I'm sure is wildly hilarious, when suddenly all the anger and guilt and sadness balled up in my stomach explodes into a constellation of dread, and I get up quickly and rush through the house, barely making it to the bathroom off the kitchen before vomiting. Then I start to cry and then I vomit again.

I hate throwing up, with a passion. Usually, when I feel sick, I refuse to give in. I wait out the pain. They say this makes a stomach illness last longer and that it's actually better to vomit and be done with it. But I can't stand the vinegary taste in my mouth, the burn in my esophagus, the fatigue in my muscles and lungs, the "Oh, hello again," of my last few meals. The last time this happened, I was eleven or so and got dehydrated after a day at Disney World. I sat on the clean white floor of our clean white hotel bathroom, and threw up into the clean white toilet (not so clean after I was done with it). The acrid smell of my last few meals mixed with the mellow scent of almonds that all hotels have. Dad and Laura, famously squeamish, retreated into the remotest corners of the hotel room and turned the TV volume to level one thousand, and I heard Steve Irwin, the Crocodile Hunter, gushing about baby rattlesnakes, which made me feel worse.

But Mom sat with me, and she pulled my hair back and braided it gently, and rubbed my shoulders, unfazed by the mess or the sounds or the smells. She bundled me up on her side of the bed she shared with Dad, in layers of white, soft, almond-smelling cotton, and made me drink my favorite color of Gatorade (red), and made Dad and Laura change the channel to a program about a middle-aged couple shopping for a beach house. And when my stomach rebelled again, and I tore out of my white nest to the bathroom, and when Dad and Laura grimaced and made snarky comments, Mom said, "Shut up; or I'll food poison you!" and rubbed my shoulders again and said, "Don't feel bad, love; you can't help being sick."

I wish this weren't my first time being sick since then. I wish I had been sick many times in the past thirteen years so she could have been there to braid my hair and feed me red Gatorade.

My stomach is empty, so now I am free to cry. I flush the toilet and cry. I wash my face and cry. I swish around some mouthwash and cry. I come back through the house and settle onto the couch, drawing a blanket around me.

"Are you okay?" Laura asks. She creeps closer, then settles onto the other end of the couch, at my feet. "You haven't thrown up since Disney World."

I pause and look at her. "Yeah. I'm okay."

"You don't seem okay. You seem..." she pauses, weighing her words, and weighs them so thoroughly that she doesn't say anything else.

"I feel like shit," I blurt.

"You shouldn't have gone."

"Don't tell me what to do."

"I'm just trying to help."

"Well, don't."

"Sorry."

134

"Fine."

"You should have called."

"You're not my mom!" I retort, and the minute I do, I regret it. It was so involuntary, that little phrase everyone uses at some time or another, jokingly, to tell someone to fuck off. But it means something else now. Laura presses her lips together, very tightly, and her face contorts a little bit, and I expect it to crumple in on itself, but it doesn't. "I'm sorry," I say. "I didn't mean it."

I'm sorry I'm sorry I'm sorry.

"I thought the same thing had happened to you," she said. "Those few hours. Theo told me not to worry. But I thought…"

Damn it; I really am Judas.

I sit up, despite the pounding in my head. "I'm sorry. I'm so sorry. I wasn't trying to hurt you."

"Right."

"I'm never trying to hurt you, Laura."

She looks at me wryly. "Right," she says again.

"You really think that everything I do is to piss you off?"

"Not everything. But most things."

"Why would I waste my whole life trying to make you mad?"

"I don't know."

"Damn." I lie back down again. "Not everything is about you."

She breaths in swiftly, and then lets the air out. "You're right."

"Yeah," I say.

"Not everything's about you, either." Her voice is small, defiant.

I stare at the ceiling now, the caverns of white spiky plaster, the black and chrome ceiling fan. When we were kids, we would lie on the floor and stick our legs up in the air, pretending that the ceiling was the floor, and the floor was the ceiling. We imagined walking upon the spiky plaster with carpet over our heads, dodging the fan that threatened to cut us off at the knees with each swift paddle, and hanging Singing-in-the-Rain-style off the pendant lights in the corner over Mom's houseplants, which grew above our heads like a jungle. Even now I feel weirdly suspended, as if all I have to do is kick off the couch and drop down into the world on the ceiling, which is as familiar to me as the house itself. If you lie down long enough, the world starts to tilt, until up seems down and vice versa.

"I just... miss you," she says. I wait for her to say more, but the only noise in the whole house is the little pull chain of the ceiling fan whacking against its lightbulbs. I pull my chin down and look at her. She stares up at the ceiling too, her head resting on the back of the couch, her face as bland as if she were sleeping. I look back up again.

"I'm right here," I say.

"It's not the same."

The house is so, so quiet, and the couch so soft, I can't feel my body. I breathe, and she breathes, and our breathing syncs up for a minute, and then separates, and syncs again, in a never-ending cycle of joining and separating.

"I remember knowing you so well," I say suddenly. I'm tired, and ill, and dizzy from looking at the ceiling and imagining the world upside down. I don't want to think about anything I'm saying; I just want to let my mouth talk and see what happens.

"You know me pretty well," she answers.

"No. Not anymore. I used to be able to say something and know you'd laugh. I used to see something that reminded me of you every day. And now, I feel like I don't know you, that I don't even remember you. I remember Mom and Dad, but I barely remember you." My mouth stops and the house is silent again. The little swinging chain isn't even making noise. We're on the couch, a single body, breathing, and it feels like we're at the center of the universe. Holy ground.

"I feel the same way about you," she says. "That's why I miss you so much."

Slowly, we start to unravel, divide into our component parts, until we're not a single set of nerves and lungs but two separate ones. Like we're oil and water and we can't mix; we were never supposed to, and the thought that we could or did was nothing but an illusion that has disappeared now that everything has settled, and the bubbles are still there.

I remember what that smell is, the familiar one that's both pleasant and sad. It's her perfume, her favorite fragrance. Vanilla and freesia and orange, clean and crisp like bleached linens. It's the first time she's worn it since… I don't even know.

"Great," I say. The world has tilted again, back to its former state, and the ceiling doesn't seem magical or mystical. It's just a ceiling, and the floor is just a floor, and the world is the way it is, and it cannot change, no matter how much I feel like I can kick off the floor and fly.

The next day, Laura and Theo go back to church for the first time. They politely invite me, and I politely decline. I spend the morning nervously tidying up the house, insisting to myself I have nothing to be guilty about, yet feeling a telepathic weight of judgment emanating from the direction of the church. When the two of them return, I serve lunch—roast pork and sauerkraut, one of Mom's mainstays—and ask them how it was.

"It was nice to see everyone," Laura says. "People said hi. Emma and Daniel enjoyed having you over the other night." Her eyes don't betray even the slightest of a knowing look, and that's the end of that.

I'm so certain that there's more to it: surely someone must have asked why I wasn't there too, or why they might have seen me one night in the back of a pickup truck with the dregs of society. Surely someone has some kind of prophecy, as some of the Christian hippies do, a message laid on their heart by the Lord just for me, something along the lines of, "Get back into spiritual shape, you fiend."

But if any of these things did happen the first week back at church, Laura and Theo don't tell me, and all the nervous energy I have is wasted, and I am disappointed at the lack of a fight.

Chapter Eleven

The day before Thanksgiving feels like the last day of summer, or the night before a surgery, or pretty much every Sunday afternoon when you're in college. There's a sense of dread in all of us, an impending break between things as they are, and things being changed. It's the first big holiday since Mom and Dad died, the first of many they will never be there for again. Somehow that seems more final than just a bunch of normal days; somehow a holiday season makes their death seem much more real. The holidays have come too soon and we aren't ready for them.

In the past, we always spent Thanksgiving with Mom's mom and Dad's parents and Aunt Sophie, at our house. This year, however, we don't have the heart to cook Thanksgiving dinner in our kitchen. So Grandma Nancy and Grandad George invite us over, along with Nanna Mae and Aunt Sophie, who plans to bring her new boyfriend for us to meet. Aunt Maeve won't be back until Christmas. It's the perfect new tradition to help us forget the old ones.

On the day, at two in the afternoon, we show up at Grandad George and Grandma Nancy's house, the house Dad grew up in. We've been here a few times since the funeral, so it doesn't feel pointedly nostalgic. The house is old and a little bland and always slightly cold, a late-Victorian foursquare that's been "renovated" one too many times. It features flimsy covered porches, two nonworking fireplaces, a single bathroom upstairs, and beige wall-to-wall carpeting that was installed when we were children, but still leaves a new-carpet smell in the air. The walls are all painted eggshell white, with generic landscape paintings on the walls like in a Best Western, punctuated only by perfectly posed family photos from decades of appointments at Olan Mills (Grandma keeps the candids in their own photo album). The furniture is all very cushy and neutral, with crocheted afghans at every turn. In the little kitchen, which still sports its 70s avocado green appliances, Grandma Nancy is hard at work mashing potatoes and whisking gravy. Nanna Mae arrived early and is spooning stuffing into serving bowls.

"Can we help, Grandma? Nanna?" I ask after we give our coats to Grandad George. I wear my short red velvet dress which I always wear to holiday events. Theo and Laura have dressed similarly formally; Laura has the black dress she wore to the funeral and her favorite teal cardigan (which I bought for her many years ago). Theo's wearing his usual uniform: gray pants and a deep blue checkered button-down, with a navy suit coat. There's no real reason to dress so nicely; we're just hanging around the house today. But Grandma seems to appreciate our attempt at formality, as grandmothers usually do.

"Oh, you kids look so nice. No, I don't need help. Just finishing the last of it. Go have some appetizers in the living room. I got those little pickles you like." Grandma Nancy is dressed to the nines as always on holidays, with black slacks and patent leather shoes and a beaded sweater the color of a good merlot. She wears lipstick as usual: a dark cherry red that, along with her curls which she keeps dyed black and her light blue eyes, have always reminded me of Snow White. "I brought Gouda cheese!" says Nanna. "Let me know what you think!" She gives us a grin that, in a flash, reminds me of Mom, and I do a double take. "Go on," says Nanna. "Go try it!"

We obey, trooping back through the dining room—the big table set with all of Grandma's dishes—into the living room, where we sit side-by-side on the beige couch. The coffee table is spread with cheese and meats and crackers, spiced olives and the little pickles Grandma promised. Grandad George is pleasantly feasting on slices of swiss dolloped with mustard.

"I asked to help too and they sent me here," he says.

"We're in good company," says Theo. He helps himself to the food first, slathering a cracker with some of the almond-encrusted port cheeseball.

"How have you been?" asks Grandad, a redundant question, since we see him a few times a week.

"We're fine," I say.

"Hard to believe it's Thanksgiving already, eh?" His blue eyes twinkle a little, but not as brightly as they used to. I don't think they'll ever be as bright again.

"I keep forgetting it's Thanksgiving, honestly," says Laura.

Then we awkwardly eat cheese and listen to the clock above Grandad's chair tick loudly and stare at the painting over the mantel, a Thomas Kinkade of a garden with a marble staircase going up into a walkway that is obscured by bright flower bushes. This painting has always maddened me; you can't see where the path is coming from, or where it is going; only the grand, be-flowered staircase, leading from nowhere to somewhere. Even as a child, I wanted to prune the bushes just a bit to get even the smallest inkling of where we are supposed to be and what we're supposed to be looking toward.

"Your grandmother is excited to host," says Grandad. "Both of them are."

We smile politely. This whole arrangement is kind of like when you're a kid and you really have your heart set on going to the beach for vacation, maybe the Florida Gulf or Outer Banks, but when summer rolls around, Mom and Dad have no money for the Florida Gulf or Outer Banks, so they take you to Erie instead, and you spend the night at a campground on Presque Isle, and they act really excited like this is the best possible vacation, but you know this is only Plan B.

The doorbell rings, and in comes Aunt Sophie with a tall, dark-haired man dressed in a burnt-orange sweater. "Sorry we're late," she says. "There was traffic." I almost laugh but choke on a mini pickle instead. The idea of there being traffic from Cainesville to Haven is hilarious. There were probably three other people going the same way. "This is Paul," Aunt Sophie says. We proceed to have small talk with Paul, in which we learn that he works at the sawmill outside of Cainesville, that he loves to hunt, and that his favorite beer is Yuengling, traits which make him no different than any other man in the county. But he, like Aunt Sophie, is a Unitarian, which makes him, like her, a rare bird, and Grandad George asks him deep questions about the meanings of the universe, in between slices of swiss cheese and mustard.

"Now," says Aunt Sophie, settling herself into the last available inches of couch, between me and Laura. Her bright turquoise earrings swing wildly, getting caught in her long dark wavy hair. "How are you guys?"

"We've been getting by," says Laura.

"You've gone back to work? How's that?"

"It's good to have a diversion. The kids are great."

"And Amy, what have you been up to?"

"Job hunting, mostly. Trying to find something in Pittsburgh. Or really anywhere."

"Very good."

Before Aunt Sophie can ask more probing questions, Grandma Nancy comes into the living room. "Dinner is served!" she says, ushering us back into the dining room where we sit at the giant table. Grandad sits at the head, Grandma next to him, Theo and Laura next to her,

Nanna at the foot, then me and Aunt Sophie, with Paul finishing the circle at Grandad's right hand. Poor Paul.

"This looks lovely, Mom," says Aunt Sophie.

"It was a team effort. Me and Mae," Grandma Nancy answers.

"Did you like the Gouda?" Nanna Mae asks.

"It was very nice," Laura says.

"Smoky," I add.

"Before we begin, shall we go around and give thanks?" Grandad says. His voice has the usual chipper quality to it, as he asks this question he's posed to us every Thanksgiving ever. But his voice cracks on the question mark, and the query hangs on the air, and no one says anything in reply. The silence wraps itself around our necks and sets anvils on our chests and ties our tongues into knots. I stare at the plate in front of me, the familiar sunflower pattern from every celebration of my whole life. I swallow, trying to breathe.

Theo rises and holds up his glass, which like all of them is filled with sparkling grape juice since Grandma Nancy prefers not to have alcohol in the house. His voice strains at first but gains strength. "I give thanks for family. Past, present, and future."

141

We raise our glasses in unison.

Then there's a gasp, and a sob, and Nanna Mae next to me puts her glass down and breaks down crying over her empty plate. Then Grandma Nancy follows suit. Aunt Sophie covers her face with her hands, the many rings on her fingers like a bejeweled mask over her eyes. Paul bites his lip and pats her back. Grandad George holds Grandma's hand. Theo, across from me, pats her shoulder. Laura and I, on either side of Nanna Mae, each take one of her hands at the same time, and she grips so tightly I feel my tendons will snap.

Theo and Laura stare at me. I stare back. I swallow and blink away tears. I don't want to do this. Not now. I don't want to have an emotional moment. I want to have Thanksgiving dinner and pretend it's the most normal thing in the world. For a few minutes, there is only the sound of sobbing and the soft clink of jewelry against china. I force myself not to fall into it. I force myself to be distracted by everything I can see: every paint stroke of the china pattern, every thread in the tablecloth. This is important; if I can't withstand this moment, I will fall apart and completely unravel. Laura seems nearly overcome, and Theo's face is red.

As the sobs melt into sniffles, then into silence, I give Nanna's hand a paltry squeeze, and with my free hand, I take the spoon of the serving dish nearest to me—green bean casserole— and pile some on my plate, then slide it toward Laura. She looks at me with a mingling of reproach and relief.

I clear my throat. "Nanna," I whisper. "Here. Have some food."

Theo, across from me, gets the same idea. "Here, Gram," he says to Grandma Nancy.

"Have some food."

They agree slowly and slightly confused, like children waking up from a nap. Little by little, each dish gets worked around the table and divvied out. Soon everyone is passing food and taking food and eating bites of the food and commenting on how good the food is, and then we're all really talking about anything and everything, except of course a few select things.

Later, we eat dessert around the table. Nanna Mae makes a pot of coffee, and Aunt Sophie brings out pumpkin pie and chocolate cake from the kitchen. Then our group splinters off: Grandad and Paul and Theo migrate to the living room to watch football, the grandmothers and Aunt Sophie linger around the table, and Laura and I find ourselves in the kitchen, washing dishes.

"I'm glad we avoided a big thing back there," I say, referring to the episode before dinner.

She nods. "Mhm." She loads dishes into the dishwasher slowly.

"The food was good though," I add, trying to bridge the awkward silence there always is between us. I turn to the sink to rinse out the gravy boat. When she doesn't answer me, at least politely, I turn back to her, and she's hands and knees on the floor, breathing heavily.

"Shit, are you okay?" I drop the gravy boat in the sink and rush over to her.

"I'm fine, I just..." She takes a deep, gasping breath in. "I just don't feel well."

I touch my hands to her head and shoulders. "What's wrong? Are you sick? Was it something you ate?"

She grips my arm, trying to pull herself up. "No, no I'm fine. Just tired."

The grandmothers and Aunt Sophie, hearing the ruckus, have come into the room, and surround us, asking over and over if she's okay.

"Geez, give her space," I say, waving my arm out like a scythe cutting wheat. "Help me get her to the couch."

Off the kitchen is the small den, which is darker and quieter than the rest of the house, still featuring paneled walls and rust-colored shag carpet. We settle Laura onto the couch. Aunt Sophie goes to get Theo.

"I'm really fine," Laura says. "I just felt lightheaded. Too much food and dessert, maybe."

The three men rush into the room, Theo first, a ball of concern. Laura repeats her refrain: *I'm fine, I'm fine. Just tired. Just overwhelmed. It's a big holiday.*

In another part of the house, the phone rings, and everyone stiffens.

"Oh gosh," Laura says. "You can answer the phone. Really, I'm perfectly well. I just need a little nap."

Satisfied, Grandad runs to get the phone, and the grandmothers and Aunt Sophie and Paul filter out, until it's just the three of us: Laura on the couch, Theo bent over her, smoothing her hair, and me in the doorway. Laura looks over at me.

"Thanks for your help, Amy. You don't have to stay. I'm really fine."

I nod, embarrassed, swallowing a lump in my throat, remembering again that it's the two of them now, and I'm the third wheel. Remembering again that I used to know her better than anyone, until I didn't.

I head back to the dining room, grabbing the leftover dishes off the table. All our wine glasses are still there, so I take them away in twos and threes to the kitchen, where Grandma Nancy and Aunt Sophie are cleaning up shards of china from the gravy boat I dropped.

In the living room, Grandad is on the phone with Aunt Maeve, who's called for her usual Thanksgiving chat. The phone is passed around the room, each of us speaking to her briefly in turn, and she seems rushed but excited to see us for Christmas. I'm the last to talk to her before I pass the phone along to Grandma Nancy.

"Amy, you really should come down and visit me," Aunt Maeve says. "I heard you lost your job, and I'm so sorry. But there's so many opportunities down here. And the weather is warm! Just imagine it."

"Thanks, Aunt Maeve," I say. "I'll have to visit soon." I say goodbye and give Grandma the phone. She begins talking and wanders off throughout the house, leaving the rest of us in the living room. Theo emerges from the den and joins us.

"How's Laura?" Grandad asks.

"Oh, she's fine. Just tired. Had a bit of a stomach bug lately."

This is news to me. I give him a quizzical look, but he becomes absorbed in a conversation with Paul and Grandad. Me, Aunt Sophie, and Nanna Mae are left to our own devices.

"How do you all like Paul?" Aunt Sophie asks us in a conspiratorial tone. She sprawls a little, relaxed, in her seat, twirling her dark curls with one hand, a glass of something that looks suspiciously like non-sparkling grape juice in the other hand.

"Oh, he seems sweet," Nanna says, winking. Her eyes are piercing bronze-green and her expressions remind me so much of Mom that I can barely look at her.

"Yes, absolutely," I echo. Trying to make conversation, (Paul is fine; I could take him or leave him, to be honest), I go on: "I'm glad you brought him," which isn't really true, but isn't untrue either.

"I think he might be the one," says Aunt Sophie. I feel a pang of pity; she's said this about a few men a few times. The youngest of Dad's siblings, Aunt Sophie has always been the stereotypical free-spirited aunt: a little flighty, never fully content, torn between the need to love deeply and the need to keep options open. Paul may very well be the one, and for her sake, I hope he is. But I also doubt it.

"Ah, how sweet," Nanna Mae answers, giving me the perfect opportunity to nod politely.

"I wish your dad could have met him," Aunt Sophie says.

"Didn't he?" I ask.

"No." Aunt Sophie takes a deep breath. "He was supposed to. Soon. And then."

The emptiness of the *and then* yawns before us, a big black hole.

"I'm sure he would have liked Paul," I venture. Dad's favorite beer was also Yuengling, I almost add, but I decide this might sound too flippant.

"He fits right in with the family," Nanna Mae suggests, nodding her head toward where the three men are engaged in deep conversation. "Did Maeve get a chance to meet him?"

Aunt Sophie raises an eyebrow, nearly imperceptibly rolls her brown eyes. "Oh yes. After the funeral. Unfortunately."

"Why unfortunately?" I ask. "Didn't she like him?"

145

Aunt Sophie's voice quiets, and Nanna Mae and I lean in. "No, she doesn't like him," Aunt Sophie says. "She said she thought I could do better. Whatever the hell that means."

Aunt Maeve isn't necessarily wrong, I think, but there's slim pickings for men in these parts, so I'm not quite sure how much better she expected Aunt Sophie to do.

Grandma Nancy comes back into the room, phone in hand, but it's clear the conversation with Aunt Maeve has ended. Grandma sits next to Grandad, and I see the slightest twitches of sadness around her mouth.

"Maeve has been trying to get Mom and Dad to move down South," Aunt Sophie says.

"What?" This is news to me. I've never even dreamed of Grandad and Grandma living somewhere else. "Why? Are they planning to move?"

"Of course not," Aunt Sophie rolls her eyes again. She's always been the 'cool aunt,' but she's never been so honest, so forthcoming, as she is now. Maybe it's her glass of non-non-alcoholic wine. "Mom and Dad want to live here forever. They always have. But to Maeve, it's all about the practicality. How easy it will be to care for them as they age. Easy for her."

"But you're here. Theo and Laura are here." *Dad's here*, I almost say. *I'm here.*

"Well, that's it too. She wants everyone to move down south."

"What about me?" Nanna Mae croons jokingly.

Aunt Sophie laughs. "I'm sure you'd be welcome too. In Maeve's mind, the more people who move out of Haven, the better."

"I didn't realize she hated it so much," I say. Little pinpricks of memory come to mind. The night she cornered Mom and Dad in the kitchen and chastised them for letting Laura and I play in the ghost town. *You can't raise your kids in a rusty town left over from the Civil War.*

"Maeve's hated Haven since forever ago," says Aunt Sophie. "She couldn't wait to get out. Literally the morning after her high school graduation, she was on a bus, taking a summer job in Philly before college. Anywhere but here."

"But Grandma and Grandad like it here," I say, still stuck on the main point. "Grandad's a pastor. He can't just leave."

"Maeve," says Aunt Sophie, "is selfish. Everything boils down to numbers, to money, to convenience."

We're interrupted by the sudden arrival of Laura, looking a little wan, but better than earlier. Everyone greets her, a wave of resounding "Hi!" and she smiles sheepishly, joining Theo on his end of the couch, insisting again and again that she's fine, just a little tired.

I want to ask Aunt Sophie more about Aunt Maeve, about what she means by everything she's said. But Grandma Nancy insists that we must all play a game, and the moment passes.

The next day is Black Friday and Laura wants to visit the dying mall with our grandmothers. I find this preposterous, so I decide to stay home and organize the dining room with Theo. The dining table is covered with stacks of mail and papers, and I want to put all Dad's books on our shelves here.

Since the funeral, Theo's been taking care of the final affairs with Mom and Dad's will. They had him added to everything a few years ago, made him power of attorney, along with their close friend Pastor Jeff. At the time it seemed nothing more than a sweet gesture of parenthood, a welcoming of Theo into the family he had for so long been unofficially a part of. But now, I'm beyond glad these arrangements were made; there's no way Laura or I could have untangled the legal knots of settling an estate.

Now, Theo directs me in which pieces of mail we can throw out, what papers we need to keep, how we should consolidate the file cabinet. In turn, I direct him on how to organize the bookshelves that flank the fireplace: nonfiction having to do with Pennsylvania history at the top, nonfiction having to do with general history in the middle, Dad's journals and notebooks at the bottom.

"So, question," Theo says as we move around books. "Are you planning to stay here?"

"What, *here*, in this house, or here in Haven? The answer is no to both."

"What's your timeline?"

"Are you kicking me out?"

"No, of course not. You're welcome to stay forever if you want. But I know you don't, so I just wanted to know your plans."

I sigh. "Well, I've been *trying* to get a job somewhere else. I've sent out a bunch of job applications. But no response."

"None at all?"

"Not a word." This has happened to me before: when I first applied for jobs after college, I must have filled out a hundred applications, and only got three interviews, only one of which resulted in a job offer. The job I was later fired from.

"I know Laura would appreciate it if you stayed," Theo says. "Even for a few extra months."

"I can't just live here and bum off you both."

"You could get a job here, and work it while you keep looking for something else."

I shake my head. I know how that story ends: get a job, get comfortable, wake up one morning and it's been ten years since I've been *back home*. "Thanks, but I'm going to keep looking."

"Okay." His voice has neither a hint of judgment nor of approval. He simply accepts my decision, and the fairness of him bewilders me. "So, you should know," he continues. "Your parents left the house to both you and Laura. Equally."

I figured that was the case. "Okay."

"Do you want to sell the house?"

"Does Laura?"

"Laura and I would like to keep living here."

I stop and look at him. "Really?"

"We'll buy out your half of the house from you."

I tilt my head. "Really."

"We've been saving for a house anyway, so we have it in cash."

I raise my eyebrows. "Well, damn."

"It'll take a few months to process everything, of course. We'll get the house appraised, draw up some papers, pay you half of what the house would be worth on the market."

"That's very generous of you."

"It's better than seeing the house go to a stranger." He shrugs.

"You really want to live here? It doesn't creep you out?" Involuntarily, I look at the urns. I wonder where they'll end up, permanently. Maybe Laura and I will split those, too. She keeps Dad for a while, and I keep Mom. We share custody, swap them every other holiday.

"It's the perfect size for us. We're not going to have scads of kids or anything." He smiles. "And there's so many memories here. There's no sense in leaving it all behind."

I wonder if this house will be like those ramshackle ancestral homes in the woods, where the same people have lived for generations. I wonder if, in a hundred years, some history-loving dad will be driving his kids through the forest, and they'll come to the top of a hill, and he'll say, "Ah, this is where the town of Haven used to be. See these patches of pavement? They used to be streets. See these foundations? A neighborhood was here. See that house? Old Lady Carlin still lives there, in the home her parents purchased from her crazy aunt." And the explorers will drive away, through the woods hiding so many forgotten stories.

Chapter Twelve

Monday morning, I wake up early. The sun hasn't even risen yet; the sky is pale gray like the day of Mom and Dad's funeral. I hate waking up this early, especially in cold weather, but there's a longstanding tradition I am keen to resurrect. For as akin to Judas as I may feel, at least there is one thing I can be faithful about again.

I dress warmly. Fleece leggings under jeans, a long-sleeved compression tee under a sweater, under a button-down flannel shirt. My thickest wool socks. I tiptoe downstairs and make myself a quick breakfast. While my bagel is toasting and coffee brewing, I pack lunch: a sandwich with leftover Thanksgiving turkey, a thermos of soup, some trail mix. The house is quiet; Laura and Theo would still sleep another hour on most days, but she has off today, and he won't go in until later. Today is the first day of deer season, and to everyone in this area, a holiday.

I finish breakfast and bundle up in my big warm gray parka, fingerless gloves under mittens, a knit headband, black and brown duck boots. I gather my lunch and head outside to the car. A light snow fell overnight, and in the still-pale morning light, each blade of grass and twig of a tree is covered with white. I catch my breath: no matter how old I am or how cold I am, the sight of snow on trees makes my heart swell with joy.

I start the car and let it warm up. I scrape the thin glaze of ice off the windshield and back window, my breath little puffs of smoke. The edge of the sky starts to turn deep purple. I drive down the back alley and turn onto Grover Street, which plummets all the way down our hill to downtown Haven. The streetlights are still on, a little constellation which is Haven sitting in the valley beneath me. I pass houses that are dark and quiet, and houses whose windows glow with sleepy, tentative lights.

As I drive through town, the streets are deserted, and the world seems fragile in the quiet, cold white. A few delivery trucks are on the road with me, bathed in smoky fumes and kicking up salt from the snowplows. I turn off into the McDonald's, which is sandwiched between a sketchy hotel and my childhood dentist's office. The drive-through line is short, with only a handful of grizzled men in pickup trucks. I order three breakfast sandwiches and a half dozen hash browns. The woman at the window—gray stringy curls, blue eyes, smoker's wrinkles around her mouth, and a blue sweater over her uniform shirt—is more chipper than I've ever been in my entire life.

"Have a good morning, hun," she says as she hands me the hot paper bag of food.

I thank her and drive on, back through town, left past the dilapidated parking garage on the corner of Fifth and Mackenzie streets, then right past the abandoned Wendy's that was closed after the health inspector discovered it was crawling with rats from the river behind it. For what it's worth, I once had a bowl of chili there that is still the best chili I've ever had, and every time I pass that building, I taste the chili on my tongue.

I'm on a straighter street now, one that draws a line between two hills along a creek bed, passing a playhouse and an old movie theater, a string of factories—some still in use and others long-forgotten—a few churches, an auto parts store. The last building within city limits is a Dollar Tree, lights shining vehemently green against the pale winter morning. Then there's a smattering of houses, and then… nothing. I'm surrounded by what was an oil field, a small plain around the creek bed, dotted with rusty remnants of giant tanks and twisted pipe. It's all fenced off, of course, but the trees they've tried to plant along the road to cover up the mess haven't grown quite enough yet, and they are scrawny and naked except for the snow.

Soon the oil field is gone, too, and I plunge into the woods. Thick bundles of brown covered with white, layers upon layers of earth and wood folded into snow. Every now and then I pass a house, a hodgepodge of wood and metal and paint, looking stark and ugly, out of place in the sparkling forest. Over the hill to my right, a tiny sliver of orange tints the sky, and the snow looks blue and purple in the shadows that change every minute.

Five miles later, there's the familiar brown sign. *Black Gold Cross, 2 mi.* I'm not necessarily looking forward to this, but hope it will be better this time, with company. I turn down the treacherous, windy paved road, eventually slowing into the gentle slope and curve right before town, and turning into the little dirt parking lot where an old man in a white SUV waves at me through his window. Grandad George. I park and get out, clutching the paper bag. He beckons to me from within the car. I open the passenger door and climb in. "Breakfast is served," I say.

"Mm. I've been waiting for ages."

"I'm only three minutes late."

"Traffic?"

"Oh yeah. Mackenzie Avenue was crawling."

We take out the food. He gets two sandwiches, and we each get three hash browns. He's brought coffee from the Clay Café, the hippie coffee shop across town with excellent brew, if a rather hokey name.

I bite into my sandwich as soon as I can. I had that bagel at home, but something about being out so early, when it's so cold, makes you feel hollow. I chew eagerly, then I realize that Grandad hasn't started yet, but has his head bent slightly over his food, whispering a blessing to himself. I chew more slowly, acutely aware and embarrassed of every noise my teeth make as they grind up the egg and bacon and bread.

"So." Grandad unwraps his first sandwich and takes a hearty bite. He chews for a minute and swallows. "So, how are you?"

"I'm fine. Thanksgiving was nice."

He gives a resigned nod. "It turned out to be a lovely day for sure. How did you like Paul?"

"Paul? Bland, but nice. How do you like him?"

He smiles. "I have qualms with his theology, but he is nice. Very good to her. And anyway, she's chosen her path. I made peace with it long ago."

After being gone for two years and letting all my beliefs out, these conversations feel so funny. My mind now, the mind of Adult Amy, doesn't think there's a difference between being Unitarian or Presbyterian, or Catholic for that matter. I've gone to enough places and met enough people for it not to matter to me. In Pittsburgh, I knew some Jews and Hindus and Muslims, none of which I ever came across in Haven. So it's weird to come back to this place, this world, where these things do matter. To Grandad George, Aunt Sophie's chosen path is a step off the right path, and he mourns her even while he loves her. I get a shiver up my spine. If it's so easy to fall off the right path, even when you think you're on it your whole life, is it really the kind of path you want to be on? The beliefs jostling around in my head and heart confirm this opinion, but something snags. As much as I want to throw out Christianity and its many flavors, something won't let me, and I feel hot with frustration.

Eventually, we get out of the car. He opens his trunk, pulling out an orange vest and handing it to me. I put it on over my coat. His own vest has his hunting license pinned to it and matches his bright orange baseball cap. Grandad takes his rifle, protected in a leather carrying case, and some small boxes of ammunition. He stores the boxes in the voluminous, many-pocketed vest, and slings the rifle on his shoulder. He won't load it until we get to our usual place.

We lock up the cars and head down the paved road, still covered with a thin layer of snow. For all the years I've joined him for the opening day of deer season, we've parked in that little lot and walked through Black Gold Cross to where the line between the township land and the state game lands is closest, where you can hop from one into the other, and as long as you're pointed into the game lands and away from the town, you're good to go.

My heart is in my throat. I'm afraid to come through here again, afraid that I will see and hear the things I did last time. But when we turn the corner onto Main Street, the town sits as it should: empty, in the new millennium. With the snowfall, it looks deceivingly like a charming Christmas village, the rows of brick buildings which I knelt and cried between just a few weeks ago, covered with a layer of glittering white.

At the end of Main Street is Petroleum Street. This one isn't in such good shape. While most of the building foundations on Main are made of brick and stone, all the buildings on this street were built hastily after 1890, when the oil-slicked creek caught fire and the flames licked up the bank to the oily roads. Half the town was destroyed. The same thing happened in Haven many times, which led to a whole three blocks on the Allegheny River being constructed in brick and stone so it wouldn't happen again. But in Black Gold Cross, people weren't as concerned with posterity. So now, this half of town is piles of rotting boards and a few miraculous rebels to entropy.

A breeze whistles through the bare trees, blowing snow off them, scattering the snowflakes in a sparkling dry mist. I get a shiver up my spine again and stand still in the middle of the street. Without trying, I look for the grandfather trees, mentally remove everything around them, look back in time. I feel surrounded by people, like in a crowded room, even though there's no one here but me and Grandad George. Like a cloud of someone else's emotions, that I've walked into. I inhale sharply.

"You all right?" Grandad asks. He turns, and his feet crunch in the thick layer of snow over the road, and the wholeness of the sound brings me back to earth a little bit. There's the sunrise again, the glitter of white snow.

"I don't know, but lately this place just... I don't know, it's weird." I have so much more to say, but there are too many words to pick from.

He takes my hand and leads me down the road, gently. "It's fine, honey. This place is haunted, in a way."

My stomach leaps. "How?"

"Suffering happened here, a long time ago. Suffering and greed. The land doesn't forget.

It's like a wound in the ground."

I swallow. I know it. "Do Presbyterians believe in ghosts?"

He looks at me shrewdly. "I can't speak for all the Presbyterians."

154

"You, then?"

"I don't believe in ghosts, strictly speaking. I believe that we don't know how powerful our emotions are, especially the strong ones. There's a spiritual element to them we don't quite understand. They hold onto a place long after we're gone."

"Like Dad always said. A print in mud."

Grandad smiles. "Yes. Your dad took it a little farther than I would have, but it was the same sort of thing."

We start walking again. We are very deep in the woods now. We pass a little fenced-in cemetery where the first settlers of the area are buried. This gravesite is the oldest in the state, west of the Susquehanna. For white people, that is. We pause briefly to look at the stones, as we always do, the names carved with flourishes, some of the words spelled archaically, under decades of moss and a dusting of snow.

We walk in silence, letting our thoughts take up space. Finally, we make our way to our usual spot, back up against two thick, twisted, Y-shaped trees. The earth slopes gently, giving us a good view of a little valley with a shallow stream at the bottom. The deer often come here to drink and nibble on the moss that coats the dark, round rocks. The stream is not completely frozen, so chances are good they'll still stop here. Grandad takes out his gun and loads it, pointing it down at the ground even though the safety is on. Then we sit and wait in silence, feeling the quiet of the bare woods wash over us, as the morning sunlight turns the layers of snow into a million colors, like a kaleidoscope.

Something about being here, about holding fast to this one tradition, even, yes, one centered on hunting and killing a thing, is grounding to me. I used to join Grandad George on the first day of deer season each year, all through elementary and high school. It was always just us on this single day, us and the woods, and occasionally a slain deer. Then, when I went to school and lived in Pittsburgh, my holidays were too busy to make the time to come with him, and I thought I was okay with that; with letting this tradition stay in the past. But now that I'm here again, I realize how much I've missed the woods, being folded into the hills and trees like being tucked into bed. I feel like a child again.

It's that feeling that makes me cry silently, my cold tears freezing on the scarf wrapped around my neck. I think about Dad, who loved that stupid, sad, rotting ghost town, and the stupid, sad, rotting town we live in. It's foolish to love something so wretched, so fucked-up, so far gone. But he did anyway, and he gave so much thought and time and energy to it anyway.

Just as he did for all the things he loved. He had compassion for each person's story, no matter how wretched it was. So did Mom, year in year out, caring and advocating for people who needed a friend, even in a system, in a town, among people, who were so broken.

We sit in the woods for a few hours, watching the sky through the trees get lighter and lighter blue, listening to the sound of the land: the trickle of water and groaning of trees and squishing of mud. Yes, in the forest, if you get really quiet, you can hear mud. Then suddenly, about two hours in, Grandad tightens his grip on his rifle. He gestures across the stream bed. A buck and two doe are just over the opposite bank, the antlers of the buck blending in with the tree branches until he gets closer. The antlers are covered with a light layer of velvet, softly shiny in the light of the late morning. The three deer move over the snow in a stately tread toward the stream where they take turns bending their long necks toward the ground and drinking. Every strand of their fur is sharp and vivid, a hundred shades of brown. Their eyes are wide and sweet, the color of dark chocolate.

"They're beautiful," I whisper.

Grandad pulls up his gun, aiming toward the buck. But his fingers aren't on the trigger; his hand holds the barrel lightly. He's just getting a closer look through the scope. "Mhm," he answers.

The deer flick their ears. They hear us, if only a little bit. They're on guard. Grandad's fingers move toward the trigger. My heart skips. But then he moves his hand again and lets the gun down.

"I like letting the first deer go, sometimes," he whispers. "They stun me a little. I don't have the heart to shoot."

I nod. I understand.

At four in the afternoon, the shadows lengthen. As the temperatures rose over freezing and dipped back down over the course of the day, the snow on the ground melted, then the moisture turned to frost again. We haven't seen any deer, apart from the ones Grandad let get away. He plans to go out again tomorrow, alone, perhaps meeting up with some friends later in the day.

We walk back through the woods out of the game lands, past the oldest cemetery west of the Susquehanna, back onto the dirt road that goes into Black Gold Cross. The trees catch the light of the oncoming dusk and make smoky blue and purple shadows on the snow. I shiver as we pass the first extant building on our way, a faded yellow house with empty windows. Then there's another, and another, the Sheriff's office with the roof falling in and the brothels with their chipped paint. Soon we're back at the street corner, in the middle of town. My eyes look for the grandfather trees again, involuntarily. There's that weight on my chest again, the intense pressure of emotions and thoughts and memories that are not my own. It wraps around my lungs, my windpipe and larynx. I take deep, gasping breaths, starting to feel numb in my fingers and feet, telling myself it's just the cold, that I will not have a panic attack in the middle of a ghost town. Not today.

"Come in the car," Grandad says. "Have a bit of coffee before you go."

I obey, feeling trapped in a big glass bubble, caught in a dream. I open the car door and sit in his SUV, but nothing feels real or solid. I dig my fingernails into the palms of my hands, count drops of water condensed and frozen on the windshield. Vaguely, I hear him load all the gear in the trunk, then he joins me in the driver's seat, offering the last of the coffee from his thermos.

"Are you okay?" he asks, watching me drink the coffee down.

My heart pounds, feeling slowly returning to my extremities. "I'm okay."

"Can I ask a question?"

"What?"

"It's a prying question. But just know I ask it in care."

Oh, no. "Sure. Shoot."

He takes a deep breath. "What happened to you, Amy?"

The question takes me aback; it has so many answers. "What do you mean?" I avoid the gaze I know he is giving me directly. I stare down at my hands in my lap, watch my fingers twist into pretzel knots around the thermos cup.

"Did something happen to you in the past five years? Before... before a month ago, I mean. Anything at all?"

"Why?"

"You're so angry. You've been so angry for such a long time."

I shrug, but my eyes smart with salty tears. He is venturing into territory I don't even know very well and I feel like a child about to be discovered in a game of hide and seek. "I don't know," is all I can say. Silence hangs between us like a heavy velvet curtain, black and ominous.

"I remember when you were a child," he says. Outside, the shadows lengthen and slowly envelop the car. "All bright and silly, full of spunk and hilarity. I remember when you were baptized, when you made your parents' faith your own. You were so full of joy, so assured."

I know what was going on in my head and heart on that day, and the memory stings. But he continues, his blue eyes crackling as he stares out the window now, remembering.

"There were times we would talk about God, you and I. Some of the things you said had me running for my money. You always had a knack for demolishing years of seminary training with a single, innocent observation. A small detail in one of the Psalms, a stray comment Jesus said in the gospels, one of Paul's metaphors that no one ever notices. No one, but you."

I had forgotten all these things about myself. I remembered Grandad and I always having spirited and interesting conversations, but I always figured it was because Grandad himself was spirited and interesting. It never occurred to me that I might be, too. Little by little, the recollections resurface, and I'm so delighted by that silly, subversive, precocious girl that I laugh before I can help it. I'd forgotten all the joy in her; I'd only remembered the anxiety, the fear, the neurotic need to figure out God so she could stay out of hell.

Grandad goes on. "You know, I always thought you'd be a pastor one day. I felt it in my bones."

I laugh more now, utterly shocked. "What?" The thought had never crossed my mind. "You've met me, right? What makes you think I'd make a good shepherd for people's souls?"

He looks at me straight, without indulging in my hilarity. "A pastor —despite the name, which implies otherwise—is not a shepherd of people's souls," he says. "Only Christ himself is worthy of that title. All of us are only people, sheep ourselves, foolish and flawed. The best pastors, ministers, mentors, know this. Or they at least try to remember. So no, Amy; I never thought you'd make a good shepherd of other people's souls, just as I don't think I am. But the reason I always thought—I knew!—you'd be a pastor was because of your curiosity, your utter unwillingness to rest until you found the truth. That, and your compassion for others."

"I'm not very compassionate," I answer.

"Of course you are! You're one of the most compassionate people I know."

"Grandad! I'm rude and opinionated, and I use way too many swear words, and I'm impatient with people. Pardon my French, but I'm an asshole."

He reaches across the car and grasps my hands, making me drop the empty thermos cup, and he looks right into my eyes now, and there's no avoiding it. "You are *not* an asshole. You care deeply about everything. You care about the truth, about the right way to be. You care about people being safe and happy. You care about people flourishing. You are *not* an asshole. But you *are* angry. Very, deeply angry. And I want to know why. I want to know what happened."

I stare at him, stunned, frozen. He's right, damn it; he's right. "Nothing happened," I say. "At least, not a single thing happened. It was… it was just everything."

"Like what?" He loosens his grip on my hands, holding them softly now as if I'm a small child with fragile bones.

"Like... all the cracks. All the contradictions." I close my eyes and think. All the stories in the Bible that said one thing about God, while there were other ones that said different things. God was love, but God was also judgment. The "truth" being a single right way to live, and if you fail or disagree in any way, you're lost. Being baptized and feeling bright and fresh and new and reborn, only to return to my stale, muddled, human state a few days later. This town, full of horror and beauty and violence and rebirth, swirls of alternating hopelessness and hope. The judgmental church people, who talk about the love of Christ while meting out punishment. Then people like my parents, who talked about the love of Christ while doing exactly the kinds of things Christ did. "Nothing is black and white," I say. "And we try to pretend that it is. All my life, it was this or that. In or out. But it's not true. There's too much, too much unknown. Too much unsure. None of us knows what we're doing. I don't; you don't; Pastor Jeff or any number of the people I looked up to. Mom and Dad. We're all just floating, living, hoping we're good enough, hoping it's all good enough." I try to pull my hands back, but he grips them, gently but firmly.

"Is that it?" he asks. "That's why you're angry?"

I'm angrier *now*, becoming more frustrated the more my mind spins in circles, the more he won't let my hands go, but yanking them away would hurt him too much. "I'm angry because there's no use! What's the use of trying to be a good person if it still ends up not being good enough? What's the use of living your whole life full of joy, just electric with love every day, just so, so beautiful every day, and then you still end up at the bottom of a ravine in the middle of the woods in a shit town? What's the use, Grandad? What's the point?" I'm shaking now, shuddering with horror and sorrow and rage.

He releases my hands and reaches his arms across to hug me, hold me. He smells like aftershave and laundry detergent and leather. I am a child again, small enough for my grandfather to pick me up and hold me, while I cry and cry.

"I'm not a pastor," I tell him, my voice muffled by his shoulder. "I don't know what you were thinking. I'm a mess. That day I was baptized? I was so full of fear. I was so afraid of going to hell. It was all a sham. I don't think I was ever really saved. I didn't make my parents' faith my own; it was always theirs. It was never mine."

He strokes my hair gently. I go on. "I never really knew God. I never really believed in God. I never—" This isn't true. Trying to confess myself to Grandad isn't working, because the confession isn't true. I *did* believe in God. I do now. It *wasn't* all a sham. Maybe some of it, but not all. This faith *is* mine. It's bedraggled and messy and quite frankly fucked-up, so it's the most mine of any faith I've ever known. The only time, the only moment, I can remember it not all being a big mess is that single moment, that single image in my mind, of the little polyester silk flag-waving, the light over each fiber bending and stretching. *God is very beautiful.*

"I'm sorry," says Grandad. "I didn't know."

How could he have? We're all just floating, trying, hoping our best is good enough. "It's okay."

We're quiet, him holding me as the forest outside grows darker and darker. But there's not a heavy curtain of silence between us anymore.

Chapter Thirteen

Time goes by, cycles of freezes and thaws, of keeping the house and combing the internet for jobs, of waiting for Theo and Laura to come home each night. I know Laura goes to therapy every week, but she doesn't try to get me to talk to Dr. Mueller again; she doesn't even mention her appointments at all. I suspect Dr. Mueller may have something to do with this.

Now it's Christmas time. I've always loved Haven at Christmas; I have to admit. The businesses that do exist always decorate their windows with lights and winter scenes, there are little Christmas trees in the parks, and the lampposts bear faded blue flags that have been wishing everyone *Happy Holidays* every year since 1993. At Christmas, everyone is hopeful, even if they have no business being hopeful.

We make plans to celebrate Christmas Eve with all the family at Grandma Nancy and Grandad George's, just like old times. Their house is big enough to fit everyone, so it makes sense for Aunt Maeve to come up from North Carolina, and for Aunt Sophie to stay over. In preparation for the impending festivities, Grandma Nancy has decorated the big tree that takes up half the living room and hung all the furry red and white stockings on the mantle of the artificial fireplace.

Our own house looks drab by comparison. Theo insisted on wrapping lights around the rhododendron bush in front of the house, but otherwise we've done no decorating. I think we keep waiting for Mom and Dad to do it in their usual way: Dad rooting around in the attic a week after Thanksgiving and bringing down boxes of stuff, Mom purging clutter in the living and dining rooms to make way for the artificial garlands, the ceramic angels, and the tiny music box village. They played Bing Crosby, *The Nutcracker*, and Phil Keaggy's instrumental Christmas album from 1999, in which he collaborates with the London Festival Orchestra. Mom lit the first pine-scented candle of the season and we all got to work.

Now, I don't even want to think about it. I don't want to go up in the attic and get all the boxes marked *Christmas Décor Fragile* and remember helping Mom pack these very same ornaments away less than a year ago. I don't want to find all the strings of lights Dad insisted were still good, even though they're missing half the bulbs. I don't want to see the ceramic angels and tiny music box village ever again.

But I also don't want to do nothing. That feels like admitting that something is so wrong we won't obey the commands of the calendar. So instead, I go to the mall to take advantage of the many seasonal pop-up shops and buy a new Christmas tree, a tiny one, for twenty dollars, a pack of blue plastic bulbs, and a short string of white lights. One night, when Laura is at her therapy appointment and Theo is working late, I assemble the sad little Christmas tree while drinking the Irish whiskey Mom saved in the china cabinet and playing various covers of "Blue Christmas" over and over. When Laura comes home, I show it to her.

"Merry Christmas." My words slur just the tiniest bit.

"Are you drunk?" she asks.

"Nope. Whaddya think?"

"It's nice." I've put the tree on a coffee table in the corner of the living room, where the white lights can shine out of the front windows, and everyone who passes the house can know that we are *Just Fine*. "Did you get a creche?" she asks.

"A what?"

"A manger scene."

"Nope." I'd forgotten all about it. Mom's manger set was a beautiful, simple collection of white ceramic figures without faces. I used to sit and look at them, and imagine their facial expressions as the Son of God, who takes away the sorrow of the world, lies before them, humble and vulnerable and so not what they expected the Son of God to be.

"There should be a creche," says Laura.

"Yes there should," I answer. "But I'm not going up into the attic."

She says nothing; just takes off her shoes and sets them by the door, then goes upstairs to their room. I hear her dresser drawers open as she changes out of the nice clothes she wore to work and Dr. Mueller's office. Then there's the unmistakable creaking of the spring that holds the trap door to the attic in place, stretching as the door is pulled down, and the ladder going up is unfolded. There are the soft footfalls of feet in socks ascending up into the top parts of the house. Then, soft thuds and the *wooshes* of cardboard being pushed across 100-year-old floorboards. The footsteps come down again, more slowly and deliberately, and the ladder is folded back up, and the spring that holds the door is retracted again, and soon Laura comes down the stairs holding a cardboard box that says *Christmas Décor Fragile.*

"I think this is it," she says. She sets the box down in front of my Christmas tree, opens it, and pulls out a figure wrapped in newspaper, from an issue of *The Oil Well* from 2009. The figure she unwraps first is a shepherd of white ceramic, unmistakable in his long robe and headdress, a wire crook in one hand. He stands tall, his other hand set against his forehead, shading eyes that don't exist. He watches and waits. Laura puts him at the foot of the tree.

"Help me, won't you?" she says.

We put it together, and, suddenly, there it is: Mary and Joseph, Jesus in his wooden manger filled with raffia ribbon, the shepherds and sheep, an angel and the three wise men. Mom always put the wise men in the dining room window on the opposite side of the house to show that, despite common lore, they weren't really at the birth of Christ, but came two to three years later, and that taking part in the myth they were present that very night is part of the grand whitewashing of the Christmas story, which was not as polished and pure and European and civilized as we like to imagine it is. Laura and I put the wise men in the dining room window.

"Now it feels like Christmas," says Laura.

"Does it?"

"It feels like Christmas will feel for the rest of our lives."

"I don't like it."

"Me neither."

We stand together at the end of the dining room, looking through it to the Christmas tree far at the end of the living room beyond. The paltry tree casts a solemn, magical glow. I remember Mom trying to teach us how to do cartwheels in these rooms long ago, how I was terrible at it and resorted to somersaulting from this room to that one until I got dizzy. I hold my breath, feeling again the weight of them here, all around us, still living and breathing in this house.

"What's wrong?" Laura asks.

"Nothing." I sit at one of the chairs of the dining table, which is cleared off now that Theo and I organized it.

Laura steps into the kitchen and comes back with a glass of water, heaped with ice like Mom used to do. She sets it in front of me. "Drink."

I lift the glass to my lips but get very little water before my lips start to freeze. "Thanks," I mumble.

She sits across from me, her back to the fireplace. The urns hover above her head, above each shoulder. "So Theo told you, then. That we want to buy the house."

"Yes."

"You don't mind?"

"It's not as if I'm planning to live here myself."

"Once we get you the money, you can go wherever you want. You could even put a down payment on a house of your own, somewhere else."

I had fantasized about this, of course. For every job I applied to, I imagined myself in a new house, a new neighborhood, a new wardrobe, new car. A new me. "Yes. I'm still weighing the options. I've been thinking of Pittsburgh, but the jobs are slim pickings. I might decide to start fresh somewhere else."

"Of course."

I put down the glass. "What's that supposed to mean?"

She inhales sharply, then exhales slowly. "Nothing. Just that you like fresh starts."

"Yeah."

"You shouldn't have drunk the whiskey. Mom was saving it."

I flick my eyes up to her. She meets my gaze, her green eyes dark, nearly black. "What for?"

"Christmas."

"Well, Merry fucking Christmas then."

"I wish you wouldn't do that."

"What?"

"Speak that way. Use those words."

"This is how people talk, Laura."

"It's not how you used to talk."

"Well," I gulp down more water as the ice melts. "I've changed."

"Clearly."

"You know what's stupid?" I slam the glass down again, a new wave of semi-drunkenness washing over me. "You know what's really *fucking* dumb?"

"What?" Her brows knit together, a fine pointed zig-zag that makes her eyes even more piercing.

"All this shit has happened to us. Between us, and then to us. All this shit we won't say. Our parents dead, just like that. Me, losing everything. You, losing... I don't know. You lost something. And the only thing you can think to say to me is you wish I didn't use bad words. Isn't that just wild?" I laugh a little bit and then realize how very thirsty I am. "Grow up," I say before drinking deep from the water glass.

She reaches across the table as if to grab my hands, but her arms don't reach far enough. She stands up and slams her palms down instead. "Shut up, you idiot," she says. "You're so blind. You think you're the only one who hurts, the only one who feels."

"I'm the only one who's honest!" I yell, standing up too. "I'm the only one who lives in the real world, not this little bubble where we just pray to Jesus and everything's okay!"

She shakes her head and laughs bitterly. "I don't know where you think we are, but this isn't that place. I don't think that."

"Yes, you do. Perfect Laura, perfect sweet Christian wife Laura."
All the things I've thought about her for years come bubbling to the
surface and the thought hits me that maybe, if I say them, this awful
pain, this pressure wrapping tendrils around my chest, will go away.
"You're so blind, you know that? You say *I'm* blind. Ha! You stay here
in this shitty town and live each day and you're so complacent with
nothing!"

"This is my *life*. How dare you—"

"You get married young and live here and work here because
you're too afraid to go or do anything else. You live with your parents
and go to the same church you grew up in and believe everything the
good preacher man tells you to believe, and you judge *me* every time I
come home, because I lost my faith, or I wasn't good enough to stay in
the club of people you think are going to heaven. You think I'm
damned, that I'm going to hell, that I'm a terrible, disgusting, fucked-
up person."

The words bubble out, fizzing, and then dissolving, and the air is
silent between us. She glares at me. "You said all these things," she
answers. "I never said a single one of them." She turns and walks to
the living room.

"But they're true, aren't they?" I yell after her. "You do think them;
admit it! You've thought them from the beginning. From the time I
went to college. From the time we were teenagers, and you were
friends with all the good virtuous youth group girls and I liked the
bisexual Christian school dropouts. From the time you got baptized at
six and I was a whole year late."

"I don't know what you're talking about!" she cries. "We're
different people; that doesn't mean I always thought you were going to
hell! Dear God, what is wrong with you?" Her tears reflect the light of
the Christmas tree. She is iridescent, translucent, fragile as a soap
bubble. I feel a sudden pang of the familiar guilt. Damn, damn, it's still
there. "Dear God," she goes on, putting her hands to her head, sinking
into the living room couch. "Why do you assume the worst of me? I
thought we were friends. I thought everything was okay. And then it
wasn't."

"You always judged me," I say. "I was always too much for you. I was always too much to be a good girl."

"I didn't care about that."

"Yes, you did. When I first started going to college, you—"

"I was afraid of losing you, okay? That's it. That's all of it. And I talked too much, and I ruined it. I was afraid because all my life I was as you say: good and sweet and virtuous. And the pressure of that hardened over me like a shell I couldn't escape: the more I did what I was told, the more people expected me to until I didn't know who I was or what I wanted. And you… you went off to school and became this worldly person, and I envied you. Oh God, I envied you!

"But I told myself you were wrong, that I was doing things the right way, so I married Theo because I wouldn't let myself have sex with him until I did, and thank God it actually worked out and he's a good man and I love him because I was too young to get married. I know that now. But I still can't exactly regret it. But I've done many things throughout my life, to you and to others, and to myself, that I do regret. And I don't know what to say or how to reconcile it, except that I know I did and said all those things because I was scared. That's all. I was so damn terrified of making a mistake. Because as you know, making a mistake isn't just messing up: it's a *slippery slope towards destruction*, no going back.

"So I'm sorry. That's all I can say. I'm sorry. I wish I were as good at being good as everyone thinks I am."

She stares at the carpet, deep brown, 2002. I remember when it was installed, when Mom and Dad took us to the giant carpet store in Erie, and let us play in the huge rolls that smelled like rubber and new nylon.

This is all too much. I can't do it. I can't think. I turn and leave, rush out of the house into the cold night air that burns my nose. I take my car downtown, mind spinning, insides screaming.

I want to hate her, still. I want to be angry. The hurt I've kept for years, the little threads of it reaching farther back than I ever realized, wants to stay knotted up in my chest. But the more I grasp at the threads, the weaker they go. She's not my enemy. There is no enemy, not really. Just misunderstanding. Just expectation. Just fear.

I hit the steering wheel, over and over. Why didn't anyone notice us two, with our neurotic yearning to be as good as possible? Why didn't anyone notice we were killing ourselves from the inside out, trying so hard to follow the way of light, and love, and belonging? Why didn't we notice each other? Why didn't we work together instead of isolating, digging ourselves deeper and deeper into twin graves?

Why didn't *they* notice? Dad, who was so observant of everything, down to the gingerbread trim on a house in a ghost town. Mom, whose fire and feist would have singed all the bullshit to a crisp if only she'd known about it. If only they'd known. If only. Why didn't we tell them? Why weren't we taught to tell them?

I find myself in front of Bobby's Bar again, in the dark, in the cold. If I try hard enough, I can pretend it's not today, but a few weeks ago, and I've just come from Emma and Daniel's, and I'm enraged at the sight of such perfect traditional domesticity. I can pretend I still don't get my sister, that I am alone in my pain, that Haven is a monolith I'd rather not dig into the nuance of. I step into the bar, and see the same people there. Katie and the others, and they greet me happily, say they've been waiting for me each night, and they order me a drink, and I drink it, and it drowns out every thought, and the weight in my chest lightens just a bit, and I think *yes, this was the cure all along.* And the room fills with people, and we dance to last year's hits, and the music is loud and throbbing and terrifying, and I am so exhilarated I scream and laugh and draw the drink and noise and people around me like a suffocating blanket.

But then I notice the Christmas lights, festooned above the bar, and I realize it's December. I remember the nativity set, the Lamb of God who takes away the sins of the world. I remember my sister, and I remember I love her. I remember that I used to believe a lot of things, but now I only believe one. *God is real.* I remember how angry I am with him, and I remember that everyone else in the world probably is too. I remember that I am in pain, and I'm not alone in it.

God is within you, a thought rises to the surface, a belief peeling itself off the table. *God is within you.* The scrap of polyester silk. *God is within you.* The Holy Spirit, like a dove, like fire coming down from heaven and burning up all the bullshit.

I find myself out on the sidewalk, in the cold, crying and crying.

"You okay?" Katie has followed me out, her cheeks and nose turning suddenly red in the cold.

"No," I say to myself.

"Come back inside," she says.

"I can't."

"Why not? Come on."

"I'm sorry. I have to go home."

"Amy, what's wrong?" She takes my shoulders, and as she comforts me, I see in her eyes the look of someone who's only ever wanted to be comforted. And I am so ashamed I can't bear to look at her.

"This isn't right. I shouldn't be here. I'm just running away."

"Running away from what?"

My pain. My life. Myself. I swallow. "God."

She laughs sharply. "God ran away from us first."

My brain is foggy, but I'm still taken aback by this. She doesn't know about me and Laura, me and Pittsburgh, me and God. "Us?"

She looks at me, her brown eyes glistening quietly in the streetlights, like so many stars in a dark sky. For a moment, she looks like the girl I remember, the girl I secretly envied for many reasons, not the least of which because she was so ardently herself, even when everyone else told her it wasn't good enough. But I also see the lines, already, of age, the weariness of being an outcast in a place where there are already far too few people. And I realize, in this moment, that she and I are more alike than I thought, than I ever wanted to admit to myself, than I even want to admit now, because doing so would put something else on the table, and I'm not ready to sort it out with all the others yet.

My heart hums. *God is real. God is within you.*

"Hey," she says, touching my shoulder. "Talk to me."

170

I look at her wildly, feeling suddenly terrified. I realize how empty town is, this late at night, and the place feels cavernous and haunted. I shouldn't be here. I shouldn't be drunk, again, in the street in the dark. I should be home with Laura, sorting things out.

"I'm sorry. I have to go." I stand and start walking, hoping the air sobers me up enough to drive home.

"Where are you going?" she asks.

"I have to go back home. I have to talk to Laura."

"Laura will be there in the morning. Talk to me." I turn back and look at her. Maybe she can see the terror on my face, because she sighs. "I'm not going to bite you."

"I can't keep coming here," I say.

"Where, to the bar?"

I nod.

She laughs. "I knew you were still a good Christian girl."

This isn't what I meant. But damn it, I have a pounding headache, and I can't think straight. "No, I mean the drinking. I keep drinking. I'm just running away." I bend at the waist, feeling suddenly sick, but I won't be sick again. I refuse. I breathe deep, trying to fend off the numbness creeping up from my fingertips.

A flicker of recognition crosses her face, a spark of realization, and I know I've told her something about herself, inadvertently, just as she did for me a few minutes ago.

I don't know what comes over me, but before I can think about it, I find myself walking back toward her, and hugging her, and she is cold and bony and frail, but she hugs me back, and we both cry silently in the frozen December air.

When I return home, the house is dark except for a single light in the living room. Even the Christmas tree is switched off. Theo sits in the corner, on his phone. "Where were you?" he asks. His face is imperceptible, which is unusual for him.

I've sobered up all the way, having spent the past hour on a Haven street curb crying with Katie and swallowing lungfuls of frozen air. "I was out clearing my head," I say. "I'm sorry."

I'm sorry I'm sorry I'm sorry.

"Is Laura still up?" I ask.

He puts his phone down and leans forward. "Why do you constantly self-sabotage ?" he asks. "For real. Why?"

"What did she tell you?"

"That you had a fight. That you were drunk and still went out. That she apologized to you for every way she had hurt you, that she thought you had some kind of breakthrough, and then you left."

I stare at the floor. Hardwood, here in the hallway. 1910.

"Did she wildly lie, or does that cover it?" Theo asks.

I clear my throat and nod.

"What do you want?" he asks. He covers his eyes, briefly with his hands. "We're trying to help you. I know it's complicated. Believe me. I get complicated. My family wins best prize at the fair for complicated. I know it's not... she's not right all the time, and neither are you. I get it. But why do you have to keep leaving? Why do you insist on going through everything alone, when you don't have to?"

The house is silent. Above my head, I hear it again: faint footsteps in between my breaths, the inhaling and exhaling of their room. "I don't know," I tell him.

"Well, neither do I. I don't know what more to do." He looks exhausted, and I realize how—of course—I should have known all his steadiness was a mask, as it always is, and he is also tired and sad and angry at how everything is.

"I'm sorry Theo," I say. I come forward a few steps. "I don't know what to do."

He sits upright again. "You can start by trying not to make things worse."

His voice nettles me. He's never spoken to me this way, not without a lightness, a sarcasm, a jovial wink, or silly expression. He's tired, and sad, and angry.

"Should I just leave, then?" I ask. "Should I just get out of your hair, get out of your life?"

"No." His face is set, dark. "Because that would make things worse."

"So I'm not allowed to leave, then? Ever."

"Not until this is all sorted out."

"What does that even mean?"

"You know exactly what it means."

I nod, give a bitter laugh. "All right then. Good night. Sorry to keep you up." I turn and walk up the stairs. As I pass Mom and Dad's room, my heart skips a beat: the door is partly open, and a light is on. I peer around the doorway and see Laura, asleep, curled up on the bed, her arms wrapped around one of Mom's pillows.

Chapter Fourteen

That night I sleep poorly, tossing and turning, mulling the day over and over in my mind, trying to untangle the knots of all that happened. Trying to sort out the people and events and the new ideas I have to acquaint myself with.

Theo's right, I shouldn't have left. I was stupid, and confused, and drunk. I really shouldn't have left. Thinking about it all smarts, stings with wave after wave of guilt, and it's different than the panic engulfing me every five minutes: it's sharper, more specific. For the first time, I told Laura what I really thought. And for the first time, she told me, and in that moment we were closer than we'd been in years. And then I left.

Why do you have to keep leaving? I don't know why. Because everything is too much sometimes; because I feel suffocated, strangled. Because I'm trying to beat people to the punch, to leave before they can judge or criticize me. Before I can scrutinize myself too much.

I was afraid of losing you, okay? I wish I was as good at being good as everyone thinks I am. So it was all an act for Laura. A sham. No, not quite that. I don't know what it is. She tried the best she could. She tried so hard because she wanted to, because it was important to her. I do the same thing, just in a different way. We're all just floating, trying, doing our best.

I keep drinking. I'm just running away. Gin on ice. Irish whiskey. I realize how much I've been using them to get through my days, each and every painful memory, every tense moment, every wave of blind panic. I've been abusing it, I realize. I'm this close to becoming an alcoholic. This thought stings too. I understand now why people like Pastor Jeff don't drink, even if they don't believe it's a flat-out sin: because sometimes it's just too easy not to stop.

I think of Katie and the others at the bar, happy to see me, waiting for me. It was such a nice feeling, to be welcomed without pretense. But maybe Theo's right; I have self-sabotaged. Because I've been welcomed by other people, too. Emma and Daniel. Grandad and Grandma and Nanna. Dr. Lynda. Pastor Jeff and Julie, if I'd let them. Theo. Laura. The welcomes weren't always perfect, but I had them.

Why do you insist on going through everything alone, when you don't have to? I don't know, I don't know. I've always been this way, since I can remember. It's my fatal flaw. I want to be independent, smart, special. But it's not just that. I don't want to need people. Needing people sucks. Until you need them.

God has already run out on us. I know why Katie thinks this. I don't blame her for thinking this. Her family ran out on her. Her friends ran out on her. Her church ran out on her. I want to agree with this statement. I did, at one point, agree with it, when I tore down everything I believed and put them on the table. But now, I have these two beliefs that won't budge. They're fixed, like a keystone in a doorway. *God is real. God is within you.* How can God be within me, a part of me, and run out at the same time?

And then there's the part I really don't want to think about: what Katie meant when she said us. A deep, unnamed part of me I've always known in some way, but found it too easy to ignore. Even during college, when I was challenging everything, I didn't challenge this. I can't even challenge it now. I don't want to. It's too much. I punch my pillow, then sit up before the weight on my chest can suffocate me.

You can't leave until this is all sorted out.

One thing at a time. I'll tackle one thing at a time.

The next morning at breakfast, my thoughts have mellowed enough. I tell Laura I'm sorry for running out, that everything was just so much, so overwhelming, that I'm glad she told me everything anyway, and that it helps.

"Thank you for saying that," she says.

"I'm tired of fighting," I say.

"Me too." Glimmers of hope surface, the sparkling of oil and water blending again.

She prepares to leave for work. "Theo's working late again," she says. "And I won't be home for dinner."

"Are you going out?" I ask.

"I'm rejoining the lady's Bible study," she answers. "With a few friends from church."

I nod. "So you're still doing church stuff. Even after everything."

"Just because I haven't always done it right, doesn't mean I don't want to do it at all." She puts on her coat and runs her fingers through her loose waves. I notice that she's put on a little bit of weight, looks much healthier than she did even weeks ago. "Just because it's messed up in some ways doesn't mean I want to throw it all out." She gives me a sad look, a frustrated look as if she wants to say a million things but can't decide which to say first.

"I know. You're right." The thought comes back to me that I have no right to judge her, now that I know where she's been coming from all these years. I can't blame her for how she's lived her life in light of it, even if it's different than how I would do it.

"Christmas Eve," she says. "There's a service at church. Would you come with us?"

I'm taken aback. I haven't been to Christmas Eve service in a few years, not since the year of their wedding, which was the last time I went to church at all, besides the funeral.

She sees what is probably a panicked expression on my face, and forges ahead. "It would mean a lot to me if you'd go."

I don't want to go. It's the sort of thing where you know putting off doing something again and again will just make it worse when you do eventually do it, but I'm too scared to jump in and try. You just have to bite the bullet. Theo's words ring in my ears: *You have to make this right. You know exactly what that means.* I think he gives me too much credit because I really don't.

"Okay," I say. "Yes, I'll go with you."

She smiles, relief and joy flooding her face, and I think everything must be worth it. "Thank you. I appreciate it." She turns to go. "Have a good day. See you tonight."

It's not exactly all sorted out the way Theo would probably like. But the two of us have an understanding now. The oil and water have melded, just a little bit. The ceiling and the floor are a little more magical, a little fuller of possibility.

Aunt Maeve comes home about a week before Christmas. I pick her up at the Pittsburgh airport, relishing the two-hour drive and the brief glimpse I get of the Steel Building between the hills as I skirt around the city. She is effervescent on the way home, bubbling with excitement and joy at seeing us for Christmas, and I catch myself thinking how happy Mom and Dad will be to see her multiple times. Then I remember what Aunt Sophie said of her at Christmas: "Maeve is selfish," and I realize I'm going to spend all Christmas looking for evidence for that, and my excitement at seeing her again sours.

Outside, the land is brown, and we haven't yet had a really good snow: just a few minor flurries since November. The ground is frozen and crisp, but the snow has been too dry and it blows away with the wind. The trees are bare, like dark toothpicks stuck in the ground, and each day has been almost unbearably gray and dreary.

"Brr. It's so cold up here," says Aunt Maeve. "Although, down in North Carolina we've had a cold spell too."

"How's everything down there? How's work?"

"Busy," she sighs, pulling down the passenger mirror and studying her reflection, smoothing her face, which is perfectly made up. "I had to pull myself away just for this trip."

"I'm glad you did. Grandad, and Grandma, and everyone are excited to see you."

She smiles, red lipstick against the whitest teeth. "How has everyone been? It's been a rough few months."

"We're getting through it," I say.

"What's it like living in Haven again?"

I exhale quickly. "Um, it's different."

"You can vent to me," she says. "I know living there isn't a walk in the park."

It's nice, as Laura says, to talk to someone who hasn't been going through it. Although this isn't exactly what she means. I tell Aunt Maeve how I lost my job and apartment (although I'm sure my grandparents told her), how frustrated I am, how things between Laura and I have been shaky for years, and how we're just now starting to get somewhere, even though I'm still confused about Haven, and family, and God.

"All of this is normal," she says. "It's a normal part of growing up. It's exactly how I felt at your age, which is why I left."

"If it's so normal, why does it hurt so much?"

She smiles wryly. "Growing pains? It doesn't make it any easier when your world is so small, when you have a whole community of people pressuring you to be a certain way. I mean, take me. I was the oldest daughter of a pastor. People were always expecting me to be a certain way. Church people are so judgmental."

"Not all of them, though," I say softly. I think of Mom and Dad, Grandad. Pastor Jeff, Julie. People in my life who were always thoughtful and loving, so quietly good that the noise of all the others, critical and self-serving, ended up drowning them out.

"Sure, there's probably a few good apples," Aunt Maeve says dismissively. "But in my experience, religion does more harm than good. I'll go to church on Christmas Eve to make Mom and Dad happy, but that's the end of it for me."

I expected her to say something like this, but it still, for some reason, hits me sharply. I've never talked to her so frankly about things; growing up, her opinions were reserved for hushed conversations with Mom and Dad, and snide comments every now and then in mixed company. I gathered from Grandad that Aunt Maeve was more or less nonreligious and that it disappointed him. A part of me agrees with her, but a part of me agrees with him, too, and I can't decide which I agree with more.

I drop Aunt Maeve off at Grandma Nancy and Grandad George's, and return home to an empty house. I make myself some coffee and turn on my computer, keen to get a few job applications in since I still haven't heard back from the bulk of them, and the one or two calls I did get ended in fruitless second-round questionnaires that apparently didn't tell the hirers what they wanted to hear.

I've been searching for jobs in the communication field mostly: where I have my degree and the most experience. Copywriting, social media management, PR. Jobs I was told were numerous in college, which I later found out means they're extremely competitive. The fact that I was fired from my previous one, due to my own hot temper and grief, instead of being let go quietly, doesn't help my case, because it's almost two years of experience I can't even cite when most jobs seem to want twenty-five years of experience.

I open my emails and scan them quickly before deleting them all. Then one catches my eye, and I delete it too fast, and I have to go to the trash folder and fish it back out. "Interview Request," says the subject line. I open the email, and it's from a small startup in Pittsburgh, wanting to interview me about being a public relations, social media "guru," as they put it in the job description. "We're a young and hungry group of professionals who want to change the world and maximize impact. Only apply if you are willing to work tirelessly, be part of a growing community, and love dogs," the description had gone on to say.

The listing sounded a little hokey and potentially toxic, and still told me nothing about the actual job, but I had applied. I could be a tirelessly-working, hungry, dog-loving social media guru if it would get me out of Haven. And here it was: they wanted to meet with me after Christmas. I email back eagerly and set an appointment. Perhaps things are finally beginning to make a turn in the right direction.

Christmas Eve, I find myself before the mirror in my bedroom, putting on my velvet red dress for church. It will be the first time I've gone to church at all in over two years, not counting the funeral, and I am oddly lacking in anxiety about it. I feel calm, hushed as if standing in the woods during a heavy snow. What I *do* have anxiety about is that it's Christmas and it doesn't seem like it should be. It's Christmas, and they're gone. And we're all pretending it will be just like always, that we'll all emerge from our rooms in our best clothes, and they will too, and we'll all drive to church together in Dad's bright blue SUV.

I smooth my hair, which feels wooly under my fingers. I try to remember last Christmas. I didn't go to church with them, instead stayed home and baked cookies, had everything all nice and festive for when they got back. The grandparents and aunts came over, too, and we laughed, and sang songs, and drank wine, and played games, and were so stupidly unaware that it would be the last time. The last real time. Even though things with Laura were still awkward, it's a good memory.

I rub some cream between my fingers and smooth the skin under my eyes delicately, copying the finely-tuned way Aunt Maeve applies eye cream when she thinks no one's looking. I trace the soft curved line of my dark brows and feel the muscles under my skin stretch ever so slightly. Then I grab my makeup bag and get to work. Soft brown shadow, black mascara, tinted cream in the lightest shade they sell, a generous layer of lipstick in just the right shade to match the dress. I'm a little too sexy for church, but it's Christmas Eve; I won't be the only one. The Christmas Eve service has a way of cleaning out all the latent and lapsed worshippers, pulling them back into the fray in the name of family, tradition, festivity. Many of them, like myself, are rusty on the etiquette: the words you can't say, the things you can't wear. I try out a few euphemisms, just in case I slip up and curse: *Darn, Shoot, Freak.* No, better keep it safe. *Fudge.* I stand up straight, compress my shoulders and elbows inward, zip my knees together, keep my hands close to my body, avoid stretching out or looking too loose, too comfortable, too sensual. Yes, me, such the tease. The muscle memory I have from doing this, unconsciously, every week as a teenager, is astounding, something I didn't even realize until now.

Downstairs, Theo and Laura are ready to go, layering scarves and hats over their coats. It's cold out, everything crystalized with a fine layer of frost. We're set to get some snow tonight, and it would be nice to have a white Christmas.

"I'm glad you're coming," Laura says. "You look really nice."

"Thanks," I smile. I pretend this is like all the Christmas Eves I remember, when dressing up and going to church on this night felt magical, and sacred; when the world seemed so big and wide and full of hope instead of fear. When the thought of catching a cute boy's eye in my Christmas best put butterflies in my stomach, when I wasn't aware of the routine my body went through each time, to prepare for scrutiny.

When they were here.

The church is swarming with people, almost as many as the day of the funeral. Outside, the church windows and Christmas lights glow brightly in the cold night, a slow breeze whistling through the streets of Haven. The dark hills stand tall and protective, sentient and steady, under the starry sky. I shiver a little in my red coat, but it's the kind of delicious shiver you get when you feel completely safe and happy, and the feeling confounds me, because I don't know if I do.

Inside, we struggle through a throng of people to find a seat. Every single person is familiar, though to me they are a distant memory, sometimes an uncomfortable one, and I have a clarity now that I didn't have the day of the funeral, so each memory seems sharper. Mrs. Carol Novak, the church secretary and evergreen event planner, who when I was thirteen told me my church dress was immodest because when I raised my arms during praise and worship, the hem lifted too far above the knee. (She told me this in love, she said, because she wanted to save me from the sin of causing a brother—any male around—to stumble with lust). She gives me a hug now, and says she's so happy to see me. Mr. Brian Mishler, a Sunday School teacher, once rebuked me as a child for teasingly saying "I hate you!" to a friend, calling it *coarse joking.* Now he shakes my hand and says I look so grown up. Emma is here, and several of my other old friends, all of them married, all of them with kids. I wave to a few of them, and they politely wave back, the look of vague recognition on their faces. When I wave to Emma, carrying little Sam, she flashes me a smile with a hint of hesitation in it, which perplexes me, but before I can wonder what it means, the service begins.

Pastor Jeff takes the pulpit, dressed in black slacks and a red checkered shirt, a novelty tie with Christmas trees on it around his neck. I am surprised how much older he looks than I remember: his beard, always neatly trimmed and groomed, is nearly gray, and his usually balding short hair is shaved completely. His face seems more weathered. I realize, with a pang, that in losing Mom and Dad, he also lost two of his best friends, and I feel bad about avoiding all his visits. Maybe he wasn't trying to confront me about my apostasy: maybe he was trying to mourn together.

The service goes along in the usual way: the worship band plays a few upbeat versions of Christmas carols, punctuated by readings from the gospels. Pastor Jeff gives a short sermon, all about the love of God, how God desires to be with us so thoroughly, that he sent Jesus to come to earth to be with us.

"God is a hound," says Pastor Jeff, "Following us day and night, whether we like it or not. Once we stick to him, he's stuck to us. God is within each of you, no matter where you go and what you do. His love is so strong that he pursues us, relentlessly."

God is within you. The second belief I have, ever since that strange night when I ran out on Laura and cried with Katie and tried to forget everything but couldn't. Maybe this way of characterizing God is aggressive and problematic, but I don't care; I kind of like it. I once heard someone say God is a perfect gentleman; he never forces his way in. He says please and thank you. He wipes his feet. But this always seemed too tame, too civilized, for me. For as much as I hate other people cornering me and trying to get a solid bit of theology out of me, I like the idea of God being wild, and rude, and intrusive. I like the idea of saying, "God, I don't know what I believe right now. I'm hurt, and I need some space to clean all this up. Please leave me alone. It's not you; it's me," and God replying, "Fuck that. I'm with you, thick and thin, whether you like it or not."

I like a God who can swear, I guess. A God who can handle the real world. A God who isn't a wuss.

The brightly decorated church, with its festooned Christmas trees and poinsettias, the sounds of music as the band begins to play again, all fade away while I realize something: I'm not angry at God. I thought I was, but I'm not. Rather, I'm angry at all the contradictions of all the people who say they love God. It's not God I have a beef with: it's the dozens of ways I've been told I must act, I must be, in order to even have a chance at a good life. The people who tell me they're sorry for my loss, but also that my parents are lucky to be dead, and we should envy them. The people who welcome me back to church, after once berating me for being a child with a body, after once bullying out people like Katie and others, and then not understanding when they think God has run out on them. Maybe I've been going at it all wrong: maybe I shouldn't be throwing out God. Maybe I should be throwing out how people have diluted and fed God to me. Maybe that's why I'm so sick. Maybe, just maybe, I don't need to be afraid of God. Maybe I don't need to be afraid of myself.

I'm startled out of my deep thoughts by everyone clapping as Pastor Jeff tells us to go and enjoy Christmas with our families. Everyone gets out from their seats, some to leave for festivities at home, some to mingle with each other. Laura and Theo dissolve away to say hello to some friends. The atmosphere is celebratory, sparkling, and hope rises in my heart, the beginnings of an epiphany. Once I get home, I'll think about this more. Maybe I'm not out in the wilderness, wandering. Maybe I've been home all along, and all I have to do is make my home my own.

"Amy?" A voice in the seat behind me calls. I turn around and see Emma, joined by a few of the other girls our age, old friends. Mrs. Gladys is here too. I'd thought she'd died long ago, but I guess not. Damn it.

"Hi!" I say, a little too cheerfully, projecting easy friendliness. But at the pit of my stomach dread rises. There's too many of them. Something's wrong. I pick up my purse and put on my coat, wrap it around me like a blanket.

"How have you been?" One of the girls asks. Sarah Eckenburg, now Ingram.

"Oh, you know," I say. They nod solemnly. "It's been a tough few months. But," I gesture to the front of the church, "It's great to be here and see everyone." This is not quite a lie, but not quite the truth.

"Listen," says Emma with concern in her voice. She grips my arm in what is meant to be a comforting gesture, but she's stronger than she thinks. "Listen, we know you've been going through a rough time, and we're here for you."

I look at them. "Thank you. I appreciate it." My voice is flat, monotone, polite.

"We would love for you to join our ladies' group," says Sarah. "It's every Thursday night. Laura comes too, and really enjoys it."

Oh yes, I'm aware. "Thanks! I might be able to come by. My schedule's a little crazy after the holidays… I have a new job opportunity—"

"We just," Emma continues, "we just know you have been struggling with what has happened, which is totally understandable. But we've all been praying for you, and we felt led by the Lord to tell you, that you don't have to turn to substances, or to unhealthy people and habits, to heal your pain. God loves you and wants to help. All you have to do is turn to him."

My body grows rigid, stiff as a ramrod. "What?" How could they know about this? I don't remember dancing in Bobby's bar with Emma staked out in the corner.

Mrs. Gladys chimes in, her voice warbling from the back of the group. "And with your sister's baby on the way, your family needs you to be strong, to take care of yourself."

The world goes still. The dread sinks to the pit of my stomach again, quiet for once. My entire body is stunned to a stop, like I've jumped from a far height into a pool and belly flopped on the surface of the water. I can't breathe.

My vision tunnels through the crowd of people to the back of the church, where Laura chats with Pastor Jeff's wife, Julie. She locks eyes with me briefly, and then she sees the group of women in front of me, and a shadow passes over her face, her eyes growing electric green with panic.

She told them. She told Emma, and Sarah, and Mrs. Gladys, and probably everyone else. But she didn't tell me.

Me, the other half of the whole. *Me*, who used to know her best. *Me*, from whom even her husband asked for a blessing to marry her.

We're oil and water. We can't mix. We were never supposed to. The ceiling is just a ceiling. The floor is just a floor. The world is the way it is, and there's no use changing it.

In a moment, Laura is at my side. "Amy, Listen—"

I turn away and walk out of the room, passing clusters of happy, smiling Christians in their bright Christmas clothes. *Peace on earth, good will toward men.* My eyes smart with stinging tears. The dread in my stomach rises and meets the fear in my chest, and they explode into lumps I swallow down my throat. I rush out of the church into the cold air. Theo is there, having pulled the car around. I walk past him, down the street.

"Hey, Amy, I'm over here!" he calls from the car. "Get in!"

"Go to hell!" I scream at him, startling the handful of people outside.

He gets out of the car, leaves it running. "What's wrong? Hey, what happened?" I keep walking, faster and faster, down the street. He jogs to keep up with me. When he finally catches up, he grabs my shoulder. "Amy, what's wrong?"

I turn and smack him across the face. He yells. I keep walking.

"What's wrong with you?" he says. "What the hell?"

I don't want to tell him. I want to walk and walk, and I want the night to melt me into another place, far away from here. But I'm too weak. I break down, bent over with exhaustion and rage, and begin to cry. "Why didn't you tell me? Why didn't you tell me she was pregnant?"

He stops and looks at me with a lost expression, like I remember him looking once long ago, a little boy whose world had crumbled around him. The mussing of his hair, and my mark across his face, doesn't do him any favors. "She wanted to tell you herself," he says.

I laugh. "Oh, okay. Right. Well, she did. She just enlisted a whole Bible study full of women to pass that message along."

"What?"

"She told fucking Emma, and fucking Sarah, and fucking Mrs. Gladys, and probably everyone else in this fucking church, in this fucking town, because that would be better, I guess than telling me!" I spit out each word, tasting more and more bitter.

He shakes his head. "There has to be some mistake. Calm down. Let's go home and talk about this."

"Don't tell me what to do. After giving me that bullshit lecture about how I had to make this all right! *Me!* When she was lying and talking about me behind my back the whole time!"

Halfway up the block, Laura emerges from the church. "Amy!" she calls. Her voice echoes down the dark street, against the houses lit up and glowing from within, where other families are spending their holiday away from prying eyes.

I step forward and lean close to Theo. My voice is low. "I will never go to that fucking house again. I will never come back to this shit town again. Tell her I'm done. Tell her it's finished. And this time, it's on her; not on me." I step back and turn away, and start walking down the street.

186

Chapter Fifteen

I call Aunt Maeve, who has just gotten out of the service at Grandad's church, and I ask her to pick me up. She arrives in the car she rented a few days after her arrival, the rates in Haven being cheaper than they would have been at the Pittsburgh airport. The car is new and smells unfamiliar and too clean. I lay against the cushy headrest.

"Is everything okay?" she asks.

"No," I say. "No, it's not." And I burst into tears and sob and sob while she drives through town, and when she pulls up in front of my parents' house, I say. "No. I'm not going back there ever again."

"Where would you like to go, then?" she asks.

"Home. Pittsburgh."

She doesn't tell me that's too far, or that we already have plans with family. She turns the car around and drives.

Christmas morning, I wake up in a hotel in Ross Township, outside the city. It was the only place for a reasonable price not booked to capacity. Aunt Maeve stayed with me, while I cried and cried and told her everything, and she held me and said nothing, only listened. Telling someone everything did not feel, as I thought it would, like throwing sparks into fumes. Nor did it feel like the release I thought it might: instead, my mind is even more tangled in knots, the situation even more hopeless.

This morning, cold gray light sneaks across the whites of the hotel bedding, Aunt Maeve's sleeping form under the thick coverlet, a mask over her eyes. I dress and head to the lobby for some watery scrambled eggs and bad coffee, joining a few other sad people spending Christmas morning alone in a hotel. I wonder why they're here, but I

don't ask. They probably wonder the same thing about me, especially
because I'm wearing my red velvet dress from last night. I take a deep
breath. Everything aside, it's liberating to be in a place where nobody
knows your name.

I check my phone, stomach bubbling with anxiety. Calls and texts
from Laura and Theo. I know Aunt Maeve called Grandad and told
him where we were, so nobody's worried that I'm injured or
kidnapped, or dead in the middle of the woods. They're worried for
my soul, probably. Worried because I'm gone and I'll never come
back. Tough.

I finish my coffee and stare out the window. It snowed last night,
less here than it probably did in Haven, where the elevation is higher.
The snow is a delicate icing on each tree branch and blade of grass and
will probably be gone by the day's end. But the sky is blue, dotted with
the remnant colors of the sunrise. Route 19, the main thoroughfare in
this part of the North Hills, Pittsburgh's northern suburbs, snakes
through the hills, connecting shopping centers and neighborhoods on
its way to the city. This is one of the most ancient roads in the area:
used first by native Iroquois, Lenape, Shawnee and others hunting in
these hills; then by George Washington on his military conquests; then
as a trolley line connecting the countryside to the city; then as the main
highway from Pittsburgh to Erie, until they built the interstate.
Grandad took this very same road once, long ago, when he first went
to seminary in the city. Of course, this hotel and the mall and the fifty
different Starbuckses weren't there then. Dad showed me old pictures
once: Route 19 in the 1920s, a sea of farmhouses and forests and
empty land, where now there are culs-de-sac and superstores. At one
time, this place was the wilderness and now isn't; it's the reverse of
Haven. You can still find the remnants: pieces of buildings hidden in
the shadows of newer ones, brick foundations hidden in the brush
between neighborhoods, original farmhouses built alongside
midcentury ticky-tacky homes, rusted metal streetlights leaning on
LED poles like kudzu vines. See, this place has grandfather trees too;
just different ones. I still love looking for the stories of people past; it's
just different people. Different land. Different stories.

189

Grandad's ancestors came from Ireland and used to live around here, a hundred and fifty years ago. They kept moving further and further north, chasing the wilderness, following this road, until one of them found themselves in Haven, just before the turn of the last century, and decided the area reminded him so much like Ireland, he had to stay there. But for a long time, many of my ancestors lived here, in the city, and built a life. This place is as much in my blood as Haven.

The Lord your God will be with you wherever you go. Pastor Jeff's sermon from the night before comes back to me and with it a mingling of anger and hope. I remember the beginning of the epiphany I had last night, before everything went terribly wrong. I remember that idea, that everything wrong with my faith isn't wrong with the faith itself, with God himself. Maybe everything wrong with it is how other people messed it up. Maybe I can have my three beliefs: that God is real, that God is within me, that God will be with me wherever I go; and these three are enough. Maybe I can acquire new beliefs daily, or never acquire any again, and that doesn't mean I'm lost. My faith may be fucked-up forever, but at least it's mine. At least it's always been mine.

As I think over these things, there's still a knot in everything: Laura. My family. Haven. The guilt of leaving when I don't want to stay. I'm so angry at everyone and everything, but Laura especially. I'm so angry that something so happy—I'm an aunt, and I've always wanted to be a fun aunt!—has been ruined by secrets and judgment and the syrupy prayers of people who insult me and think it will comfort me.

"Merry Christmas." Aunt Maeve joins me at the table with a cup of coffee. "How'd you sleep?"

"Pretty well," I say. "Thanks for coming down here with me. I'm sorry to ruin your Christmas."

"Hey, it's just been that kind of year, huh? Don't worry about it; I was getting antsy in that place anyway. It kind of smothers you, you know? Like a hug that goes on for too long."

I nod. "And no one else gets it. No one else sees how small the world is up there."

"Some people are just blind," she says. I'm a little surprised at her bluntness, but I guess she's right. "Listen, honey," she goes on. "Don't give a damn what everyone else says. You're a strong and confident woman; you can do anything. Take this new job, find yourself a place to live, live your own life. You can even come down and stay with me if you want."

I smile a little. "Thanks." I fiddle with the plastic spoon I used to stir my coffee. "I just can't believe she didn't tell me. I thought we were getting close again."

"It's not your fault," Aunt Maeve says. "Something happens to people's brains in that town, especially if they're religious. It's a cult mentality: anyone in the community is good, anyone outside is bad. And if you are different at all, you're out."

I cock my head. "Mom and Dad weren't that way."

Aunt Maeve smiles a crooked, sharp smile. "Your parents were wonderful people. But…" she pauses to collect her thoughts, and in that small moment, everything inside me churns with rage.

"But what?" I say, a challenge.

"But they were too invested in their own interests to think about the big picture. You. Laura. The future of our family, the chance to live a better life in a better place."

"They liked their life."

"I'm sure they did," she says. "I mean, your dad was a brilliant man. A little nutty, of course, with his ghost-seeing, but brilliant. Your mom was such a firecracker, so passionate. But just think how much better those passions could have been put to use somewhere else. Can you imagine the ways your dad could have grown the study of history if he'd worked at a big university? Can you imagine all the positive changes your mom could have made if she was a social worker for a big organization, in a big city where people really need people like her? Their talent was wasted in a place like Haven. And what's more, they robbed you girls, too, of the opportunities for jobs and education and better social circles."

I feel hot. All the things she's saying have knocked around in my
own head now and then, but hearing them said out loud is different. I
realize, now, how pretentious they sound. "I don't know," I say. "Dad's
whole body of work was about the stories of forgotten places. Ghost
towns. Northern Appalachia. Post-industrialism. He couldn't have
done that anywhere else. And Mom worked in Haven because people
in Haven, as you said, don't have the same opportunities. They were
exactly the people who needed her help."

"That's the guilt talking," says Aunt Maeve. "The Stockholm
Syndrome. At some point, you can't think about the things that hold
you back. You have to help yourself. You have to do what's best for
you."

I realize, in an instant, that she and I have not been discussing the
same things, and the difference between us yawns so wide and obvious
that I can't believe I didn't see it. I think of Grandad on that day we
went hunting. *You care so much. That's why you're angry.* I think of
Aunt Sophie on Thanksgiving. *Maeve is selfish.* I think of Dad. *We
have to remember, or no one else will.*

I nod and paste on a smile. "Yeah, true," I say to Aunt Maeve.

We spend Christmas day buying some clothes at the only store
that's not closed, and sight-seeing around the city. Much of it is stuff I
never had the time to do when I lived here last time: skating in Market
Square, shopping at the Strip District, riding the Incline and seeing the
city spread out like a quilt over the hills. Aunt Maeve goes back up to
Haven the day after, and I find a cheap temporary apartment in
Shadyside, which I can rent by the week until I find something more
permanent. She promises to bring back some of my stuff from the
house—most of which is still packed from the last time I left a place in
a hurry—and to bring back my car, once she's returned the rental.

The next few days I spend alone in Shadyside are the most oddly
wonderful days I've had in a while: I buy my daily necessities at a
small shop down the street, I walk through the neighborhood that in

itself feels so still, even though all around it the city hums with the traffic of people hurrying to hospitals, museums, and universities. The houses, built so close together, press in protectively. The shops along Walnut Street hum with light and life. For the first time in months, I am independent. I can breathe. The world isn't simple, black-and-white, but there's a comfort in it. A comfort in multiple possibilities.

There's a difference, too, from the last time I lived here: a nearly imperceptible shift. Mom and Dad are gone. I have no ties, anymore, to anyone else. As complicated as that whole thing is, it makes me free. My success or failure now has no bearing on what I have to prove to someone else; my way is only for me. I never realized what performance meter I had in the back of my head until it was gone and there's so much extra room in my brain now. I find myself spending time at bookstores and the library, reading everything historical I can get my hands on. Carnegie and Frick, the great floods, steel and immigrants and labor and strikes. This all held my fascination when I lived in Pittsburgh before, but this time it seems crucial, like oxygen or sunlight.

A few days after Christmas I go to the interview at the hungry, dog-loving startup, which is in a small open-concept office on the third floor of a dilapidated building in Oakland. I can see three hospitals and three universities from the same window, one of which is the university I went to, and it feels very circle-of-life. Andre, the CEO, who's also my interviewer (and, I think, the person who empties the trash cans each evening), is a few years older than me, smartly dressed, with a sharp haircut.

"We started this company about a year ago," he says, "and it's growing fast. We really liked your experience, and you have a good energy."

I don't know what this means, but I don't care. It's the first time a job has really wanted me since… forever. Even at my previous job, I could tell I wasn't the first choice. And that was before I called my boss a bitch. Andre promises to call me later with their decision, and I get the call within an hour of getting back to my apartment: I have joined the ranks.

Everything is aligning, settling into place, and I am so alight with excitement I want to call someone, tell someone, celebrate. But there's no one to do that with. I've pushed them all so far until it was easy for them to push back, and now we're all too far away.

On New Year's Eve, Aunt Maeve arrives at my apartment driving my car, with some boxes of my most important stuff. I drive her to the airport for her flight back to North Carolina.

"Well, that was an eventful Christmas," she says. "Everyone says hello, if you want to know."

I don't especially, but I do feel bad for ruining Christmas. "How's Grandad and Grandma? Nanna Mae?"

"All fine. Missing you. Not quite understanding. I told them it was between you and Laura, no hard feelings on them."

Grandad will be calling me. I can feel it in my bones.

"Oh, God, can't believe I almost forgot this," she says, ruffling through her purse. She lays an envelope in my lap while I drive. "Theo gave this to me for you."

"Thanks."

"So Laura is pregnant then, huh?"

"Yep."

Aunt Maeve shakes her head. "So young. Of course, your mom was that age when she had you two. At the time it didn't seem young. Now it seems *very* young."

"Did she say when she was due?" I ask, surprising myself. "I didn't hear."

"Beginning of May."

Laura was pregnant this whole time. No wonder she was beside herself during that first week after the Terrible Friday. No wonder she was sick and pale and tired. She must have been frightened out of her mind; pregnant for the first time, with no mother to turn to, no one but Theo to tell. She could have told me, of course. But I didn't even notice. How could I have not noticed?

We arrive at the airport. I pull into the lane for departure drop-offs and park. "Thanks for everything, Aunt Maeve," I say.

Happy to help. Call anytime, and come visit anytime you want to get away." She looks at me, a brief note of regret crossing her face, darkening her brown eyes. "I know exactly how you feel." I smile and hug her goodbye. I watch her wheel her suitcase into the airport, swishing offstage as briskly as she came in. I don't think she knows how I feel, not exactly. Not anymore.

I'm not supposed to linger in the drop-off lane, but I keep the car in Park and open Theo's envelope. I'm afraid if I don't now, I'll lose my nerve and shut it in a drawer somewhere. And then, I'm glad I didn't do that: out pops a check, a huge check, for my half of the house. I know I'll probably have to sign some papers or something so the house is fully, legally theirs, but we're square. They have what they want and I have what I want.

Along with the check, there's a letter. I don't read it; instead, I fold it and the check up again and stick them in the envelope. I drive back to the apartment and prepare to ring in the new year alone.

Little by little, life starts to knit together into something solid, then into something familiar. I start my new job as a copywriter at the little startup, which is fun and scrappy and exhausting. A week later, I sign a lease for an apartment in Squirrel Hill, the first floor of an old brick house near Frick Park. It's painted with soft whites and blues, white tile in the bathroom and kitchen, a sliver of a lawn in back. There are two bedrooms, and I plan to get a roommate for one of them... a roommate who won't kick me out at a moment's notice.

At the beginning of February, I call my friend Joy, who I haven't spoken to in months.

"Holy cow, Amy," she says. "It's good to hear your voice."

"Yours too." The complete goodness of her floods me with, well, joy, and I cry. I should have been talking to her this whole time. "I'm sorry. I'm so sorry." The familiar chant rings in my head, but it's softer now, less accusing. "I should have listened to you. I should have moved in with people I knew or waited for you to be done with grad school, so we could live in a flat in Berlin or Helsinki."

"You were exactly where you were supposed to be," she says. "And I'm almost done with grad school. Berlin or Helsinki is still an option."

"I should have called you. I'm so sorry. I didn't mean to ignore you. To push you away. I'm so sorry."

"Hey, it's okay," she says. "Talk to me." Her voice is so full of tenderness and understanding, and I feel so ashamed that I cry again. I remember the last time someone made that invitation, *talk to me,* and how I was so afraid to. But I'm starting, step by painful step, not to be afraid anymore. The knots unravel, little by little.

I tell her everything, but with her, unlike Aunt Maeve, I can be even more honest, and again I wonder why I didn't want to talk to her before. I realize how much my conversations with Aunt Maeve had the veneer of disparagement over them. Aunt Maeve was trying to do what she's always done: convince me to leave, to agree with her, to leave everything behind, and move on toward things she thought were more important. It's only when I talk with Joy that I realize what it's like to have someone talk with me to understand, and to support, and to love. The difference is astounding.

"When you're done with school, come back to Pittsburgh," I say. "You can live here."

"It's not Berlin," she says. "But I guess it'll do."

And for the first time in a long time, or maybe forever, I feel completely seen, and completely loved, and I realize what I was so afraid of for so long: being honest. Being honest about my whole self, even the ugly and uncomfortable and untidy parts. I've always assumed that being honest would mean being alone, but now I see that it doesn't have to.

One evening, I get a call from Theo. Maybe I'm going soft, but I answer it.

"Amy?" He sounds shocked, as if he didn't really think calling me would work.

"Hi."

"How are you? Are you okay?"

"I'm doing great, actually. New job is awesome. New apartment is wonderful."

"I'm glad," he says. "Truly. I assume you got my note, either that or Aunt Maeve deposited the check."

"Yes, I got the check. Thank you."

"You didn't read the note."

I pause. I don't want to tell him the truth, but he'll know if I lie. Turns out, the pause is answer enough.

"I'm sorry how things happened," he says. "Please try to understand."

"I do."

"You don't sound like you do."

"No, I do. There are just some things that I can't get over."

"Amy, I'm going to be a *father*," he says.

"I know. Congratulations."

"I'm freaking out."

"You'll do fine. You're practically a second father to me."

"Laura's freaking out."

"She'll be fine." I try to keep my voice light, but it cracks. "She's the mother I never had."

He sighs the familiar sigh that says *Amy is incorrigible.* "She would like you to be around."

"Why doesn't she tell me that herself?"

"Because you won't answer the phone."

"Why didn't she tell it before?"

"Because..." Theo pauses, and when he speaks again his voice is tired. "She was scared. She didn't know what to do. And she was too proud to admit it."

"That answer isn't good enough. She was just fine telling everyone else in town."

"Not everyone else in town. She only told the women in the Bible study. She didn't want them to corner you. She was concerned about you, at the end of her rope, and confided in them. They thought the pregnancy was common knowledge. It was a misunderstanding."

"They had no right—"

"You're right! They didn't. They were fools, and they were self-righteous, and they stuck their noses in where they didn't belong. We all know this. Laura knows it too, and she won't talk to them about it anymore."

"Wow, I'm impressed."

"Please," he pleads. He sighs again. "Can we please move on? I don't know what happened, now or in the past. I'm sorry for hurting you. We both are. I want to move on. We want you to be around for our kid, Amy."

"I said I'm not going back to Haven ever again, and I stand by it."

"Amy, this is ridiculous. What will you do when one of your grandparents passes away? What will you do when Laura has the baby, when we have the rest of our children? What will you do if there's, God forbid, another accident, or an emergency? Are you really going to stay away forever, to banish yourself from your own family?" I'm silent. His voice breaks. "Damn it, do you really hate that she married me that much?" His voice is thick, and I am horrified that I might have made him cry. I inhale sharply, taken aback.

"God, it's not about you, Theo. I love you. You're the only person in Haven who doesn't drive me crazy."

"Well, it started when we got married. You were fine until then."

"No, it wasn't that."

"She told me you had an argument."

"It's not about you. It's about her."

"What about her?"

"We're just different, and I didn't realize it until we got older, and she was this good virtuous girl and I was a rebel, and she judged me for it, and I judged her back, and she loves Haven, and I don't, and we're on separate paths, that's all, and there's no shame in that."

"There's being different," he says, "and there's being outright antagonistic."

"I don't know where it started," I say. "Honestly, I don't. Maybe it was always there. Maybe we weren't ever intended to be the best of friends; we just acted like we were until it was too painful to act anymore."

"You're not friends, though," he says. "You're sisters."

This idea makes me breathless with longing, a deep and raw and heartbreaking longing to know her so well, to love and be loved by her so well again. "I'm not good enough for her," I say. "I never was. I ruined getting married for her. My questions were too much for her. My self was too much for her."

"That's not true at all," he says.

I know, from the conversation I had with her a few months ago, that he's right: that's not the whole story. There was another side of it that I didn't know: her story, her half of the whole.

"There's too much to sort out," I insist. "It's too much to deal with."

"At some point," he continues, "you have to decide to let everything go and love each other anyway. Maybe you'll never sort it out from the beginning. Maybe you just have to start over."

I want to know how people do that. I want to know how to start over. But deep down I know the answer: you have to want it enough. You have to want harmony more than you want the pain. And although it would be nice to kiss and make up, to be honest with her, the memory of Christmas Eve in the church still stings. Laura betrayed me, and it hurt. It reminded me, yet again, that I'm not good enough to know her better than anyone. There will always be someone else, someone more righteous and holy and pure than I, who deserves to know my sister as well as I used to. And that stings like hell.

"I'm not ready yet," I tell him. "I need time."

"Do you know why they wanted to meet you in Grove City that weekend?" he says.

"What?" I am startled.

"We asked them to plan a day. To meet you, to shop, to have dinner. It was going to be a surprise. They didn't even know. We were going to tell you all the news."

I swallow, silent, my heartbeat in my ears.

He clears his throat. "Well, don't take too much time, okay? If there's anything our family knows, it's that time is short."

He hangs up before I can answer.

True to my gut feeling, Grandad does call me. Feeling rather guilty about my call with Theo, I answer this call too. I apologize to Grandad for hurting him and Grandma Nancy and Nanna Mae, tell him I needed space, that I feel better now than I have in months. I expect him to chastise me, to call me back to the place I belong, to make peace with my sister. I expect his voice to have a touch of gruffness in it, of disappointment, the kind of tone he has when he talks about Aunt Maeve's life in North Carolina, or Aunt Sophie's Unitarian boyfriend. But it doesn't. He's kind, and understanding, and it's almost worse.

"I've thought so much about what you told me that day in the woods," he says. "About how you felt it was all a sham."

I've thought about it too. I've thought of little else. "Yeah. I'm sorry if I shocked you with all that."

He laughs, a round and deep, full laugh. "Shock me! Oh honey, you really underestimate me. I am not easily shocked."

I make a skeptical face, which of course he can't see.

"I realized," he goes on, "that I don't believe you. I don't believe it was all a lie, that you didn't mean it. Because I just keep thinking about that sharp little girl who used to argue with me about God. She used to *teach* me about God. And I simply can't believe she didn't really mean it."

The table of beliefs rattles because he's poking at the very thing I knew as I was telling him all those things in the woods: that even while I was confessing my apostasy to him, it didn't seem right; it didn't seem honest. It wasn't all a sham for me. I meant everything I believed, in the best and most imperfect way I could. And just because the meaning of it has since changed, doesn't take away the fact that it meant something. It doesn't take away the fact that it still means something and has always meant *something*. I was just afraid of the changes.

"Yeah," I tell him. "I think you're right. I'm still too much of an asshole to be a pastor though."

He laughs again. I'd stay on the phone forever if I could keep making him laugh. "Whatever you say dear; whatever you say. Just let me tell you one thing."

"What?"

"Don't ever make the mistake of thinking that you must be alone in your doubts. Because you're not. You never are."

Chapter Sixteen

It's the end of February by the time I get around to unpacking the last of the boxes Aunt Maeve brought from up north. By now, Joy has decided to move back to Pittsburgh with me, at the end of April, and I start buying up furniture from flea markets and thrift shops to fill out the apartment. I make friends with some coworkers and reconnect with a few of my old friends, mostly casual acquaintances, the kind who won't pry any more into my recent loss than to say, "That's so terrible; I'm so sorry," and move on. I keep working. I start going to yoga class, and burst into tears multiple times right in the middle of Pigeon Pose, and people tell me this is normal. I read more about Pittsburgh, learning about each layer of the strata, each forgotten street corner, and building, and bridge. I adopt a cat named Boots, who's the perfect tuxedoed gentleman. It's because of Boots that I finally get around to unpacking that last box: unsatisfied with all the catnipped toys I've given him, he insists on sitting on it, and I decide to be magnanimous and empty out the box for him to fully enjoy.

At first glance, the contents don't seem very important and obviously weren't important enough for me to need them until now. Some extra bedding, some towels and books. But wedged into an empty spot on one side are two things I didn't pack. One is a square velvet jewelry box. In it is a collection of heirloom jewelry: a gold Claddagh ring, a silver bracelet stamped with the image of a thistle, an emerald pendant on a silver chain, diamond studs. A little piece of paper is folded up among it all. *I know you always loved these,* it says in neat print. *I thought you should have them.* Laura's writing. This is some of Mom's jewelry, some of the pieces I always loved to play with before she caught me and told me they were too old or fragile. The gold ring is from one of Grandad and Grandma's trips to Ireland; the silver bracelet an heirloom from Mom's Scottish side of the family; the emerald pendant, Mom's birthstone, from one of the birthdays in which Dad bought Mom a present, but Laura and I took credit for it. The studs are probably from one of their anniversaries.

Theo and Laura must have finally cleaned out Mom and Dad's room, organizing the clothes, the jewelry, the little papers on the desk. I feel a pang of regret. I'm sorry I wasn't there to help. I'm sorry you had to decide what to keep and what to give away, all your own. I'm sorry I didn't see her favorite dress and his trusty old work shoes one last time. The old chant again. I wonder if Theo and Laura will use the room now, if the baby will occupy their room now, or even mine.

The other foreign item in the box is a journal with a black leather cover. One of Dad's. A sticky note is on the inside, with Laura's writing again. *This is from the year we were born. I thought you would like to read it.*

She knows me well, of course. I turn each page carefully, savoring each word, trying to imagine them in his voice, trying to remember his cadence. I realize how hard it is to recall someone's voice after so long, and it frightens me. I trace the lines of the sketches he made, the familiar lines of buildings and hills and waterfalls he later took us to.

In March of that year, I read about the day he and Mom bought our house:

Moving day in the new house. A 1910 American Foursquare. Currently the color of pistachio ice cream, but Maggie intends to paint it peacock blue. I intend to get it sided. Beige, maybe.

Mom won.

First order of business: painting the dining room, which has redneck wallpaper. Antlers and leaves. No joke. Maggie keeps asking me if there are ghosts here. I keep reminding her that they're not "ghosts:" they're the imprints of memories left behind, like a footprint in mud. She keeps saying it's easier to call them ghosts, but I have a feeling the people at church would be less than enthused to hear about that.

To answer her question, No. I haven't seen any of these imprints yet, although the street has a few. But this house feels nearly new. Not a lot of life has happened here, despite the age. There aren't a lot of memories in it yet. Hopefully we'll change that.

The fear, constant and pressing, gripping my ribcage, has begun to loosen a little, really loosen. Dad was my age when he wrote this: my age when he bought a house and started a family. In my head, he was always old, and mature, and assured, but that's how we always think of our parents. It's comforting to think of him as a nerdy, scrappy new husband, who hid parts of himself from the church people just like I do.

This funny thing happened when we were unpacking. We were in the dining room, and suddenly, I felt like we weren't alone. There was this heaviness, but not a bad heaviness. It's only a bad heaviness in Black Gold Cross or the other ghost towns, and even then, it's not heavy all the time. It was the kind of feeling when someone is happy or sad, and you feel their happiness or sadness so palpably that your own heart seems like it will burst. Like a cloud of someone else's feelings, that you walk into.

Breathless, I turn the page.

But it's not scary. It's never scary for me, even when Maggie says it should be. At any rate, I felt this. And I looked into the living room, and I could sort of see the outline of a woman. Not the full image, not clear enough. I couldn't see her hair or clothes, or even most of her face. Just the eyes. And I felt really happy for her, and also really sad. I felt like I knew her, but also that I didn't know her. Maybe she's a new ghost. Maybe she's someone I don't know yet.

I shiver, hair standing on end, my apartment feeling suddenly very empty and quiet. Boots startles me by jumping in my lap, and I scream. "Damn it, Boots!" Then I laugh and cry and hug the cat despite his desperate efforts to get away.

Dad would tell us about his beloved imprints of lives past, those memories still stuck in the air or on a building or tree, until it seemed so innocuous, so commonplace, as normal as looking for grandfather trees. But now, reading it in detail, I know why he kept it hush-hush around the church people. The Christian hippies would say he was witnessing spiritual warfare between the powers of good and evil; the recovering fundamentalists would say he was being courted by the occult like those poor Harry Potter fans; and the ex-Catholics… well, depending on the Catholic, they might be totally fine with it.

But I don't remember him apologizing, or trying to rationalize, or trying to pray away whatever it was that made him so fascinated, so in love with the past that he could sometimes see it. He just let it happen, made jokes about being a time traveler. He was himself, and he also loved God, and he was completely unbothered by anyone who might say those two things couldn't go together.

I wish I would have picked up on that more. I wish I would have stopped tying myself in knots worrying so much, trying so hard to be good that I eventually gave up. I wish I had stopped to notice and remember, the way he tried to teach me to.

A few days later, I get a letter, which is unusual, as my address is still so new. I'm still getting junk mail from the last guy who lived here. But there it is: an invitation to Laura's baby shower, at the end of March, to celebrate the arrival of her baby girl. Baby girl. I'm going to be an aunt, to a niece. There's that longing again: that deep raw desire to be a part of things, to belong, to be a sister, a daughter, an *aunt.* I wonder who is throwing the shower for her. It should be me, and that's no one's fault but my own. I put the invitation in a drawer with Theo's note, and don't look at it again.

I keep reading Dad's journal, savoring each page, making a meal of it.

Maggie is having twins, he says almost twenty-five years ago, in April. *And we're trying to get as much done on the house before they arrive, but it seems unlikely that we'll even get around to renovating our own room. There's just so much to do, and the time is ticking down for Maggie, before the doctor insists she go on bedrest. I am learning so much about what pregnant women are not allowed to do, and some of it seems spurious. According to Maggie, pregnant women aren't even allowed to look at paint samples, because it might make the baby colorblind. Who knew!*

On Sundays after church, we walk around Black Gold Cross. I love it so much there; you can feel the history, feel the energy. It hums with life. Most people drive by it without a second thought. I'm going to make it my goal, once I finish this damned Ph.D, to turn this place into a state park. I'll consider my career, my work, all of it, worth it if I can just do this one thing.

I swallow. Of course, it's no surprise he loved Black Gold Cross. I'm more surprised he didn't know what a lost cause it was. Even then, and especially now, it would be better to bulldoze the entire ghost town and put plaques down, or something. Even twenty-five years ago, another wood frame building blew down every time there was a spring storm, the old houses were riddled with graffiti and animal shit, and the police were busting drug dealers using a Civil War-era general store as a crack house. Even then, Black Gold Cross was more of a community leach than a tourist destination; an unwanted, unloved place. Of course, that's why he loved it so much. I'm sorry, for his sake, for everyone's sake, that he didn't accomplish what he wanted to. I'm sorry that no one will remember it the way he used to.

I think of the last times I was there, with Grandad, and before that, the terrible night I barely remember, with Katie and the others, and the time before that, when I was alone. None of those times were very pleasant, and I wonder if it was like that for him, too. It doesn't seem so; it seems like to him, each moment of vision was a gift, an adventure. Maybe it could be that way for me.

The days get warmer, and in mid-March, the eternal give and take between winter and spring begins. Some days are warm and sunny, the scent of earth making everyone ridiculously cheerful; other days, I wake up to a foot of snow and know everyone I meet that day will be in the worst mood.

Joy and I video-chat often: it's so good to see her, even digitally. Her pixie-cut short hair she dyes a different color every few weeks, her large blue eyes that hold so much emotion, so much space and understanding, even through a screen. She asks me good, hard questions, picking apart all the knots in my mind. She's like Grandad George in that way. I ask her about California, which she says is far too hot for her cold Pennsylvania blood, and the people far too crazy.

"A good crazy, though," I say, smiling wryly. "You like it."

"I do. It's my kind of crazy."

"You should stay there, then, shouldn't you?" I say with a sudden insight. "Why would you move back here? That's where you should be. There's not nearly as many opportunities for you here."

She shrugs. "I love it there, though. Pittsburgh is my home. My family's all there."

"But it's so cold. And the people are the wrong kind of crazy."

"Don't you want me to come back?" she laughs.

"I do, I just don't want you to move here just for me. I want you to do what's right for you."

"What, do you want to move to California, then?"

A year ago, a few months ago, I would have said yes. But the answer isn't yes. "I think I need to stay here," I say. "I want to stay here. Pittsburgh is my home." This is the truest, most honest fact, and it rings through me like a tuning fork. I'm being honest now, and the words don't come as easily at first, but the weight on my chest is feeling lighter.

She smiles again. "Yeah, idiot; Pittsburgh is my home too, which is why I'm coming back."

"Okay," I say, relieved. "Okay, it's settled."

"You know," she says, "Being in the place you belong and being with the people you love aren't always mutually exclusive."

I nod thoughtfully. "In my experience, they are."

"Well," She shrugs again. "Maybe it's time for a new experience."

I tell her about Dad's journal, about the way he could see history sometimes, the ways I think I'm similar. True to Joy's nature, she doesn't act out in disgust: she thinks it's the coolest thing ever.

"Dude, you should totally go to grad school! For history!" She says this as if it's the most obvious fact, as if telling someone they should stop running red lights.

"It's just a hobby. My degree isn't even in history."

"That doesn't matter in grad school. As long as you're smart, someone will take you. You have a gift. You'd have such a one-up on all the other schmucks. It's like a super-power."

I laugh. "Not exactly."

"It brings you joy. It connects you to yourself. You should think about it."

And so, for the first time, I do. Maybe I'll be a history nerd like my dad after all.

Each day of the month of March gives me intense anxiety because each day gets closer and closer to Laura's shower, which I haven't RSVP'd for, and which is burned to my brain anyway, even though I haven't looked at the invitation since I received it. Some days, I am so angry and upset about everything, and I insist I won't go; I'll keep my promise to myself and never drive up to Haven again. Other days, my yearning not to banish myself, as Theo put it, from my family is so strong, and the image in my head of being the smiling, supportive sister I should be, the one I should've been all along, that I nearly pick up the phone and say I'll come. But then, I am always reminded there will be so many people there whom I don't ever want to see again. But then, I think of my grandmothers, how disappointed they will be if I'm not there, how disappointed they will be not to see me for a long time. But then. But then. But then.

Three days before the shower is to be held, I'm sitting in traffic on my way home from work. It's an unseasonably, hopefully springy day, sunny and warm, and the forsythia have bloomed, tufts of delicate yellow among the brutal browns and beiges of rock and concrete. I'm in the thick, standstill traffic on Fort Pitt Bridge going into town, my car windows open, the radio playing mellow instrumental folk, which I remember, with a sudden pang, was always Laura's and my favorite thing to listen to together.

As if on cue, my phone rings, and it's her. I begin to shake, my palms getting clammy as I grip the steering wheel. Her, after months of no contact; she gave up trying to call or text in January. I let the phone ring and ring, before finally turning it off so I can listen to my music.

Then traffic moves again, and someone behind me honks because I'm going too slow, and I get a flash of sudden memory, and realize this has happened before. I was on this bridge, in traffic, stopped, letting the phone go to voicemail, five months ago.

A cold, prickling feeling descends upon me, and I begin to sob and pound the steering wheel and scream the worst words I know. This can't happen again. Maybe it's an omen, maybe it's nothing at all, but I'm tired of living this way. I'm tired of letting calls go to voicemail and blaming someone else when I miss the chance to talk again.

I veer into another lane and punch it across this bridge and onto Veteran's Bridge, pulling forward north and out of the city. The traffic is thick but I keep moving, slowly at first, and then faster and faster, breaking free of the clogged roadways, until I'm on open highway, up and into the wilderness. Outside, a storm is kicking up: wind rustling the trees and trying to blow my car from side to side, sky marbling with dark clouds. But in the car, everything is silent except for the ring of the wheels on the highway, and in the silence I listen, I notice, and I remember.

God is real.

God is within you.

The Lord your God will be with you wherever you go.

All the things that made me so angry with God, all the contradictions, iron out one by one, and I can see them, in my mind's eye. A vast map of knots unknotted, stitches unraveled, tears repaired. If I try to zoom in, try to pick at a particular problem, answer a particular question, it doesn't make sense again. But in the grand scheme, it does. Like an impressionist painting, like embroidery.

Everything works out. Everything will be okay. All I have to do is listen, notice, remember. Each day.

I'm sorry. I'm sorry. I'm sorry.

That voice, chanting *I'm sorry* over and over again, wasn't mine, I realize. I wasn't Judas; I didn't have a penance to serve. It wasn't my fault. The voice was God's, so sorry because my heart was broken. So in pain because I was in pain. I was praying all along, in my head, without even knowing it. All along, I was speaking to God, and God was speaking back. My faith was never a sham, even on that day I was baptized in the river in a desperate attempt to feel bright and new and reborn. I had meant it in the best way I could. Every stage of my faith, every step of it, when I felt like I was playacting, when I thought I had taken everything out and put it on a table, believing and disbelieving nothing, what just another part of the journey of my soul, not the end of it. I had seen the layers people wrapped around the Divine, and thought that peeling back those layers meant I no longer believed. But that's not true: peeling back those layers means I can know the Divine for its own sake. My questions are big enough for God. I don't have to be afraid, even if all I end up doing is asking questions for the rest of my life.

Suddenly, I am rolling into Haven, established in 1859, Population 10,452, and I realize that the weight in my chest, the dread in my stomach, the grip on my ribcage, is gone. There is no fear, only more and more love, and more and more longing to love as much as I can until I can't.

I park behind the house and run down the back walkway. I let myself into the back door and nearly run into Laura. We stare at each other.

"It's you," she says. "You're here."

"I am."

"I called you a little while ago."

"I know. I just… came here instead."

She's very pregnant. I thought that would scare me; that I'd see her and assign an unspoken judgment on myself. But it suits her. Despite everything, she glows. She wears a light pink dress embroidered with colorful flowers, soft black leggings, suede slippers. She looks so happy, so bright.

"I should have answered your call," I say. "I'm sorry."

"It's all right." The sky grows darker, tree boughs tossing wildly. Thunder cracks. Before I can say anything else, she holds up her phone. "Theo's at work. He says there's a tornado warning."

I laugh. "Of course there is."

I follow her through the kitchen, the beginnings of dinner on the counter, to the basement door, where steps lead down to the small cellar Mom and Dad tried in vain many times to refinish into an art studio for Mom's many artistic hobbies. The only problem, of course, was that in a basement, there's no light. We turn on the fluorescent lights, sit on puffy chintz chairs Mom found at a flea market, light a few candles in case the power goes out. Upstairs, the house whistles in the wind.

"I'm sure it'll be fine," says Laura. "We're on a hill. The wind is more dangerous than anything. Hopefully, no windows are broken."

I hug her, desperately, tearfully.

"Don't worry, I'm sure it's just a small tornado," she says. She tries to keep a straight face but erupts into laughter.

"No, you idiot. I missed you."

"I missed you too."

"I'm so sorry. There's so much, I just—"

"Listen," she holds up her palm, shushing me like a small child. "Let's just start over. Let's take the best parts of us and keep them. And let's throw everything else away. Let's pretend that the year my baby is born is Year Zero and time starts from now on."

I study her. She seems taller than me though I was always taller. Older than me though we're twins. Her eyes are a soft and vibrant green like a polished emerald. Her face wears a new expression, more solid, more secure.

"I'd like that," I say. "I love you."

211

"I love you too."

Above our heads, the house shudders, and the fluorescent lights go out. We hold hands. The shadows of candlelight flicker across the cinderblock walls, which Mom painted bright cornflower blue long ago. I can't see the color right now.

"How are you?" she asks.

"I'm doing really well. Better than I have in a long time."

"Good."

"Joy is going to move in with me in April."

"Wonderful; I'll finally get to meet her."

"I might go to grad school for history."

Her face softens. "Good." The sound of rain, then of hail, pelting the roof three stories above. "Theo got a promotion."

"Good for him."

"Our grandparents are doing well."

"I'm glad."

"I'm going to be a *mom*."

I grin. "I'm going to be an aunt."

"We've named her already. We haven't told anyone."

"You shouldn't name babies before they're born; you should get to know them first."

"That's ridiculous!"

"No, it's not! What if she comes out, and you have this name all ready to go, and she hates it?"

"Her name is Maggie Amelia."

"Well, that's a name that will suit anyone."

"Did you get the things I sent you?"

"Yes. Thank you."

"Dad's journal?"

"I loved it."

"It was nice to read it. It was nice to know they were like us, sometimes. Just trying to figure things out."

"Seeing ghosts."

"Well," she rolls her eyes. "Imprints. Footprints in mud."

"I like it. It suits him."

"It suits you."

"Thank you for the jewelry."

"There's more of it. You can look through the rest. We reorganized the house."

"I can't wait to see it."

"Hopefully the storm doesn't knock it down."

One of the candles burns out. I light another one.

"How is it, living in the house?" I ask.

"They're in everything," she says. "A memory everywhere. But it's okay. It's good. We're making it our own, too."

The wind begins to die down, little by little.

"Are you coming to the shower?" she asks.

"If you'll let me."

"You were invited."

I shrug.

"They're not coming, you know," she says.

"Who?"

"Those women. Emma, Sarah."

"They're your friends."

"Not anymore. Not after Theo and I left the church."

"What!"

"We're taking a break. We talked to Pastor Jeff about it; we'll probably return someday. The drama isn't about him, of course."

"What happened?"

"Emma, Sarah, Mrs. Gladys, they all got mad at *me* for getting mad at *them* for cornering *you*," she says, laughing. "It was the dumbest thing. Like middle school all over again. I told Mrs. Gladys she should be ashamed of herself; she's pushing eighty and acting like she's twelve."

"You said that?" I'm astonished.

"She was due for a chastising. But I shouldn't have said it. But I don't care. Theo and I were perfectly content to keep going but they made it weird. Spread rumors about me at the women's group, stupid stuff like that. It's utterly ridiculous. No wonder Mom got fed up with the people at church sometimes. People can't merely be annoyed; they need to come up with a spiritual reason for why they're right and you're wrong, and why you need God's forgiveness and they don't. There was really no talking sense into them, so I stopped trying."

"I'm sorry." It's weird to hear her talk like this; she sounds like me, all cynical and irritated by other people's stupidity. It's amusing.

"We go to Grandad's church now. It's different from what we're used to, but he's good. Of course." She meets my gaze in the dim light. "I'm so sorry about Christmas Eve. I shouldn't have even…"

"Hey, this is Year Zero," I say. "Time starts from now on."

The wind dies down. It stops raining. Eventually, the power comes back on. We emerge from the cellar, me helping Laura up the steep stairs, since her center of gravity is a little off. The house seems fine; we walk around the outside, and although the lawn is littered with small pieces of debris, tree branches, and hail, everything looks okay. The sky has that beauty of something that has gone through hell and come out the other side; it's still mingled with dark clouds, but they are blowing away, and the air is heavy with moisture, the renewed sun infusing everything with miniature rainbows.

"Glad your new home wasn't damaged," I remark. "I hear the previous owner was a real bitch."

She rolls her eyes. "A piece of work, for sure." She sends a text to Theo, letting him know we're all right.

We go back in the house and Laura picks up the dinner preparations where she left off. I walk through the house, observing the changes. Most of the furniture is the same, but it's been rearranged, more conducive to the flow of Theo and Laura's lifestyle. Some of the bookshelves have been moved from the dining room to the living room, so the former has more space for the computer desk, a new bench in place for Laura's teaching supplies. The urns still sit on the dining room mantel and they look familiar and comforting. I stand in the living room and on a strange whim, I lie flat on the carpet and stick my legs in the air. I breathe in, breathe out, remembering some of the poses from my yoga class. The luminous, post-storm light filters in through the windows. The floor is the ceiling, and the ceiling is the floor. All I have to do is kick off the floor and fly.

My eyes travel across the carpeted ceiling into the room beyond, where a dining table suspends from above and a black wrought-iron chandelier grows up from the spiky plaster floor. The chandelier reaches just to the waist of a man standing—

I scramble upright, the world tilting on its axis. I sit on the carpet of the living room and peer into the dining room, where right at the other end of the house, two people are painting the wall. Well, they're not really painting the wall. They're making the motions of painting the wall, but it's already painted. Two twenty-four-year-old Irish Americans, one pregnant, with long auburn hair sticking out in all directions, one with brown curls and a not-quite-completely formed worry line between his eyebrows. I stare at them, mesmerized, rising slowly to my feet, blinking but afraid to look away. I creep closer, silently, step by step. I hear Laura, still, in the kitchen, chopping vegetables, the breeze outside playing with the earth again, scandalized birds complaining about the storm. And still, the two people are there, painting the wall. And the sight of them, again, so young and full of joy and *alive*, makes me so happy and so sad that I laugh and cry at the same time.

Then the one turns, as I know he will, and looks right into me with his gray-brown eyes. He can't see all of me: just the outline, just the eyes. Eyes that he doesn't yet recognize are half his. I'm just a memory, just the shadow of a memory that hasn't been made yet, a print in mud not yet stepped in. He feels happy for me, and also sad, just as I feel for him. I'm a new ghost, someone he doesn't know yet. And he's an old ghost, someone I know very well, better than I used to.

Then the woman drops her paintbrush, and he turns to help her, and they're gone.

Chapter Seventeen

"Okay, do you want roasted potatoes or mashed potatoes because I have a craving for both—" Laura comes through the hall to the living room to ask me and finds me standing there staring at the other end of the house, where I've been standing and staring for a few minutes, even after the people had gone, trying to see if I could conjure them up again. "What's wrong?" she asks.

"You won't believe me."

"What?"

"You'll think I'm a heathen, and I'm sorry but you'll just have to trust that maybe I am and that's okay."

"What?"

I point through to the dining room, to the opposite wall at the end of the house. "Remember that part of Dad's journal, when they first moved in and were painting the redneck wallpaper?"

"Yes?"

"And he saw one of his imprint ghost footprint women?"

"Yes?"

"It was me. I was her."

"What do you mean?"

"I just saw them."

"Who?"

"Mom and Dad. I just saw them, painting the wall. Well, not really painting it. And he saw me, and I could tell. I was the woman. The new ghost he hadn't met yet."

Laura stands still with me and stares at the wall too.

"What was it like?" she asks.

I tear my eyes away from the wall, finally, and look at her. "That's all? You're not going to accuse me of being a heathen?"

"No," she smiles. "I believe you. I believed all the things he said, so why wouldn't I believe you?"

216

The ceiling and floor have swapped, indeed. I'm about to press the issue, when there's the sound of a car roaring into the driveway behind the house, and we see Theo through the window, tearing it down the walkway to the back door.

"What's wrong?" Laura cries as he comes into the house.

He gasps for breath. "You have to hurry! You have to see this—hi Amy, welcome back, it's about time!—come on, get in the car, we have to get there before everyone else does!"

"Where?" we ask, but he doesn't answer, just hurries us up through the yard to the car, pulling and then pushing Laura along as gently as he can with all his agitation. Finally, we are in the car and he's speeding down Alice Street so fast I feel my lunch start to come back up.

"This is absolutely nuts. Andy—he's the main photographer for the paper—he was chasing the storm because he also has a sick sense of humor and he gets these great pictures, well while we were all in the basement of the office, he was out taking pictures. Idiot of a man. Well, he found this."

"What? What is it?" Laura shakes her head. "Please calm down."

"Black Gold Cross!" He blurts out. "It's completely gone!"

"What do you mean, gone?" I ask.

"Just… gone. There was a microburst. It flattened the whole town. Nothing's standing. Nothing at all. You have to see it."

"You've seen it?" Laura presses him.

"Yes, it's so bizarre."

"Why the hurry? Won't it still be there?" I ask.

"They're blocking off the main roads to keep people from gawking."

"Aren't you the press though?" I reply.

"I'm very pregnant," says Laura. "Please drive gently."

He tries, but he can't help himself. We speed through town, avoiding shingles and pieces of brick and stone blown into the roads, skirting the road crews and fire engines gathered around damaged areas. We speed down Mackenzie Street and plunge into the wilderness, through the forest dotted with sprouting neon green leaves.

The familiar old sign, *Historic Black Gold Cross, 2 mi.* is bent a little bit, although this could be from anything. Theo cuts a hard right, and Laura yells in protest. The car struggles over the rough, twisting road, around tree stumps and boulders. We make the sharp right turn into the little parking lot where a small crowd has gathered, including a police officer and some volunteer firemen. We join the little knot of people—law enforcement don't exactly know whether to keep people away or let them in yet—and there it is. Or rather, there it isn't.

In my mind's eye, I see the town: Main and Petroleum streets making a sideways T, the crooked train station, the empty shopfronts, bank building with its granite stoop, the ostentatious brothels, and the rickety defiant church, all on the edge of Seneca Creek, in a little hollow of the land, surrounded by hills and endless forest.

Now, it is, as Theo said, all gone. It's all flattened in a nearly perfect, mile-wide circle of devastation, the trees just beyond the parking lot pushed straight down like a pile of pencils, every building crumpled like a miniature put under a hydraulic press, the ground one big patch of debris. Just like that.

Maybe to an outside observer, this is nothing special. A storm happened and a ghost town was flattened. It happens every day, probably. But to all of us here, there's something more about it. There's something about nature taking back the thing that once caused it so much devastation: this town and others like it, bleeding the earth dry, setting the creeks on fire, burying people alive in mud and sludge. There's something about our history ending right here, right now, having nothing physical to look back on, no foundation to stand on. Year Zero. The future can be anything now. There's something about how the town, once so thick with ghosts and stories, has now come tumbling down, emptied out to make way for something else. It feels lighter here now, as if the place could float.

For a while, we're speechless, staring and wandering through the debris. I pick my way down Main Street, gingerly, where I used to run pretending I was a bank robber, where at the former street corner the granite stoop sits, once a lowly place for people to step on, now the tallest point in Black Gold Cross. I begin to laugh. I laugh harder and harder, feeling lighter and lighter.

"Laura, look!" I laugh. I step up to the top of the granite and the wreckage of the ghost town is laid out before me. I jump, pretending, for a split second, to fly. I am suspended above the earth, weightless and alive, peering down at the world, a bird's eye view of my sister, of Theo, of the random collection of people who are my countrymen. Then I come back down, landing on my feet on a pile of rotted boards. I laugh and laugh, giddy.

Laura starts laughing too. We grab hands and spin in circles. And Theo joins us and we dance on the rubble of the ghost town without knowing quite why, except that it seems like the right thing to do.

That night, the end to probably the weirdest day of my life, we spend hours at the dining room table, lingering over dinner and dessert, talking and talking, telling stories, remembering. I don't know what it is, but suddenly every wonderful and important thing I can think of spills out of me, and I just want to keep talking and being talked to. Grandad and Grandma and Nanna Mae come over, and they're so happy to see me and I to see them, and we sit up long into the night, being together, being happy.

When it's finally time for bed, Laura shows me to my room, which they cleaned up and reorganized, but which still has my dresser and bed, a tidy stack of my boxes piled against the wall waiting for me. Theo and Laura have moved into the master bedroom, completely rearranged with their furniture and stuff, and Laura's old room has been repainted and decorated with soft earth tones and woodland animals, awaiting Maggie Amelia.

I drift off to sleep, half wondering if this is all a dream, knowing that it's not, my eyes leaking tears, because I know I'll have this happiness for the rest of my life.

The next morning, I leave the house for Pittsburgh. I'm going to grab an overnight bag, and Boots, and return later in the day. I'll be the loving and supportive sister at Laura's shower. I'll be the fun aunt, the aunt who doesn't only pop in for the highlights.

"See you later," Laura says when I leave. "Can't wait to meet your cat."

"He's excited to meet his Aunt Laura." I grin.

I set off down the hill and through Haven, which is blossoming before my eyes with spring. It's only the end of March, but we will have an early spring; I can feel it. I drive out into the wilderness to meet up with the interstate, my eyes swelling with the beauty of the countryside. A thousand different shades of feathery green grass, sharp dark tree branches carrying frothy white and pink and yellow blossoms. Bridges over creek valleys, brown ribbons over green, as the land swoops down and rises again in mound after mound, layering against each other mile after mile until it disappears in the horizon, into the bright blue sky, cloudless for a rare moment.

And in this moment, I feel a new belief peel itself off that table. But it doesn't calmly join the other beliefs in my head. It's not gentlemanly. It's not ladylike. It's not polite. It's an asshole. It wallops me, striking me between the eyes and staring me right in the face, daring me to doubt, daring me to claim it isn't real. Daring me to wrestle with it, to punch at it and be punched by it day after day.

You are loved.

You'd think it would be easy to accept this: that no matter what happens, what I do or say or think, no matter what questions I ask, that I am loved. On the surface, it seems like a simple, uncomplicated belief, perhaps even a little too easy, too irresponsible. But damn, if it isn't the most challenging belief of them all. I didn't realize how little I truly believe that I am loved no matter what until I'm met with the choice to believe it. Because if I believe it, there's no cosmic locker combinations to unlock, no perpetual anxiety to stave off, no penance to serve. Nothing to do, and only one thing to be.

You are loved.

I see it all in a flash before my eyes. Black Gold Cross. Ghost towns. Grandfather trees. Headstones. Granite. Oil. Water on fire. People who aren't alive anymore, a whole slew of them, pioneers and train conductors and loggers and riverboat captains and oil barons and sex workers and ministers and Civil War vets and doctors and nurses and freed slaves and church people and indigenous tribes and soldiers and fathers and mothers and children. My Dad. My Mom. Everyone who came before me. A whole world, beloved and wonderful and wide.

You are loved.

The ghosts and angels and demons. The life and death and resurrection. The things I can't explain but know they're real. The pain in the earth, like a scar. My handful of beliefs, like a salve. The handful of beliefs, all I have to make sense of everything.

God is real. God is within you. The Lord your God will be with you wherever you go. And you are loved.

"Okay," I say. Before I can say anything else.

About the Author

Hannah Allman Kennedy grew up among the oil ghost towns of Venango County, Pennsylvania. She earned her MFA in creative writing from Carlow University of Pittsburgh, Pennsylvania, attending residencies both at Carlow and at Trinity College in Dublin, Ireland. She holds a B.A. in writing from Geneva College. Hannah is a lover of old things, hikes, good coffee, good yarn, and peonies. She lives with her husband in Pittsburgh, where she teaches writing and works as a freelance writer and web designer. She can be found online at hannahakwrites.com.

Made in the USA
Las Vegas, NV
05 December 2021

36108042R10125